THE STAR MIRROR

THE
STAR
MIRROR

The Extraordinary Discovery of the True
Reflection between Heaven and Earth

MARK VIDLER

Thorsons
An Imprint of HarperCollins*Publishers*

Thorsons
An Imprint of HarperCollins*Publishers*
77–85 Fulham Palace Road
Hammersmith, London W6 8JB

Published by Thorsons 1998

1 3 5 7 9 10 8 6 4 2

© Mark Vidler 1998

Mark Vidler asserts the moral right to
be identified as the author of this work

A catalogue record for this book
is available from the British Library

ISBN 0 7225 3720 4

Printed and bound in Great Britain by
Creative Print and Design (Wales), Ebbw Vale

FOR ISLA AND KATY

CONTENTS

ACKNOWLEDGEMENTS

Special thanks to Sheila Knight, Richard Vidler and Julia Wells.

In addition to thanking Michelle Pilley, Lizzie Hutchins and all the team at Thorsons for their skills, enthusiasm and seemingly endless commitment to hard work, I am also indebted to the following people for their assistance: Bill Stainthorpe, Nick Valentine, Bill Salisbury, Bernard Rosewell, Tristan Forward, Vieve Forward, Jo Edwards, Teresa Jones, Gregory Jones, Kat Pebbles, Tony Wayte, Phil Bryant, Jerry Herman, Robert Strauss, Johnny Moreland, and the authors of *The Orion Mystery*, Robert Bauval and Adrian Gilbert.

Sincere thanks to my literary agent Caroline Davidson for her invaluable guidance through all stages of the work.

Above all I would like to say thank you to my partner Sally Stafford. I couldn't have written this book without her.

INTRODUCTION

Shortly before completing this book I bought two large maps of the central Australian desert. I had not seen these maps before and I knew little about this region of Australia. The maps are called Operational Navigation Charts and they are designed for aeroplane and helicopter navigators. For obvious reasons the designers of these charts have been particularly concerned to identify the whereabouts of all the highest points of land and to give details of the topography in general.

Before returning to my office with the charts I drew a particular shape on a piece of paper.

The two charts are now spread out in front of me, covering two square metres on the wall. I have located the three highest mountain peaks overlooking the entire region of central Australia and joined the three summits together to create a single shape. The shape created on the map is the same as the shape I drew earlier.

I already knew the shape, but I had no prior knowledge of the region. In the world of geometry the shape itself is unusual and seldom occurs at random between three points.

We will find this shape in the Americas, China, India, Europe, Africa and in the middle of the Pacific Ocean, and when the journey is complete we will have visited many of the world's greatest ancient sites and the world's highest mountains. The vehicles transporting us from place to place will be the brightest stars in the sky today.

STARS IN THEIR EYES

'If we come to think of it we
have been living in a world of
Astronomical Myth until
yesterday.'[1]

This is really a story about the present day, but it begins many thousands of years ago, when gods were in the stars and our ancestors worshipped the sky.

The pattern of stars in the night sky changes very little over the millennia and therefore the sky today provides images shared by humanity since the dawn of recorded history. At some unspecified time in the past the starry vault was divided into 48 constellations and each group of stars was given a title. With only one exception these names are still used to define the star groups in the present day. Yet who among us can locate half a dozen of these ancient constellations? Even eminent astronomers are said to share this problem of identification. Patrick Moore observed, 'I know a number of eminent professionals who would be quite unable to go out on a clear night and identify the various star groups.'[2]

Although the night sky is not particularly well known today, our ancient ancestors lived in awe of the stars. They worshipped the lights in Heaven, seeing them as a direct reflection of the Earth.

This passion was most keenly felt in ancient Egypt. The first Pharaohs were said to be direct descendants of star gods and goddesses who floated in boats across a celestial lake of stars. The great lake was just teeming with gods, according to Egyptian (and later Greek) beliefs. The entire celestial lake was seen as a beautiful naked goddess and the Earth beneath her was seen as a beautiful naked god. The sky goddess was called Nut, the Earth god was called Geb; they were twins.

Figure 1: Nut and Geb

Nut and Geb gave birth to the great star god Osiris and his sister Isis. In the mythology of ancient Egypt Isis and Osiris were the first gods to walk the Earth in mortal form, but destiny would return the couple to their true home in the stars. Osiris was symbolized by the Orion constellation, the brightest group of stars in the sky, 'with the greatest number of stars above the 2nd magnitude',[3] and Isis by the brightest single night-time star, Sirius. The voyage of Isis and Osiris across the sky can still be seen on clear winter nights.

The idea that a god is moving around 'in Heaven' has been prevalent for a long time, but the 'Heaven' and the 'God' discussed in modern theology cannot be identified or measured. Exactly the opposite was true in ancient Egypt. The god Osiris was a physical manifestation, untouchable, but visible each year in the night sky. Thus, in ancient Egypt, 'God' was actually on view in the sky, a concept now lost to us when we look at the stars.

It was only when somebody looked closely at the body of Osiris in Heaven that the full extent of this ancient devotion to the Orion stars was recognized. The modern perception of the ancient world was recently shaken by an extraordinary individual insight.

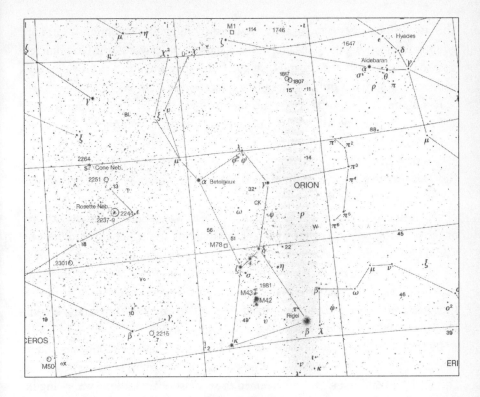

Figure 2: Orion

A STROKE OF GENIUS

An Egyptian-born engineer called Robert Bauval had been studying ancient Egypt for several years. He had a particular interest in the layout of the three large Giza pyramids. One night, camping in the desert, Bauval and a friend were looking at the stars of Orion. His friend pointed out that the three brilliant stars in the Belt of Orion appeared as a straight line, but if you looked very carefully you could see that one star was in fact slightly off the centre of the line. The light dawned on Robert Bauval.

The pattern of the three stars in Orion's Belt is almost identical to the layout of the three main Giza pyramids. They are the mirror image of each other.

Nothing like this had ever been considered before, but Bauval demonstrated the three large Giza pyramids provide a direct reflection of the stars of Orion's Belt.[4]

3

This astonishing discovery suggests the three monumental pyramids at Giza are symbols representing three specific brilliant stars. In other words, the Giza builders were so enraptured by the sky and their god Osiris they attempted to provide a map of the central stars in Orion by *using pyramids as symbols of stars*.

It was already well known that the ancient Egyptians built numerous temples and pyramids pointing to the stars, but these alignments were horizontal, i.e. along the ground, pointing to the horizon. This form of research had been pioneered by Sir Norman Lockyer, whose classic work *The Dawn of Astronomy* (Macmillan, 1894) clearly shows that ancient monument builders were working on points and lines defined first in the sky, then back on the Earth.

The method employed by the ancient architects was extremely simple. Lockyer only had to follow the baseline of an ancient building to the horizon and there he would find the sun rising at the summer solstice, or a brilliant star rising, or a similar notable celestial event. Although some errors have been found in this early work, Lockyer (and Professor Nissan in Germany) discovered that the ancient Egyptians had used the horizon as a celestial marker and oriented their buildings according to a stellar lore. Lockyer had found a code in the stones.

In 1894, when he first published his findings, the academic world was almost entirely unprepared to accept that any co-ordination existed between the temples of ancient Egypt and the sky; it just seemed too fantastic. Yet Lockyer was doing no more than following a straight line described on the ground by the ancient surveyors and architects, and he repeatedly discovered 'by alignment' our own brilliant sun at the solstices or the equinoxes, or other celestial alignments, including several to the star Sirius. In many cases (including the Giza pyramids), when the line described by the building was extended to the horizon it located a point due north or due south, due east or due west. Nevertheless, academics at the time dismissed Lockyer's findings as 'coincidence' or 'chance' or 'serendipity'. In fact he was ridiculed.

But Lockyer had really uncovered a form of antique communication in which the structure of a building could be used to define something greater, beyond the structure itself. His study suggested the ancient Egyptian pyramids and temples are akin to symbols in a mute and misunderstood astronomical language.

Since Lockyer's day an immense amount of work has been conducted in this field. Now, all over the world, ancient structures are yielding their stellar secrets. There is little doubt that ancient monument builders from Egypt, England, Scotland, Ireland, Wales, France, Germany, Iran, Iraq, the Lebanon, Israel, Turkey, Tibet, China, India, the USA, Mexico, Peru, Cambodia and many other locations were all primarily concerned with astronomical phenomena when they designed and built their monumental structures.

In all cases it appears these diverse ancient cultures were preoccupied with the sky *for a good reason*. This book is written in pursuit of that reason.

THE ORION MYSTERY

When Robert Bauval and his co-author Adrian Gilbert published *The Orion Mystery*, the mute and misunderstood stellar language of the ancient Egyptians had found its modern voice. The old horizontal measures recognized by Sir Norman Lockyer were superseded by the vertical plans of Robert Bauval.

Robert Bauval showed how the layout of the stars in Orion's Belt directly reflects the layout of the three large pyramids on the Giza plateau. Thus the star Alnitak symbolizes the Great Pyramid, the star Alnilam symbolizes the second pyramid and the star Mintaka symbolizes the third pyramid.

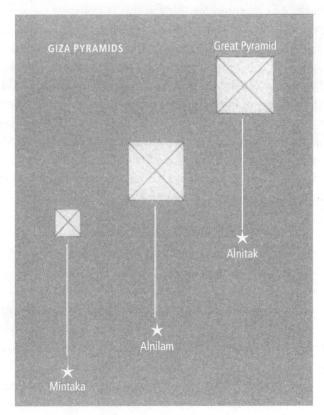

Figure 3: Three pyramids = Three stars

The Orion Mystery was published exactly 100 years after Sir Norman Lockyer's *The Dawn of Astronomy*, but the academic world was equally unprepared to accept Bauval's findings. Was an earlier error repeating itself? Academics were certainly intensely critical of the astronomical theories outlined by Bauval and Gilbert, despite the visual evidence.

For example the Egyptologist Robert Chadwick, writing in *KMT: A Modern Journal of Ancient Egypt*, says: 'At first glance the similarity between the arrangement of stars and that of the man made structures is quite astonishing.' None the less, he concludes:

'This supposed match up is serendipitous and may be attributed to chance rather than some kind of master plan devised by the ancient Egyptians of the fourth dynasty.'[5]

Chance is an odd thing, but not that odd. Chance can be measured, it is therefore scientific[6] and this important fact lies at the heart of Robert Bauval's discovery.

The three stars, Mintaka, Alnilam and Alnitak, are the most notable isolated line of three brilliant stars on the entire celestial sphere. They were worshipped for at least 3,000 years and they are found at the very centre of the great star god Osiris. In turn three monumental pyramids were created by the people who worshipped these brilliant points of light, yet Egyptologists state that the direct duplicate pattern of random stars in the sky and pyramids on the ground at Giza was not created with intent, but can be attributed to 'serendipity'.

The numerical odds that the 'serendipity theory' is correct are not good at all. Try throwing three tennis balls at random onto a tennis court and wait for them to come to rest. Now worship the three randomly arranged balls for a time. Next, throw three more balls onto another tennis court. Are the patterns you have created on both tennis courts the same? The chance comes in at thousands to one, yet these are the odds some Egyptologists advise us to bet on.[7]

Certainly the idea that pyramids were built as star replicas does not slip easily into the portfolio of agreed theories that the pyramids were tombs built for the Pharaohs. None the less astronomy is a very exact science and the ancient Egyptians were very precise astronomers.

To the casual observer the alignment of a square-based building precisely to a star or to the cardinal points of the Earth may pass almost unnoticed, yet it requires great skill to make these alignments. You simply *have to* make accurate observations from the sky in order to define the cardinal points of the Earth, there is no alternative. So how good were the Egyptian pyramid builders when it came to making these astronomical observations?

A GOOD PYRAMID

Many eulogies have been written about the phenomenal accuracy achieved in the construction of the Great Pyramid at Giza and most accounts confirm the following:

a. The base of the pyramid is a perfect square (accepting a tolerance of one part in 7,000).
b. The square base of the pyramid is perfectly level (accepting a tolerance of one part in 10,000).
c. The square base of the pyramid is perfectly aligned to the cardinal points of the Earth (accepting a tolerance of one part in 6,000).[8]

To give an idea of what the word 'tolerance' means in the measurements listed above we really need to go for a walk in the countryside. Imagine yourself on a great hill surrounded by a distant flat horizon. Take a matchstick out of your pocket and hold it up so that it crosses the horizon. The width of the matchstick can now be compared with the complete circle of the horizon that remains.

The Great Pyramid is aligned so precisely that you will have to split your matchstick in order to define the north point on the horizon with the degree of precision achieved at Giza.

RIGHT OR WRONG?

The Giza builders were extremely gifted astronomers. They also worshipped the stars in an area of sky called the Duat. The Orion stars are the brightest group of stars in the Duat and the three Belt stars are the brightest group within Orion. The three Giza pyramids directly reflect the layout and magnitude of the three stars in Orion's Belt, and consequently 'serendipity' is hardly a reasonable explanation for such a correspondence.

But perhaps there is one serious objection to Robert Bauval's star correlation theory and it concerns the use of symbols. If the Giza designers were sufficiently immersed in symbolism to conceptualize three pyramids on the ground representing three stars in the sky then they have cleverly presented the world with a conundrum. Why did the ancient Egyptians create pyramids to symbolize stars? Why not be more direct and create a star shape on the ground instead? Isn't a pyramid the wrong shape to symbolize a star?

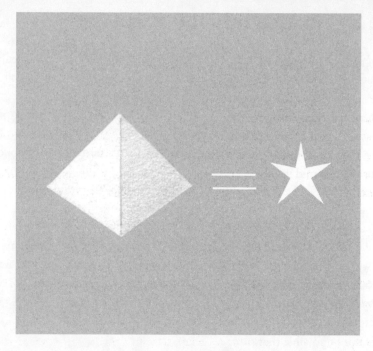

Figure 4: Pyramid = Star

The standard Egyptian rendering of a star remained almost unaltered in artwork for over 2,000 years of Egyptian history *(see Figure 5)*. So we are bound to question why a star-shaped object in the sky is replicated by an essentially triangular object on the ground.

Figure 5: The traditional star symbol in ancient Egypt

The same problem arises if the star correlation theory is translated into words:

STARS ARE PYRAMIDS   is incorrect.
STARS ARE STARS   is correct.

If the ancient Egyptians were communicating through astronomy, and if architecture was a form of language, then what kind of language were they really using?

One possible solution to this enigma is found in the shape of the pyramid. Perhaps the pyramid itself was used to point *to* the stars, rather than resemble them in shape.

POINTING TO THE STARS

Over 100 years ago Sir Norman Lockyer timidly inserted this suggestion in *The Dawn of Astronomy*:

'It is not impossible that some of the mysterious passages to be found in the pyramid of Cheops may have some astronomical use.'[9]

One hundred years after Lockyer's insight our most modern encyclopaedias now acknowledge that the Great Pyramid was designed to point to the stars. *The British Museum Dictionary of Ancient Egypt* confirms that the shafts within the Great Pyramid are directed to the sky for 'some astronomical function'.[10]

A major advance has taken place.

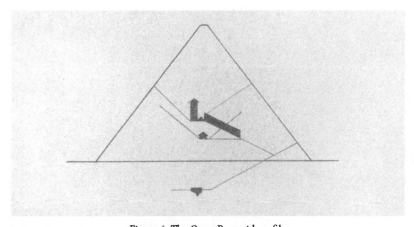

Figure 6: The Great Pyramid profile

In fact the ancient architects have designed a cross-section resembling a sextant *(see Figure 6)*. So the Great Pyramid can be recognized as an astronomical instrument – an extremely large astronomical instrument, but none the less one designed to point to the stars.

The dark bands on the illustration show all the angled shafts so far discovered within the building. The lines point at the sky and each line locates a different point on the celestial sphere. But all the pyramid lines are connected. This is a crucial technical point.

There is a line outside the pyramid joining all these interior angles together.

This line is found in the sky. It is called the meridian. The meridian is an imaginary circle of longitude[11] on the celestial sphere used by every astronomer today in order to define the location of all stars.

Archaeo-astronomers have followed these lines from the Great Pyramid to the stars with spectacular results. To summarize the progress achieved in this field of research so far, Figure 7 shows how four Great Pyramid angles once co-ordinated with bright stars. These alignments are discussed in *The Orion Mystery*. (The stars all move uniformly over long periods of time due to precession and this is discussed in more detail later.) As a result of the long-term motion of stars on the celestial sphere it is possible for an archaeo-astronomer to recognize something greater than chance creating the four alignments shown in the illustration.

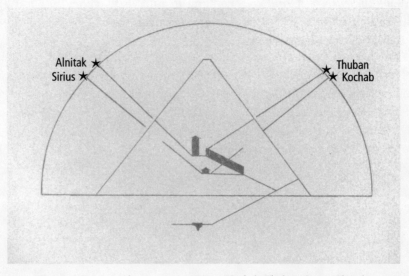

Figure 7: Four star alignments in 2450 BC: Kochab, Thuban, Sirius, Alnitak

Owing to precession these stars were only synchronized with the Great Pyramid star shafts for a short span of time in 2450 BC. The date 2450 BC was thus recognized by Robert Bauval[12] as the epoch in history when this co-ordination between star and pyramid occurred.

All four of the synchronized stars played a significant role in the theatre of the ancient Egyptian gods:

a. Thuban was the pole star in ancient Egypt.
b. Kochab, a brilliant star in the Little Bear, figured in Egyptian artwork.
c. Alnitak, in Orion's Belt, symbolized the Great Pyramid according to the star correlation theory.
d. Sirius, the brightest star in the night sky, symbolized Isis, the sister and wife of Osiris.

So the three Giza pyramids not only look like Orion's Belt in plan view, but the Great Pyramid actually points to the night sky in a synchronized manner, and in doing so once identified the star Alnitak, its own reciprocal in the star correlation theory.

This co-ordination quite clearly suggests that the Great Pyramid architects were illustrating something (perhaps a mythological theme), using the Great Pyramid blueprint as a vehicle. In fact the lines from the pyramid into the sky form a terrestrial cord binding Isis and Osiris in the heavens, a couple who were tragically separated during their life on Earth.

The star synchronization in 2450 BC also involved the pole star, around which the gods were seen to travel.

There is much to be witnessed in this process of star alignment, but first I must explain how this strange linear language operates. It is a very clever process. Understanding the method of stellar alignments brings with it an awareness of the highly sophisticated methods employed by these gifted astronomers and architects from 5,000 years ago, but perhaps more importantly, it allows us to follow ancient lines of communication only recently recognized.

A MEETING WITH THE MERIDIAN

The Great Pyramid designers used the angles of the building to define stars when they crossed the meridian in the sky. The Great Pyramid can be imagined as a lighthouse shining at night and each carefully constructed angled shaft can be envisaged as a spotlight with a laser beam pinpointing a specific interval on the meridian ruler above. Therefore when I refer to a star 'spotlighted' by the Great Pyramid I will always mean the brightest star to fall into alignment with a particular pyramid angle.

Imagine the meridian line as a ruler arching across the sky like the vapour trail of a modern jet. The jet first appears at a point due south on your horizon, but it is travelling due north, leaving a straight vapour trail behind it. In doing so it will inevitably pass vertically over your head. When it has disappeared at the point due north on your horizon the vapour trail left behind is a visible line in the sky. This is your meridian. (The vapour trail will disperse, but your meridian line remains constantly above your head.)

Although the Earth is always turning, the meridian of the observer is permanently fixed against the apparently mobile sky and consequently stars appear to travel in parallel lines across it. Each star will appear to travel across the meridian ruler at the same point every day.[13] (If the sun did not obscure the stars during the day, an observer would see the same stars returning to the same place on the meridian ruler every time the Earth turned through 360°.) Therefore astronomers can identify the position of every single star in the sky by their exact position on this ruler. Each star is given a measurement and these numbers precisely define where the star can be found on the meridian of the observer.

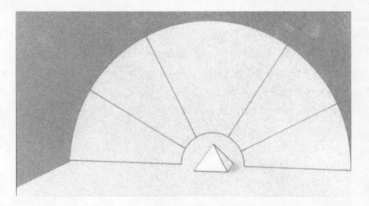

Figure 8: A 3D view of the meridian over Giza and the pyramid spotlights

How to Find a Star

The entire sky is imagined as a sphere surrounding and containing the smaller sphere of the Earth. The two spheres are placed one inside the other. Lines of longitude and latitude are imagined on the Earth's sphere, creating a grid. Precisely the same grid is drawn on the celestial sphere, offering a mirror image of the Earth's grid drawn over the sky.

From a purely geometric point of view the sphere of stars and the sphere of Earth are identical. Consequently the precise position of a star on the celestial sphere always corresponds with an equivalent location on the terres-trial sphere. (In other words, any star passing vertically over your head is given precisely your own latitude, but in the case of the star this latitude is measured on the celestial sphere.)[14]

To define the brightest star aligned with one of the Great Pyramid's spotlights it is only necessary to follow a straight line on the designers' blueprint. The line identifies a precise location on the meridian where stars are measured. The brightest star to pass onto the meridian ruler at the specified point is thus defined as the 'aligned star'.

This method of identification, in which a single star is defined by its celestial latitude, was recognized by Professor Badawy and Virginia Trimble in 1964 and later followed by Robert Bauval.

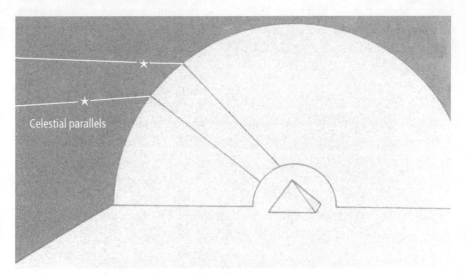

Celestial parallels

Figure 9: The lines of celestial latitude crossing the meridian
and encountering the pyramid spotlights

And from the process of joining the Earth and the sky in this strange manner something unexpected is revealed in the minds of the people who designed the Great Pyramid. The designers were using the pyramid to connect points of light on the celestial sphere that might otherwise remain unconnected. This is exactly how written communication takes place.

It is thought that written language was created around 3200 BC. The method adopted was the same as it is today – people first communicated in writing by placing various symbols on straight lines.

To discover the stars representing the god Osiris and his wife Isis both defined by straight linear spotlights from Giza suggests that the Great Pyramid architects were, and always have been, communicating by placing symbols on lines. In this case the lines are defined by the pyramid designers and the symbols are stars.

The Great Pyramid builders left nothing to account for themselves – no records, no plans, no formal communication at all. The Great Pyramid contains no hieroglyphic texts[15] and no murals. It is apparently a mute monument. Yet here we see the pyramid itself pointing to stars, placing stars onto lines. Is this perhaps a form of writing, a manner of speech?

A NEW DISCOVERY

I was studying the symbolism associated with the Great Pyramid star alignments when something struck me:

Not all the angles had been investigated.

As yet only five Great Pyramid angles had been examined, but the pyramid has a total of 11 angles defining points on the meridian over Giza.

If my hunch was right, then the other angles might also locate stars.

This was uncharted territory.

Using the familiar section view of the Great Pyramid, I extended all the architectural features to the meridian. The pyramid now had a total of 11 spotlights, including one to the vertical, i.e. the point on the meridian 90° above the pyramid.

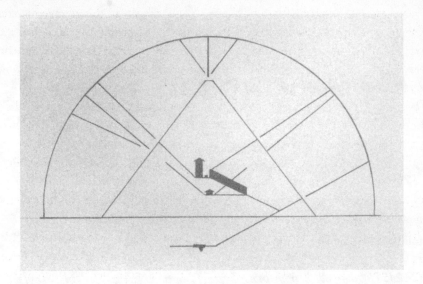

Figure 10: The 11 Great Pyramid spotlights

I decided to research the new Great Pyramid angles, following each one like a laser beam into the sky in 2450 BC. I wondered if it was possible that these angles were also constructed to point to the stars and co-ordinate with the alignments already discovered.

I started by following the straight line up the gnarled old north face of the Great Pyramid.

I was about to stumble over something incredible.

REACHING THE POINT

*'Over many years I have
searched for the point where
myth and science join.'*[1]

I followed the line up the north face of the Great Pyramid.

*In 2450 BC the spotlight from the north face of the pyramid located Bellatrix, one of the
seven brilliant Orion stars. The alignment was precise to within a sixth of a degree.*

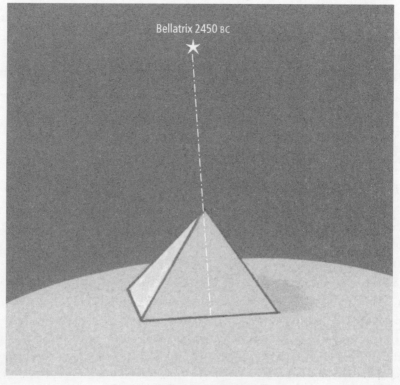

Figure 11: Bellatrix alignment, 2450 BC

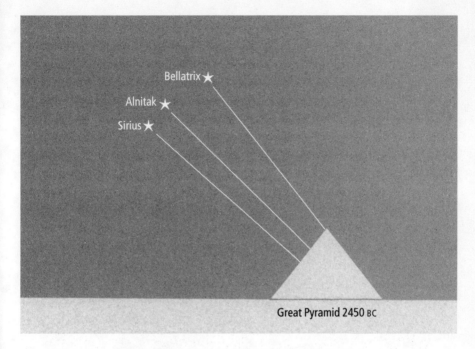

Figure 12: Spotlights on Sirius, Alnitak and Bellatrix

I was amazed. I checked the figures again. The co-ordinated alignments of Alnitak and Sirius were in place, so I followed the angle of the north face onto the meridian ruler. There was Bellatrix, by far the brightest star on this celestial parallel, the brilliant shoulder of the giant Orion, a second bright star representing Osiris.

The accumulated star alignments on the south side of the Great Pyramid in 2450 BC now created the pattern shown in Figure 12.

Bellatrix is ranked twenty-sixth in the league of brilliant stars. It is slightly brighter than Alnitak. The alignment of the spotlight was on the correct degree; indeed, the alignment was accurate to a sixth of a degree. This line passing up the centre of the enduring old north face of the Great Pyramid was, it seems, also designed to point to Osiris in 2450 BC.

So the Great Pyramid defines the location of three brilliant stars on the meridian. These spotlights do not locate the stars simultaneously, but they locate a precise parallel and therefore the brightest stars to be found on each parallel.

I was tremendously encouraged by this finding because the Great Pyramid alignment to Bellatrix could have been observed in 2450 BC. Any person standing at the base of the pyramid at that time could have followed the line of sight defined by the north face and, with this perspective, crossing the very apex of the Great Pyramid they would have found Bellatrix, passing in the night. In a matter of minutes, following Bellatrix, the star Alnitak would have fallen into alignment with the 45° shaft, and then Sirius would have followed, falling into alignment with the lower southern star shaft. Surely this was not serendipity at work, but rather a very cleverly prescribed plan beginning to emerge.

I had tried only one of the six new pyramid spotlights and immediately encountered one of the seven brilliant Orion stars. My next move was to check the south face of the Great Pyramid. I followed the spotlight onto the meridian ruler and I found the brightest passing star on this parallel was Yildun. Yildun and Kochab are two bright stars in the same constellation, the Little Bear, thus the Great Pyramid located two stars in the Little Bear and two in Orion.

(The very tip of the tail of the Little Bear is represented by Polaris. Yildun is the next bright point of light in the bear's tail and Kochab represents its brighter eye. A spotlight on Kochab had already been established by Bauval.)

I had now discovered two star alignments from two pyramid spotlights, but I had yet to fully understand what I was uncovering. I decided to look at another pyramid angle.

This time I followed the angle of the famous ascending passage and Grand Gallery from within the Great Pyramid. Extending this angle onto the meridian the spotlight from the ascending passage located a star called Gacrux.

Gacrux is ranked twenty-fourth in the league of brilliant stars; it belongs to Crux, the smallest of all the constellations. Although small, Crux is by far the brightest little area of stars in the entire night sky, resting on the starry bangle of the Milky Way. Gacrux has four brilliant neighbours forming a kite shape in the sky (not visible in London or New York), which cluster together to form Crux, the Cross.

I mentioned earlier that Orion is said to be the brightest group of stars in the sky. This is because Orion is the constellation with the greatest number of stars above the second magnitude. But this method represents only one way of defining the brilliance of a constellation. The method adopted by the astronomer Michael E. Bakich places Crux at the top of the list of bright constellations. This is because the overall brilliance of Crux, by area, is greater than Orion.

With the addition of this alignment to Crux there can be little doubt that the Great Pyramid was designed to locate some of the brightest stars in the sky in 2450 BC:

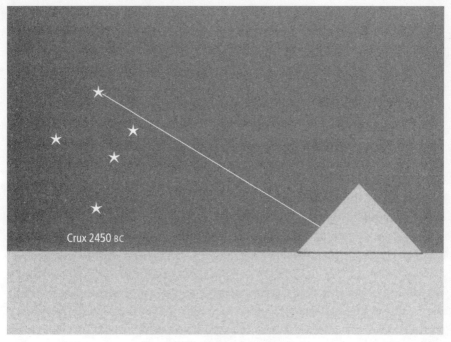

Figure 13: Spotlight on Crux, 2450 BC

a. Sirius is the brightest star.
b. Orion is the brightest constellation (using one definition).
c. Crux is the brightest constellation (using a second definition).
d. An unusually bright pole star is also located, Thuban.

Bearing in mind that in total seven bright stars had now been identified accurately by this alignment process, it became increasingly clear that whatever else the Great Pyramid might be, it was indeed a very carefully constructed star pointer.

I continued my research by looking for the brightest star at the base of the meridian ruler, where it meets the horizon due south of the Great Pyramid. Here I followed the spotlight to find Alpha Horogulum, the brightest star in the constellation Horogulum.

I was not overwhelmed by this alignment. Horogulum is not a bright constellation and I was unable to find any particular significance for this star at the time, but the picture being created by the Great Pyramid had yet to fully reveal itself.

I continued the search for stars, this time following the spotlight to the northern Giza horizon. Here I had a surprise.

The brightest star reaching the northernmost point on the Giza horizon in 2450 BC was the star Alwaid, a brilliant and significant star representing one eye (or tooth) of the massive snaking dragon called Draco. I recalled Sir Norman Lockyer suggesting this star was another manifestation of the stellar goddess Isis.

A pattern was emerging. In 2450 BC the meridian angles of the Great Pyramid located:

a. Two stars in Orion.
b. Two stars in the Little Bear.
c. Two stars in Draco, the dragon.
d. The Cross.
e. Sirius, the brightest star in the sky.

We will return to the eyes of the dragon later, but it is worth mentioning here that the dragon is a fabulous constellation. It is truly immense and curls around the northern sky dividing the Great Bear (Plough) from the Little Bear. There is a stellar link with mythology here in the coils of the dragon, because the mythical creature creates two distinct loops. Within the first coil is the north pole of the zodiac (the ecliptic pole) and within the second coil is the entire constellation of the Little Bear, including the brilliant star Polaris. This arrangement results in the tail of the Little Bear and the tail of the dragon meeting at the tips.

There was now only one pyramid spotlight left to study in this research: the Great Pyramid vertical. Was there a brilliant star passing directly above the pyramid, synchronizing with all the other star spotlights?

I did find a brilliant star above the Great Pyramid in 2450 BC and something wholly unexpected came with the discovery of this star. There is a window in the heavens, a window that has not been opened for a very long time.

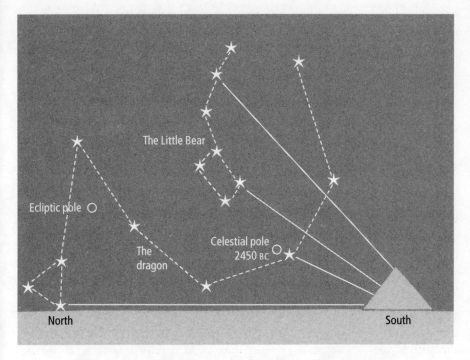

Figure 14: The dragon in relation to two north poles on the celestial sphere

STRAIGHT UP

It was only when I followed the vertical spotlight from the Great Pyramid that the complex nature of this ancient astronomy became apparent.

The celestial sphere of stars and the terrestrial sphere of the earth are a matching pair of grids, therefore to find the most brilliant star passing over the Great Pyramid in 2450 BC one simply transfers the latitude of Giza straight to the sky. Giza is at 30° north,[2] so the most brilliant star passing vertically over Giza will be on the meridian ruler marking the parallel +30° on the celestial sphere.

I followed the vertical spotlight and the most brilliant star on the thirtieth parallel in 2450 BC was Melkalanin, ranked fortieth in the league of brilliant stars.

Figure 15: Vertical spotlight to Melkalanin

In a sense I had reached the point of the Great Pyramid for the first time. I felt sure that I could have safely predicted that the vertical spotlight would locate yet another brilliant star and I was not to be disappointed. But when I came to study Melkalanin I found something more than an unusually bright star.

Melkalanin

Melkalanin is the second brightest star in the constellation of Auriga, the charioteer. This constellation is found directly above Orion in the sky; in fact Orion points to Auriga with his raised limb.

With this, the eleventh alignment, it seemed logical to conclude that all 11 angles had been designed and built with knowledge of this astronomy, and a truly remarkable achievement it is.

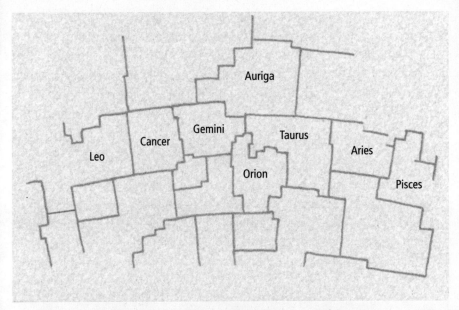

Figure 16: Modern day constellation borders around Orion

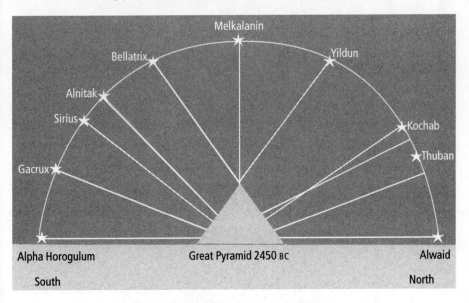

Figure 17: The full 11 alignments in 2450 BC

But I was totally unprepared for what followed.

I began to wonder if these star spotlights had any common meaning. The co-ordination of all 11 architectural angles with the sky further exposes the brilliance and remarkable facility of the Giza designers, but it did not reveal a *reason* for this astronomical work.

A NEW VIEW OF THE STARS

I bought a new star atlas published by the Institute of Physics. The atlas is the first of its kind. It provides maps of the celestial sphere printed directly from photographic negatives. (Three of these maps are reproduced in Appendix IV.) The photographic negatives provide the 'retinal image' of the brightest stars in the sky. At last with the help of these fabulous negatives I could study the night sky accurately in a book.

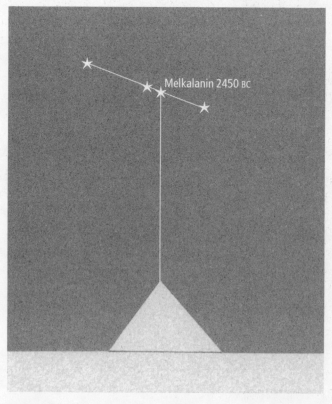

Figure 18: Four neighbouring bright stars in a line over Giza in 2450 BC

The new star atlas gave me the opportunity to consider the vertical alignment of the Great Pyramid to the star Melkalanin in more detail. Following the direction of Orion's arm, pointing over the Milky Way heading north, I found four bright stars in a perfectly straight line! These four stars are all in the constellation Auriga and the brightest of them is Melkalanin *(see Figure 18)*. (Auriga is the mythological charioteer who drives a four-horse chariot.)[3]

It is highly unusual to find four neighbouring random points in a straight line and all the more unusual when the points are some of the brightest stars in a single constellation above the raised arm of Osiris.

It seemed the Great Pyramid was pointing to Auriga, just like the Orion constellation itself. The Great Pyramid was also pointing vertically at *geometry*, at a straight line appearing vertically above Giza in 2450 BC.

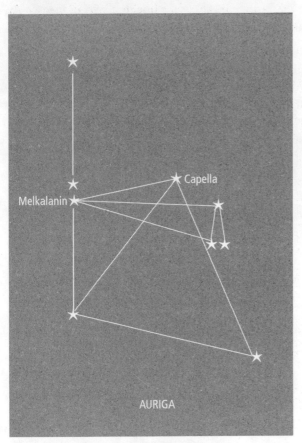

Melkalanin is a very bright star, but only the second brightest in the Auriga constellation, for Auriga includes the sixth brightest star in the heavens, Capella. Capella was the brightest star passing over Egypt in 2450 BC. These stars in Auriga (retinal image) are shown in Figure 19 and Figure 142.

Figure 19: Map of Auriga's brightest stars, creating one straight line and a series of isosceles triangles

I couldn't help noticing the three bright stars clustered beside Capella formed an isosceles triangle. When I measured the triangle in the star atlas with dividers it seemed to be exactly isosceles!

I became intrigued. Is it possible the constellation Osiris/Orion was visualized as a man pointing at geometry in the stars, and the point of the pyramid was doing the same? Wasn't the pyramid's vertical spotlight locating exactly the same stars as the outstretched limb of Osiris on the celestial sphere?

Then I finally saw the pattern. It was a great moment. I took only the three brightest stars in Auriga and joined the dots.

The three brightest stars in Auriga form an isosceles triangle!

Bearing in mind these are random points, only associated by their brilliance, it is unlikely for them to generate an isosceles triangle because an isosceles triangle always has two sides and two angles equal. Such a triangle will not generally occur if you aimlessly throw three balls into a tennis court.

Intrigued, I now looked at the other stars in Auriga. I found the fourth brightest star. To my amazement, the four brightest stars in Auriga form a cross *(see Figure 21).*

Why do these random points produce isosceles triangles? Why do Orion and the Great Pyramid point to these geometrically ordered stars?

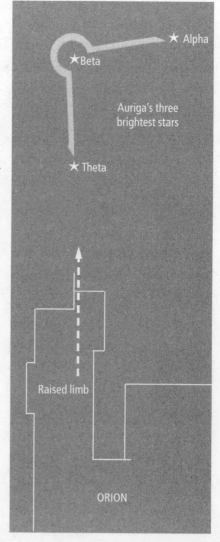

Figure 20: The Auriga triangle above Orion

26

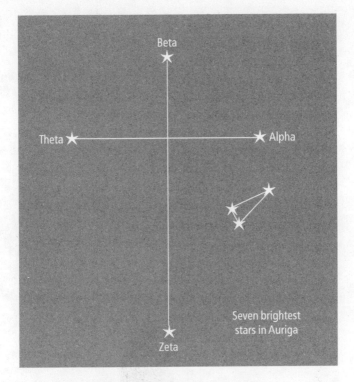

Figure 21: The four brightest stars in Auriga form a cross

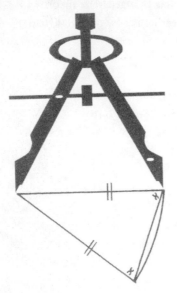

Figure 22: The nature of isosceles triangles

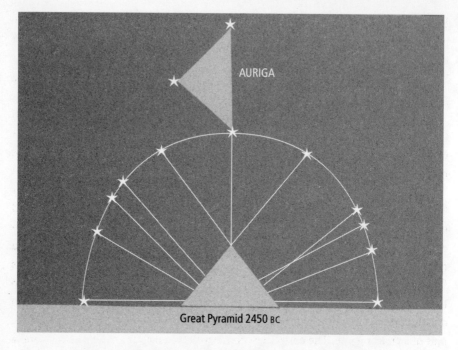

Figure 23: All the star alignments of the Great Pyramid in 2450 BC, including the vertical to an isosceles triangle

The symbolic picture has changed. The incorrect symbolic equation ('stars are pyramids') worrying me earlier is now correct. The stars *and* the pyramids are both isosceles forms.

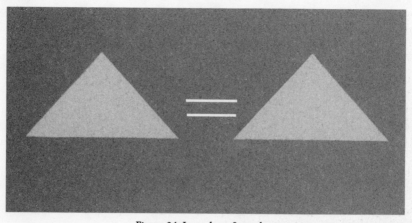

Figure 24: Isosceles = Isosceles

I had studied semiology (the study of signs), but I had never seen anything as striking as this before. The triangular star symbols on the Giza plateau clearly present the isosceles triangle as a motif and now the same motif had appeared directly over Egypt in 2450 BC. The Great Pyramid had once actually pointed directly to this geometry.

Add to this isosceles geometry a straight line of four bright stars in Auriga (with the Great Pyramid spotlighting the brightest), and you have the rudimentary parts of a language of symbols, lines and isosceles triangles. We direct each other on the roads today using the same symbolic geometry.

Signs and symbols are a complicated area of study, well beyond the limits of this book. Forms are associated in 'paradigms' which are, if you like, clusters of related parts. A paradigm can be created anywhere. For example, if you wander up a deserted street and see three tennis balls forming an isosceles triangle on the ground you may think little of it. If you continue strolling and find another three tennis balls forming another isosceles triangle it may strike you as odd. But if you continue up the street finding a third and a fourth and a fifth isosceles triangle it would be fair to conclude that the tennis balls did not fall off the back of a lorry. Perhaps they are part of a child's game. The collective geometry between all the tennis balls creates a semiological paradigm. The symbols related to Giza so far had the beginnings of such a structure.

I retraced my steps, returning one by one to the other stars spotlighted by the Great Pyramid. I knew now that I should follow the line and look for geometry in the sky.

I started with Alpha Horogulum.

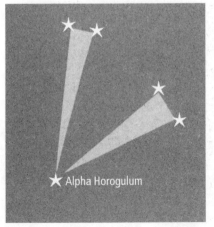

Taking the brightest stars beside Alpha Horogulum, I drew two isosceles triangles (see Figure 25).

Figure 25: Horogulum triangles and brightest stars

I moved to the northern horizon, following the spotlight once again to the dragon's eye and the brilliant star Alwaid. Could I expect a further isosceles triangle of bright neighbouring stars?

Alwaid has a partner called Eltanim. These two stars represent the two bright eyes of the dragon. Joining these stars together with the third brightest star in the head of Draco, I found:

The three brightest stars in the head of the dragon form an isosceles triangle.

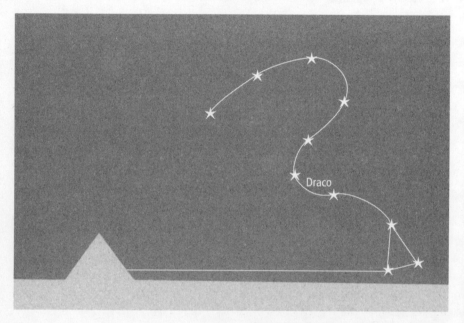

Figure 26: The brightest stars in the head of the dragon

I had discovered:

An isosceles triangle of neighbouring bright stars on the northern horizon.
An isosceles triangle of neighbouring bright stars vertically above the pyramid.
An isosceles triangle of neighbouring bright stars on the southern horizon.

Then the penny dropped.

The three stars in Orion's Belt also form an isosceles triangle.

30

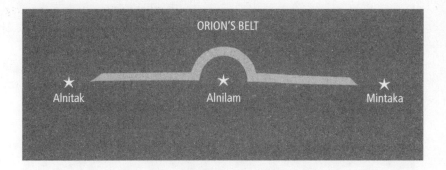

Figure 27: Orion's Belt isosceles triangle

It was a remarkable moment. Quite suddenly the complex nature of these star spotlights became apparent. This was coincidence, but it was a pre-planned coincidence. The pyramid was definitely locating bright stars grouped in isosceles triangles in 2450 BC.

Naturally I continued investigating each one of the brilliant stars spotlighted from the Great Pyramid. I needed to ascertain whether any of the other 11 spotlights had also located a cluster of three bright stars in an isosceles triangle.

The process adopted for finding the brightest stars is very simply achieved using modern computer systems. By setting a magnitude limit on the computer, one effectively lifts the veil of background stars, thus revealing the pattern created by only the very brightest stars in one area of the sky. The arrangement of these stars can then be checked in the star atlas. Imagine a dark blanket has been thrown over the sky and only the very brightest lights can penetrate it.

Using this method, I followed the next spotlight to the star Gacrux, in the little constellation Crux:

The five brightest stars in Crux form two overlapping isosceles triangles (see Figure 29).

It struck me as unusual to go looking for isosceles triangles of stars and immediately find this form once again pointed to by the Great Pyramid. Remember that in each case I am using only the very brightest stars surrounding the aligned star, with no exceptions. Thus one is bound to ask why so many groups of stars illustrate the same geometric form and, furthermore, why was the Great Pyramid pointing to them?

I moved on to look for isosceles relationships around the star Yildun, the star spotlighted in the tail of the Little Bear. Once again I was amazed by what I found:

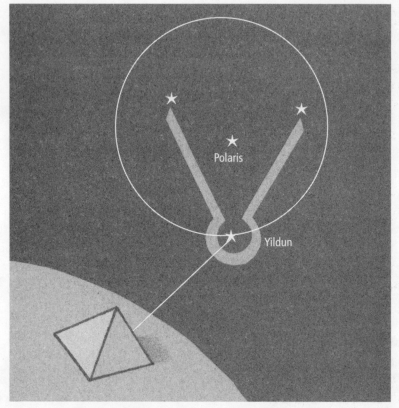

Figure 28: The three brightest stars surrounding Polaris

The three brightest stars surrounding Polaris form an isosceles triangle and Yildun is at the apex of the triangle.

Here was yet another isosceles triangle of stars and yet again one star in the isosceles triangle (Yildun) was spotlighted by the Great Pyramid in 2450 BC.

Could I expect to find this unlikely geometry yet again? I moved on to the star Thuban, the pole star of the day.

Once again the dark blanket was cast over the sky and the same motif appeared:

The first three stars to shine through the blanket beside Thuban form an arrowhead pointing at Thuban.

There is no mistaking this little triangle beside Thuban, although it is impossible to see in polluted sky. Three small distinct lights shine out against the dark background,

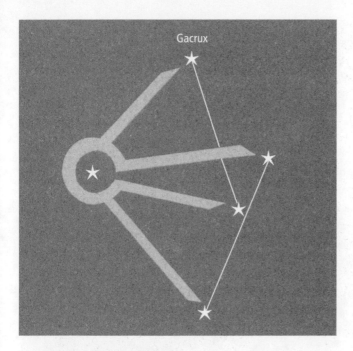

Figure 29: The brightest stars in Crux

forming a triangular pointer of three stars aimed directly at Thuban, the bright pole star of ancient Egypt.

The geometry discovered at the end of each pyramid spotlight in 2450 BC left me in no doubt that I was beginning to uncover something which nobody had come across for a long time. I could hear the message from these brilliant astronomers ringing in my ears. 'These stars are geometrically ordered,' I heard them say, but they were not whispering through some mystical cloud of ether, they were using a geometric language, a mathematically clinical language, a language of straight lines and isosceles triangles.

Figure 30: The triangle beside Thuban

Language is code and here I had found a simple code, a form of words, but not words as we know them. Yet, by repeatedly pointing to the same simple geometric form in the heavens, the Giza designers insist on our attention.

These initial discoveries were only the beginning of an unforgettable epic adventure involving more numbers than I can reasonably include in the text. More detailed study notes for all the material in this book can be found in the appendices.

Once all the alignments from the Great Pyramid in 2450 BC had been accumulated and transferred to a single image spanning 24 hours, the correspondence was truly remarkable *(see Figure 31)*.

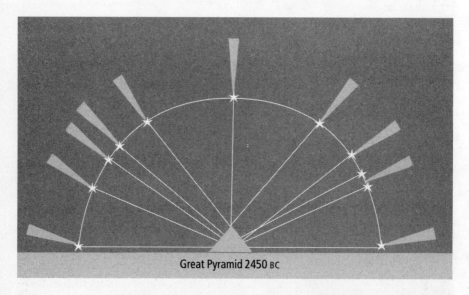

Great Pyramid 2450 BC

Figure 31: The 11 spotlights to isosceles triangles

It was only much later that I came across a hieroglyph from ancient Egypt *(see Figure 32)*. One of the earliest ever recovered, it is said to predate all the pyramids. Its meaning is still unknown.

Figure 32: The triangular glyph, *c.* 3000 BC Egypt

There does appear to be a great rift in history, a blank space in which ancient wisdom appeared, was strangely recorded and then disappeared again.

ROMANCE AND GEOMANCY

The alignments and measures I am discussing certainly suggest that ancient wisdom is not a fairy tale. Credit for these calculations rests firmly in the ancient world.

Many ancient arts and sciences have been all but lost in the course of history – alchemy, soothsaying and topomancy to name but a few. But these archaic sciences are still studied outside the mainstream and one of the strangest and most antique is geomancy.

When I started reading Nigel Pennick's book *The Ancient Science of Geomancy* (CRCS Publications, 1979) I could never have predicted where it would lead me. I was suddenly struck by a phrase reportedly used by the geomancers themselves. It was simply three words:

'Stars are mountains.'

This apparently meaningless phrase struck a chord because it so neatly expresses Robert Bauval's star correlation theory:

'Stars are pyramids.'

And we can all see 'Pyramids are mountains.'

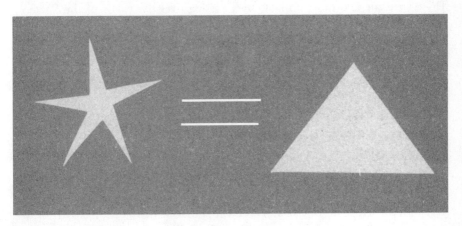

Figure 33

Indeed, the symbols of stars and mountains at Giza precisely illustrate the geomancers' strange expression. In fact the Egyptian pyramids have long been called 'the mountains of the Pharaohs' because they look like mountains.

So there are three famous man-made mountains on the Giza plateau laid out in the configuration of three famous stars. The man-made mountains at Giza are symbols of stars and the Giza designers have therefore made a symbolic record of the words of the geomancers.

STARS AND MOUNTAINS

These geomancers' words, the memorable phallus of Geb, the antique expression 'As above, so below', Bauval's star correlation theory and the 11 star alignments discussed earlier all lead to one end: they express a link between Heaven and Earth.

Could the pyramids therefore be defining a *vertical* matching of stars and mountains? Or again, are stars and mountains actually related by their positions on the respective spheres? A picture came to mind. The pyramid reaches vertically up to a brilliant star above, 'catching' the passing star. But if you reverse the image, do the stars reach down to catch the mountains? Was the Great Pyramid, in a strange manner, offering itself as a mountain, ready and in position below the consort star Melkalanin?

Extremely notional as this idea sounded, I nevertheless resolved to put it to the test. The Great Pyramid was positioned below the bright star Melkalanin. What about the other brilliant stars? To test the theory, I began with Capella, the very brightest star passing over Egypt, and with Melkalanin, its brilliant neighbour. These were the two most brilliant stars passing over the heads of the Pharaohs between 3000 BC and 2500 BC.

I was astonished by what I found as I tracked the progress of these two stars moving north over Egypt. I traced each vertical position perfectly. I watched Melkalanin approach the vertical over Giza. At the same time Capella approached the vertical over Mt Katherine.

Finally the star Melkalanin achieved a perfect vertical alignment with the Great Pyramid and *at precisely the same time in history* the star Capella reached a perfect vertical alignment with Mt Katherine, the highest point overlooking all Egypt. The matching of the two vertical star alignments, when placed in the context of precessional motion, is truly remarkable. The two verticals are matched on one particular year with a discrepancy of one arc minute, that is, one part in 21,600 parts around the horizon.

Having set out in search of a mountain and star alignment, inspired by the symbolic language at Giza, you may imagine my exuberance at discovering this near faultless duplication. The vertical location of the two brightest stars was perfectly twinned with the greatest pyramid and the greatest mountain in Egypt, but only for a few fleeting years.

And so the measure between the site of Giza and the location of Mt Katherine was established in the sky by the two brightest vertical stars in the heavens. The latitude of the two sites differs by 1.5°, and therefore the stars Melkalanin and Capella measured out precisely this distance on the celestial parallels as they passed over the two great Egyptian mountains.

The precise vertical matching of the two brilliant stars and the two mountains occurred at the very time when the pyramid shafts began to synchronize with the sky. (The parallels separating Melkalanin and Capella at this time measured 1.5° accurate to a few arc seconds. Further discussion concerning the timing and precision of this alignment is found in Appendix I.)

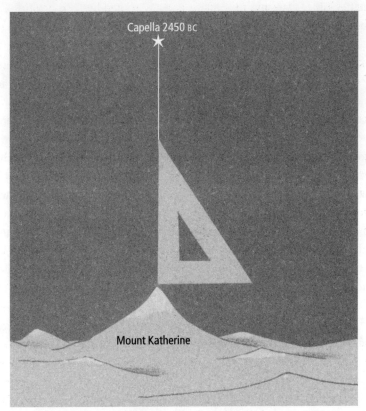

Figure 34: The vertical between Capella and Mt Katherine in 2450 BC

It struck me as extremely unlikely that I should go in search of a star to match a mountain and immediately stumble over the very summit of all the land in Egypt.

So the geomancers' apparently witless expression 'stars are mountains' had become charged with meaning. It had changed into something we can read in our own numerical language:

Capella	28°30'	=	Mt Katherine	28°30'	
Melkalanin	30°00'	=	Great Pyramid	30°00' (less one minute)	

Brightest star = highest mountain

The equation is no longer mystical, it is mathematical.

With this discovery I realized that the relationship between stars and mountains symbolized at Giza, recited by the geomancers and signified by the union of Nut and Geb appeared to be based in the real world rather than a world of fantasy, on mathematics rather than myth.

The ancient window on the heavens was beginning to open.

An Eye to the Sun

The language of geometric symbols had led me from an isosceles triangle at Giza to an isosceles triangle in the sky, and back down to another isosceles (shaped) mountain on earth.

I felt bound to investigate this relationship because *it is real*, it is an archaeological artefact. The symbols had led me to suspect a vertical alignment of star and mountain, and that is precisely what I found between the brightest star and the highest mountain. How could I ignore such astonishingly precise mathematics when the monument defining the relationship between Earth and sky is itself an extremely accurately measured man-made mountain symbolizing a star?

I had little idea what I would find next, but I realized I could now follow the same procedure with other brilliant stars. I decided to check the vertical alignment of the third star in the Auriga triangle shining above Egypt.

The third bright star in Auriga passed over the Tropic of Cancer in 2450 BC.[4]

Figure 35 shows the vertical alignment of three brilliant stars forming a massive isosceles triangle passing vertically over Egypt in 2450 BC.

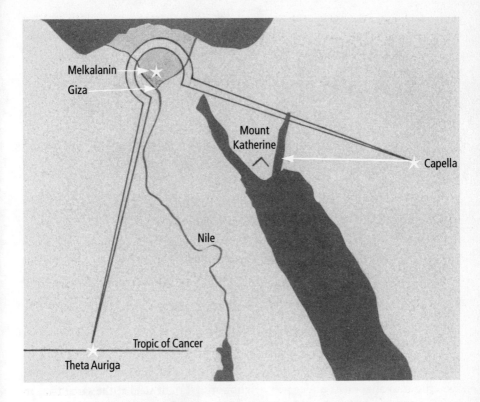

Figure 35: The three brightest stars in Auriga defining three 'high points'

The three stars form an isosceles triangle with the apex over the Great Pyramid.

The Tropic of Cancer is a parallel of latitude on the earth, but it defines the high point of the sun in the sky.

In summary, the three brilliant stars in an isosceles triangle directly above Orion/Osiris were passing over Egypt in 2450 BC synchronizing with the Earth atlas as follows:

One star passed over the highest pyramid in Egypt.
One star passed over the highest mountain in Egypt.
One star passed over the high point of the sun.

The highest mountain was directly under the brightest star. The window on the ancient heavens is a mirror, revealing a reflection, above as below, a reflection of stars and mountains.

39

✳ 3 ✳

ON TOP OF THE WORLD

*'I have wished to know how
the stars shine. I have tried to
apprehend the Pythagorean
power by which numbers
hold sway above the flux.
A little of this, but not
much, I have achieved.'*[1]

FIRST IMPRESSIONS

I was deeply impressed by the synchronicity bringing Mt Katherine and the Great Pyramid into alignment under two neighbouring bright stars at the same time in history. The vertical alignment of Capella and Mt Katherine was surely known, measured and recorded by the Giza designers. Clearly, such a hypothesis flies in the face of agreed history. Kepler could not measure the sky to an accuracy of one arc minute,[2] much less define the summit of a remote mountain with this degree of precision.

None the less it appeared the Giza designers were not only accurately defining geometry between the brightest stars in the sky, but were also drawing attention to the vertical link between Capella and their national high point Mt Katherine. As if to signal the mountain/star alignment at this time each of the pyramid spotlights located groups of neighbouring stars forming isosceles triangles. The pyramid vertical therefore suggested that the triangles in the sky are connected to the triangles on the ground.

40

DELTA MEANING TRIANGLE

Isosceles triangles are used relentlessly in the architecture on the Giza plateau. Furthermore, the same formation is repeatedly pointed to in the sky, from the Belt of Orion to the head of the dragon. But the same shape is also visible on land – the Great Pyramid itself was built at the apex of the Nile Delta,[3] which forms a massive isosceles triangle. Seen from the air, it appears as a huge green triangle surrounded by pale sandy desert where the Nile river enters the Mediterranean Sea.

Does this basic geometry spread naturally over the land of Egypt as well as the sky above? Do Nut and Geb carry the same pattern of 'geometric genes'? Are the ancient builders asking us to recognize these geometric shapes in order to convey some long-lost wisdom binding Heaven and Earth together?

Such an idea is not without precedent. The ancient Chinese art of feng shui has been described as 'a science of surveying in which symbols are used'.[4] It involves celestial and terrestrial symbols to such a degree that it has been described as 'terrestrial astrology'.

How did such complex concepts arise in antiquity?

Stepping back into Egyptian mythology we find Nut and Geb, the sky and the Earth, born together and then torn apart. They were born as mates (indeed, Figure 1 shows the phallus of Geb actually penetrating the sky), and the noted scholar of Egyptian mythology and language R. T. Rundell Clark explains,

> '...the essential event connected with Nut and Geb was their separation. The belief that Earth and sky were originally one and were rent apart is one of the basic myths of many races.'[5]

MEASURE FOR MEASURE

Very gradually I began to realize that the pyramids are actually vehicles carrying information. In many respects the Great Pyramid is like a book. The ancient designers have *written a message* in it, yet we can only read it once we are released from late twentieth-century historical dogma. In other words, we need to forget the common image of Cheops, a dumb, despotic Pharaoh,[6] commissioning such a structure for his own glorification. Once the pyramid is understood as a complex astronomical device, such an idea appears unlikely. Cheops, who 'was not religious' according to his grandson, and who 'closed the temple',[7] is hardly likely to have created the largest astronomical monument on Earth, far less have the inclination to align it 11 times with isosceles triangles of neighbouring stars precisely when Capella passes over Egypt's highest mountain.

After two years of research I had accumulated sufficient information to convince myself that the Pharaoh Cheops described by Egyptologists played but a small part in the design of the Great Pyramid (if he played any part at all). The sophisticated series of astronomical alignments show that the Egyptians were defining the sky on the meridian with far greater accuracy than the Greeks at the time of Ptolomy, nearly 3,000 years later.[8]

The reason why I have attempted to illustrate the highly sophisticated nature of the astronomical design of the Great Pyramid very early in this book is because the 11 astronomical 'spotlights' from the Great Pyramid ultimately reveal an extremely profound relationship between Earth and sky. However, if we remain irretrievably attached to the belief that no scientific sophistication could possibly have existed on Earth over 5,000 years ago, then the information that follows will make little sense.

There is now ample evidence indicating the presence of a sophisticated global understanding in prehistory. The pyramid shape, for example, is repeatedly found in ancient architecture around the world – in Africa, South America, North America and Asia, as well as the Middle East. The Sumerians, Egyptians and Olmecs built pyramid shapes. So did the Incas, the Aztecs and the Mayans. Silbury Hill in England is a stone pyramid covered with earth. Antique pyramid shapes are found at Cahokia in Illinois, USA *(see plate 8)*, and a truly massive rash of pyramids lies across the Pyramid Fields near Xi'an in China *(see plate 9)*. Isn't the pyramid an unusual shape – almost useless as a functional building, highly laborious to create and requiring stringent standards of engineering? Yet the common view of ancient history is that these disparate cultures, despite their isolation and their ignorance of each other, all became dedicated to the construction of similarly shaped, near useless, gigantic buildings. Is it rational to suggest the buildings have the same unlikely shape by chance?

Without exception these global pyramids were laboriously constructed from earth, clay bricks or solid stone and their interiors are entirely inhospitable. They were built as immutable mountains; they were built to function in the long term, to survive millennia, to provide a record. The pyramids of the world are parts of a whole, but to read their collective record requires a paradigm shift.

Until Robert Bauval made his discovery, the equation 'stars are mountains' had been sitting unrecognized on the Giza plateau for millennia. The scientific knowledge achieved in the past is manifest in dramatically clear geometry and in astronomy, but current dogma so often prevents the correct interpretation being made.

Legominisms

'A certain possibility is introduced from a realm where the impossible doesn't exist. It is something new which doesn't belong to the cause and effect of this world, and therefore changes the entire situation. The doing of this and how it is done is unseen; but, in general, it is then necessary that something should be seen, manifested, so that the particular new thing should be able to operate in the visible world among people with ordinary perceptions.'[9]

And it's a relief to know this near fantastic form of communication can be described more succinctly as follows:

'...legominism; i.e. a symbol that somehow encapsulates the meaning of what it is that is to be conveyed to the future.'[10]

But is there really anything here to be 'conveyed to the future'? Are the pyramids really symbols in an immutable language? Why should we believe such a thing?

Love and the Stars

There is almost boundless evidence in the written words, in the murals and in the architecture of ancient Egypt showing how the ancient Egyptians loved the sky with great passion. In my opinion this was a very real love, a very religious love and a profoundly moving love. It literally created the power to move mountains in a manner never witnessed before or since.

The love of a god is perhaps the greatest love of all. Those who feel this love build great churches and cathedrals, great mosques and temples, often with huge domes or spires. This is exactly what happened in early Egypt. The pure love of the star gods was very potent in those days.

Each large ancient Egyptian pyramid has a temple at the base; a pyramid is a religious and stellar monument at one and the same time. At Giza the god Osiris in Heaven is immortalized in the pattern of the three pyramids on Earth. This symbolism demonstrates the love of Earth and sky united. Nut and Geb are to-gether forever. Osiris is immutably recreated on the Earth. Osiris is wanted forever, for eternity.

But this love was not based on whimsy. The ancients were aware of something. Their monuments have purpose, they communicate an ancient faith and they use geometry as a means of expression.

43

In order to define the precise time in history when a single star passes exactly over a mountain summit a very detailed understanding of both the celestial and terrestrial spheres is required. So, in allowing myself to believe that the alignment of Capella over Mt Katherine was a known event synchronized with the arrival of Melkalanin over Giza, I had to attribute the Giza designers with knowledge akin to our own. This paradigm shift is the essential ingredient in our study, but it is so difficult to procure from present day culture. Perhaps I have dwelt too long on this single issue, but I am trying to emphasize that some vital aspect of our ancient history is missing. There is empirical scientific evidence that our ancestors understood the globe of stars and the globe of the Earth in uncanny detail. But the evidence is not written down ... it is older than writing. The communication is geometric and it is highly sophisticated. It requires our own levels of sophistication to understand it – and this is at the heart of the challenge.

LOOKING FOR CLUES

The first place to investigate the formal use of ancient geometry on Earth is perhaps the Giza plateau itself. Here at Giza there are three vast pyramids that together (in plan view) form an isosceles triangle. But a single natural high point overlooks the pyramids. *The relationship between the natural high point and the pyramids is strictly geometric, forming an equilateral triangle (see Figure 36).* So the three man-made high points are integrated *by geometry* into the local topography.

The use of high points appears to be significant:

a. The stars are high points.
b. The local peak is a high point.
c. The pyramids are high points.

The isosceles and equilateral geometry linking all these high points creates a literal pun realized in physical form. Many historians attest to the fact that this form of punning was well used by the ancients in literature.

But Giza is located at the apex of a vast river delta (the Greek Triangle), so once again the isosceles symbolism spreads naturally from the equilateral triangle on the Giza plateau over the surrounding land.

Looking at the Nile Delta, I began to wonder if the 'high point' was symbolized by more than just a mountain or pyramid peak. The positioning of the Great Pyramid at the apex of the Nile Delta suggested the terrestrial geometry employed by

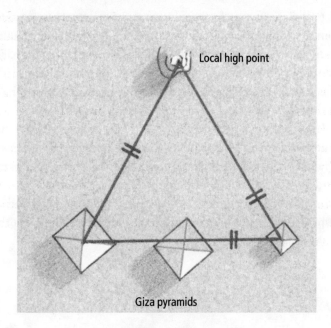

Figure 36: Giza equilateral triangle

the Giza designers extended to other forms of point. I became drawn into a closer study of the topography of Egypt in general.

A GEOMETRIC EARTH

Giza is situated on the thirtieth parallel[11] north of the equator. In order to study the topography in some detail I used the 1:1,000,000 Operational Navigation Chart of the area.[12] I followed the thirtieth parallel from Giza across the chart and shortly found myself at the northernmost fingertip of the Red Sea.

Visualized as a linear symbol the Red Sea is by far the largest and most singular straight pointer of water on the planet Earth, and it is pointing directly towards the Nile Delta, terminating on the thirtieth parallel. So the fingertip (or high point) of the Red Sea just reaches up to the latitude of the Giza pyramids.

Giza latitude	29°59'
Fingertip latitude	29°59'

One might pass this off as a chance event, but there is another geometric point. Moving from the horizontal to the vertical on the chart, the meridian due south of the Red Sea fingertip leads directly to the Valley of the Kings *(see Figure 37)*.

Giza and the Valley of the Kings are linked by a right-angled triangle. The right angle itself is found at the 'high point', i.e. the northern extreme of the extended fingertip of the Red Sea.

Terrestrial geometry may look strange, but this is, none the less, a right angle aligned to the meridian, linking Egypt's two most famous ancient sites.

I took a pair of dividers and placed one point on Mt Katherine, the highest point in Egypt, and the other point on Giza. Swinging the point from Giza down along the Nile, I landed on the radical kink in the river where the kings and queens of ancient Egypt were buried. There is an isosceles relationship between these three points.

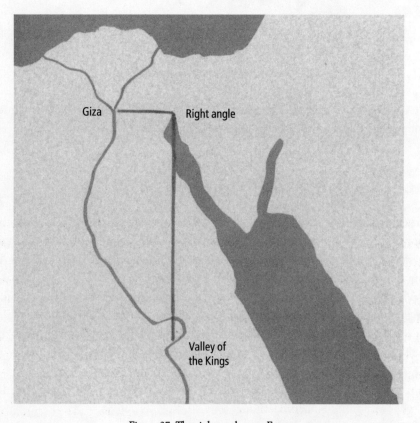

Figure 37: The right angle over Egypt

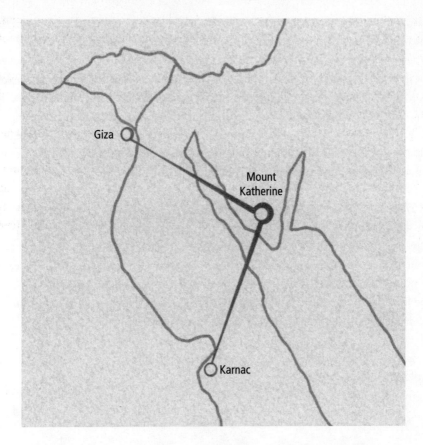

Figure 38: The isosceles relationship between geographic features in Egypt

I was beginning to develop a theory that the isosceles pattern of stars in the sky should be translated on the Earth below in order to discover the heavenly mirror of myth: as above, so below.

In order to test this theory further, I studied the relief on the Sinai peninsula. The peninsula itself strongly resembles an isosceles triangle pointing due south, and in the apex of the triangle Mt Katherine overlooks the entire area of Egypt and all the land from Mecca to Jerusalem and beyond. Thus the highest point in all Egyptian topography is itself located on a geographic point, and exactly the same sentiment is beautifully expressed by the Giza pyramids located on the point of the Nile Delta.

My research was now directing me to an inevitable conclusion. The sum total of isosceles shapes accumulated around Giza was part of a larger manifestation. The pyramid was pointing at isosceles triangles in the sky and replicating the pattern on

Earth *because the pattern is found on the Earth as well as in the sky*. So I must now look for the *replica* of the isosceles triangle of stars and find it on the ground.

Having isolated Mt Katherine, the highest point on the Sinai peninsula, I looked for the next highest massif in the area. I measured out an imaginary circular blanket 200 miles in diameter. I centred the blanket over Mt Katherine and dropped it. Opposite Mt Katherine, across the Gulf of Aqaba, there is a second great mountain range. This was the next range to appear on the blanket. The magic blanket revealed the two highest points in the range. I joined these two points with Mt Katherine (about 80 miles away) and a moment of truth had arrived.

These three high points form an isosceles triangle.

It is easy to prove that three small points (each the size of a full stop) thrown at random onto a sheet of paper a yard square are highly unlikely to generate an isosceles triangle. The odds are really terribly small when the scales are considered. None the less, the crosses marking the three high points on the Operational Navigation Chart define the three corners of an isosceles triangle very precisely.

I was astonished by this isosceles geometry between mountains even though I was looking for it.

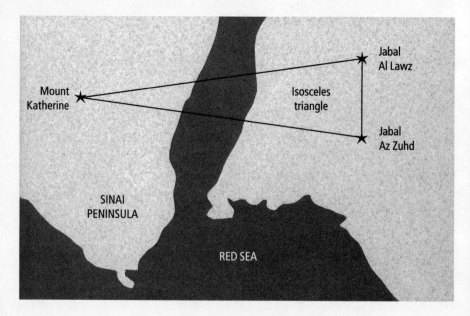

Figure 39: The isosceles apex at Mt Katherine

As you may witness, up in the sky beside Capella are three bright stars forming a perfect isosceles triangle. I was looking for the same motif beneath these stars. The triangle above Mt Katherine was therefore mirrored by a triangle of mountains I had discovered on the ground.

If you throw three tennis balls onto a tennis court, the chances are stacked against them coming to rest in an isosceles triangle. But if you play long enough the isosceles triangle will eventually occur. However, the geometric coincidence around Mt Katherine is not simply an isosceles triangle connecting three high points.

Throwing tennis balls onto a tennis court once again, how long would it take to generate an isosceles triangle in which two of the balls in the triangle run parallel with a single white line marked on the court? To achieve a random isosceles triangle is difficult, but to align that triangle with a single line on the tennis court is extremely unlikely. So the following observation struck me as quite startling:

The two mountains creating an isosceles triangle with Mt Katherine are resting on precisely the same meridian on earth.

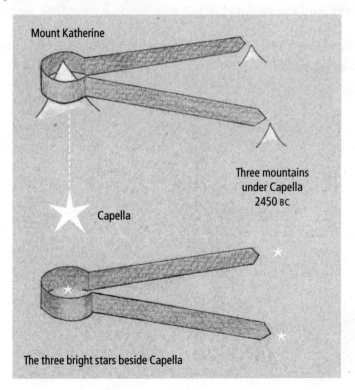

Figure 40: The duplicate symbolism between stars and mountains

49

In this manner the three mountain peaks generate an arrow shape pointing very precisely along the Earth parallel (an alignment also found with the Sphinx and all the pyramids at Giza).

The isosceles triangle formed between the three natural mountains and the meridian alignment of the triangle they form is so very accurate on the navigation chart that I could find no fault at all in the geometry on this scale.

So, although the isosceles triangle of predominant mountains is real, and perfectly natural, it is also very precisely geometric and aligned on the Earth's grid according to the charts we fly by.

High points, just like all random points, should not group together in this manner repeatedly. By grouping the pyramids in an isosceles triangle at Giza, the monuments to Osiris directly reflect (and draw attention to) the unusual isosceles nature of the peaks neighbouring Mt Katherine. In other words, travelling from Giza to the star Melkalanin and across to the neighbouring star Capella and on down to Mt Katherine was a simple linear journey interrupted by right angles. Arriving at Mt Katherine we find three neighbouring points forming an isosceles triangle perfectly aligned to the Earth's meridian. In turn, at Giza, there are three pyramids aligned to the Earth's meridian forming an isosceles triangle between them (and a further equilateral triangle with the local high point). Isn't this akin to a simple form of geometric proof?

LAND LANGUAGE

Imagine three random brilliant stars outshining all the stars around them.

And imagine three random massifs, grander and taller than any others around them.

Now imagine the odds of the three stars and the three mountains creating isosceles triangles one above the other.

The pyramid designers drew attention to these anomalous triangles by pointing at them with straight lines, thereby providing us with a view of the sky and the Earth not commonly held today. But the geometry is very real, and our own maps and photographs attest to it. The fact is that the brightest three stars in Auriga do form an isosceles triangle *(see Appendix IV)*, and the highest points on the highest massifs overlooking all Sinai and Egypt also form isosceles triangles *(see ONC H–5)*.

Because the odds of three neighbouring random points falling into this shape are low, and because the odds of that triangle aligning precisely to the meridian[13] are literally thousands to one, the question raised by these alignments is really whether the Earth and the sky have the same design. Or again, are the mountains and the stars bound together in a pattern with one image reflecting the other?

If such a pattern does exist, the pyramid builders could illustrate it to anyone following a line into the sky. By following the line and then returning vertically to Earth, the geometry of mountains reveals a mirror image of the geometry of stars.

Terrestrial and celestial geometry may seem strange, but are strangely real, as our own highly accurate charts verify at Sinai.

MT NEZZI

I noticed one other point at this stage in the research and this becomes increasingly important later.

Mt Nezzi, a great isolated peak, overlooks the Nile Valley for hundreds of miles in both directions. It is the singular peak overlooking all the antiquities of Karnac, the Valley of the Kings, the Valley of the Queens and the immense span of history interred across this ancient land.

I realized that Mt Nezzi is by far the highest point overlooking the pronounced kink in the Nile river where these antiquities are located. In turn, as if in mirror image, the Great Pyramid is the high point overlooking the Nile Delta, and in mirror image again Mt Katherine overlooks the triangular point of the Sinai peninsula. The relationship between these areas is again isosceles *(see Figure 41)*.

I have placed a question mark on the illustration. At Giza and also at Mt Katherine the high points can be joined together to create isosceles triangles, as we have seen. The question mark is asking whether the same isosceles geometry also exists at Mt Nezzi. By strange coincidence it does.

To define the highest points around Mt Nezzi I used the imaginary blanket once again. I dropped it over Mt Nezzi and the surrounding area. As the blanket descended, three high points were the first to appear beside Mt Nezzi:

The three highest points neighbouring Mt Nezzi form an isosceles triangle.

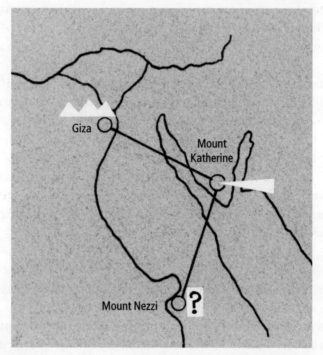

Figure 41

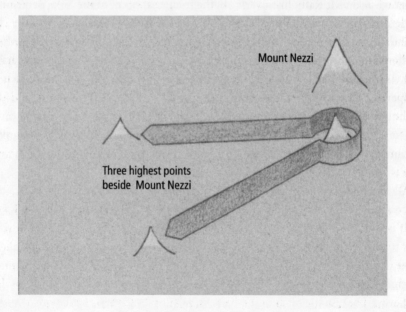

Figure 42: The isosceles triangle at Mt Nezzi

A skilled technician could not define an isosceles triangle more precisely than it appears on the 1:1,000,000 Operational Navigation Chart. The three points beside Mt Nezzi on the chart are precisely isosceles.

I was not familiar with the concept of terrestrial geometry before I began this research and I found the whole idea very unusual. There is a principle underlying all research of this kind in which the odds of chance are used as a yardstick, a form of measure. Geomancers were well known for their habit of studying the pattern of random points. They threw pebbles onto the ground and 'read' the formation of stones. Where and how did this odd habit develop? I have spent some time throwing three pebbles onto the ground myself and have produced a few isosceles triangles, but it becomes clear that isosceles triangles between neighbouring random points are unusual – or at least they should be.

MOVING EARTH

I have, in some sense, now reached the beginning of the story I am telling. I had managed to accept something that many students of the Great Pyramid have accepted before me: I had come to understand the Giza pyramids were originally designed by highly sophisticated architect-astronomers. These people remain unidentified in our conventional historical chronology and they appear to predate ancient Egypt as we currently understand it. I had learned to believe the precise mathematics repeatedly demonstrated by the Giza designers were a clear indication of their intellect. As Plato said, 'The ancients were wiser than us.' And with this new perspective I began to wonder even more about the pyramid's purpose and the facility of these architects to communicate through time.

The 11 pyramid spotlights pinpointing celestial triangles in 2450 BC were synchronized with the mountain alignment under Capella but *only at one time in history*. This is another crucial technical point.

All the alignments of the pyramid spotlights only took place owing to the process called 'precession'. Although a line on the Earth may be fixed, the Earth itself is subject to gyrate in space, causing the direction of the line to alter in relation to the stars over very long periods of time. Consequently every single alignment to a stellar triangle I have discussed so far no longer exists. The moment of synchronization has long since passed, and Capella no longer passes over Mt Katherine, because the pitch of the Earth in relation to the stars has altered.

Precession

There is considerable evidence suggesting the precession of the Earth's axis can be seen as a great hinge upon which the religions and mythologies of the ancient world hung. Precession causes the figures of the gods in the sky to rise and fall as if they were travelling on boats, but the waves in heaven last for thousands of years.

The changing view of the stars occurs because the Earth is rotating on two axes simultaneously. It rotates around one axis every day, but it rotates very slowly around a second axis about every 25,800 years. The precessional motion of the Earth around the second axis passes unnoticed in a single lifetime but dramatically affects the view of the heavens from the Earth over long periods of time.

We need to understand precessional motion in order to understand the full complexity of the Giza designers' achievement. If you were to go to the north pole with

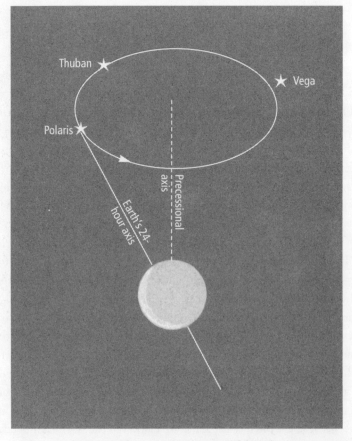

Figure 43: The precessional motion of the pole

a mirror and place it on some level ice, the mirror would reflect the image at the celestial pole in the sky directly above.

If you were to then return home and the mirror image were miraculously relayed to you each time you looked in a mirror at home, then a single bright star would always appear very near the centre of your mirror. This is Polaris, our current pole star. Polaris is by far the brightest star ever to appear centrally in this mirror, but it has not always been there.

If your magic mirror were to remain fixed in the polar ice, reflecting the celestial pole indefinitely, Polaris would be seen to gradually move out of the mirror. It would not move back into the centre of your mirror until one full precessional cycle had passed.

So the gradual (but constant) precessional motion of the Earth's axis in space affects the view of the sky above the pole. If extended into space, the principal axis appears to roll around the star field in a slow circle.

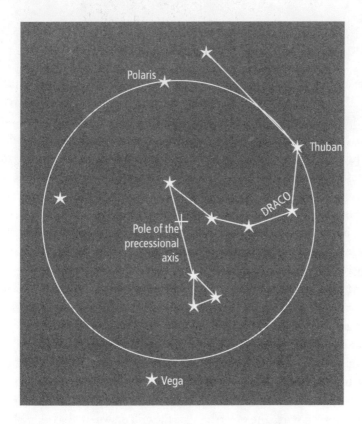

Figure 44

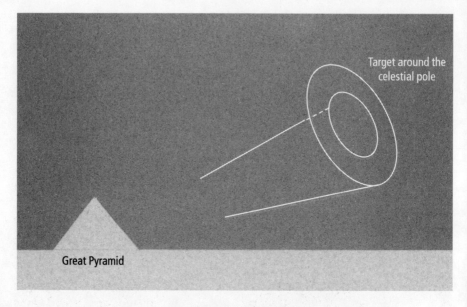

Figure 45: The polar target

There are very few brilliant stars like Thuban appearing above the Earth's pole. In fact, Thuban and Polaris are the two brightest stars ever to appear so near the centre of the mirror during the entire precessional cycle.

Clearly the pole was an important focal point for the ancient Egyptians. Two shafts from the Great Pyramid act as spotlights directed towards it. As the Earth turns these two pointers create a target around the celestial pole *(see Figure 45)*.

It is important to realize that stars have remained in the same pattern since 2450 BC,[14] but because of precession, the *location* of the pattern has gradually moved on the celestial grid. In other words, the celestial grid lines are not fixed against the starry background. They are directly connected to the Earth sphere, continually mirroring the lines of longitude and latitude on the Earth. The precessional motion of the Earth therefore carries the grid lines on the celestial sphere across the fixed star background.

Because this is such an important factor in the discoveries that follow, I will describe precession in a little more detail. The precessional motion of the celestial grid can be easily simulated outdoors using a wire grid. When the Orion constellation is passing across your meridian you can hold a wire grid at arm's length against these seven bright stars. The wires simulate the grid drawn on the celestial sphere by astronomers. The vertical wires represent the meridians of longitude on the celestial

 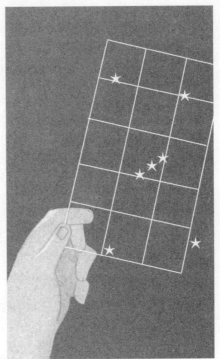

Figure 46

sphere and the horizontal wires represent the parallels of latitude. If you extend all the vertical lines upwards, they are pulled together, gradually converging until they meet at a single point. This is the celestial pole, directly above the Earth's north pole.

In order to simulate precessional motion the wire grid is gradually tilted whilst moving it up, then tilted the other way whilst moving it down again (47° separate the top and the bottom of the cycle).

Star Epochs

To take precession into account, astronomers completely redraw their star charts every 50 years or so. This is why star charts are referred to by their date, i.e. 'stellar epoch 2450 BC' or 'stellar epoch 2400 BC', etc.

The position of every single star is thus altered, not in space, but in relation to the surface of the gyrating Earth. The celestial lines of longitude and latitude[15] move across the face of the stars like the hands of a very slow clock.

So the grid lines are in perpetual long-term motion in the sky, *yet around 2450 BC the Great Pyramid co-ordinated all at once with the bright stars by defining their parallels at that single time.*

When this precessional point is grasped the unlikely nature of an accident co-ordinating the Great Pyramid's spotlights with a fine mix of the brightest stars in the sky during one epoch is more clearly recognized.

And now, none of the stars pointed to by the Great Pyramid in 2450 BC are related in the same manner on the celestial grid. Their previous alignments over the Earth are but a distant memory. The Earth has moved and the sky grid has changed.

So the Great Pyramid provides an architectural record of the mirror between star and mountain in one specific stellar epoch. To make such a record in architecture is a great wonder.

And then I looked again through the ancient window to the heavens and the light from Polaris dawned on me.

Polaris is the brightest star ever to appear in the centre of the Great Pyramid target.

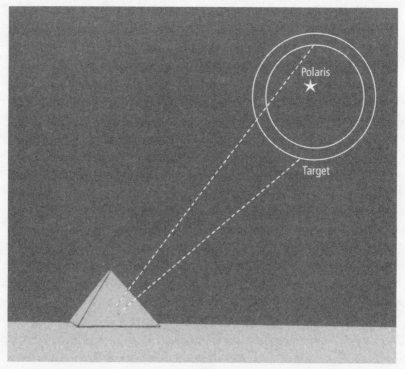

Figure 47: Polaris is now on the bull's eye of the Great Pyramid target

✳ 4 ✳

HEAVEN ON EARTH

*'For how can one catch
time on the wing?'* [1]

The precessional movement of the celestial pole creates an apparent wave motion in the sky. This motion can be speeded up on a computer and when the sky is mobilized in this manner the carousel of zodiac animals comes to life, with the mythical creatures appearing to scurry up and down as if they were climbing and descending ladders. This effect also causes the precession of the sun at the equinoxes, which move around the zodiac, a cycle commonly known as 'the precession of the equinoxes'.

At present on the day of the spring equinox the sun appears against the background of Pisces stars, but the equinoctial point is moving gradually into the constellation Aquarius. The sun at the solstices is always 90° from the sun at the equinoxes, consequently the precession of the equinoxes could as easily be referred to as 'the precession of the solstices'.

MOVING THE SUN

I set the computer to speed up through time and watched Thuban move away from the pole in 2450 BC. At the same time the solstice sun moved away from the forepaw of the lion, Leo. The sky grid continued to move and after thousands of years the celestial pole could be seen approaching the star Polaris. But I could not help noticing the movement of Orion and the solstice sun together in this sequence.

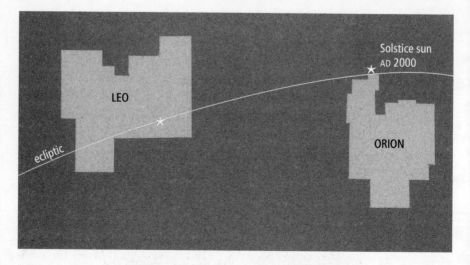

Figure 48: The travel of the solstice sun to Orion

Owing to precession the location of the solstice sun shifts from left to right, moving about one degree every 72 years. Today, the solstice sun has just reached the uppermost point on the Orion limb, at the junction between Gemini and Taurus, having precessed some 60° along the ecliptic from Leo in 2450 BC *(see Figure 48)*. (These geometric twentieth-century constellation boundaries are based upon the more fluid earlier definitions of the antique constellations.)

Here I noticed something that proved to be of immense importance:

The first stars in the Orion constellation have just reached the top of the meridian ladder.
The uppermost tip of Orion's raised limb has therefore just reached the 'high point' on its
precessional cycle.

The entire constellation of Orion stars will pass through their precessional high point (or culmination) in the coming millennium.

ORION, OSIRIS: MYTH AND REALITY

The origin of the name Orion 'is said to be rooted in the Akkadian Uru-anna, the Light of Heaven, originally applied to the sun'.[2]

For the Egyptians, Osiris was not only envisaged as Sahu[3] in the Orion constellation, but was also sometimes the corn god stuffed with seeds (said to be the first

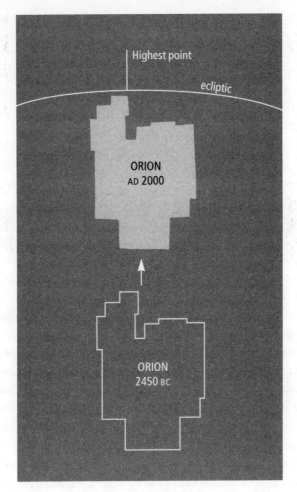

Figure 49: The top of the ladder, AD 2000

'corn dolly'). On other occasions he was enmeshed in bandages (said to be the first mummy) and at other times he sat with a crown on his head and the scales of justice before him (said to be the first judge). In some more explicit ancient stone statues he is seen with an erect phallus (said to be many things, most notably a symbolic progenitor).

But the most enduring image of Osiris is found in the Orion constellation. Both the Greek images of Orion and the Egyptian of Osiris show the constellation as a man with a belt at his waist, two bright shoulders and two bright knees, shins or feet, depending on the image you choose. But there is a further consistent feature in this body of stars and it glitters on to this day.

The Anatomy of Osiris

The dagger of Orion is well known – a brilliant line of glittering jewels hanging down between the legs of the giant. There are many bright points in the dagger, all resting on a straight line. These points merge together into three distinct lights, appearing equidistant and in alignment. With a good sky a fourth point of light is added to the top of the dagger. By 'top' I mean extreme north, and here is the nub of the matter:

The dagger of Orion is now aligned on the celestial meridian –and thereby over the Earth's meridian – for the first time in recorded history.

I considered this alignment. To begin with, it is odd to find so many points of light clustered like little eggs stuck on a single invisible line in the sky, but really unlikely to find this line pointing straight up the meridian to the brightest star ever to appear over the pole. Not only this, but the event coincides with the arrival of the first Orion stars at their highest point, and the pole star reaching its highest point, and the highest point of the sun reaching the raised limb of Orion.

A judgement about these coincidences became possible later, but first I noticed that the Egyptian god Osiris doesn't actually wear a dagger. I was drawn to wonder what this straight line of stars between the legs of Osiris might symbolize in the liberal and symbolically attuned minds of the ancient Egyptians.

The brilliant red jewel at the centre of Orion's dagger is called the Orion nebula. This 'sky where blood is sprayed'[4] is referred to by modern astronomers as 'the birthplace of stars',[5] or 'the fish's mouth'.[6] I couldn't help but wonder about this modern classification, because the Pharaohs believed themselves to be the direct descendants of Osiris, and *The Book of the Dead* is very concerned with the 'seed of Osiris'.

All this led me to wonder if the dagger of Orion could be readily considered as a phallus. If so, its alignment on the meridian today is the first erection Osiris has had for over 10,000 years! Hardly the behaviour of a sex god.

The phallic line of stars is now bolt upright, following the meridian of the Earth. However, the phallic image is perhaps more feminine than masculine, or both, because the 'birthplace' is centrally placed on the line.

I saw a connection here, because after death the Pharaohs travelled to Osiris with hopes of being reborn as a star. Could there also be a further connection with the arrival of the solstice sun on the raised limb of Orion and the arrival of Polaris over the pole?

The erection of stars in Orion also led me back to the straight line of four stars in Auriga discussed earlier. Where is this straight line today?

The straight line of four bright stars in Auriga now rests perfectly over the meridian of the Earth for the first time in recorded history, directly above the summer solstice sun in AD 2000.

These four stars are now defined in *The Guinness Book of Astronomy* as follows:

Beta Auriga 5.59 (RA)
Theta Auriga 5.59
Delta Auriga 5.59
Pi Auriga 5.59.

These four stars in Auriga are really perfectly aligned above the centre of the summer solstice sun, just one minute before the current summer solstice.[7] During the next few years precession will carry the celestial grid across them and the line of four will then shift fractionally on the grid to 6.00 RA (90°). In fact this alignment of the stars in Auriga occurs in the first ten years of the new millennium and precisely as the phallus of Osiris stands erect.

An incredible coincidence has occurred. When the sun reaches the summer solstice in stellar epoch AD 2000 it appears on the raised limb of Osiris. The phallus of Osiris is erect and the four bright stars in Auriga (directly above Orion) fall into perfect alignment with the solstice sun. The line of Auriga stars now also points up the meridian to the brightest pole star in history *(see Figure 50)*. If the ancients were interested in celestial geometry, as the evidence suggests, the night sky today provides a fabulous example of it.

The ancients may well have foreseen this pattern. For not only were both Auriga and Orion spotlighted by the Great Pyramid under the last bright pole star, but the brightest star of the four in Auriga appeared vertically over the Nile Delta apex in 2450 BC. In other words, the ancient Egyptians drew attention to this remarkable line in Auriga over 4,500 years ago, although only now do these strangely regimented four stars fall into perfect alignment with the Earth's grid.

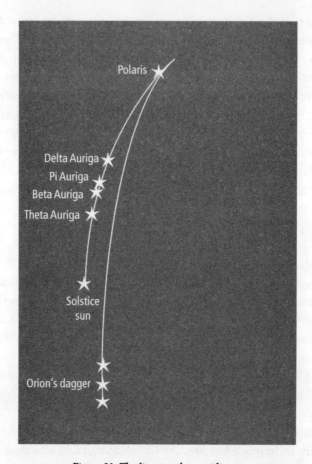

Figure 50: The lines on the meridians

The Son of Osiris

In trying to fathom what the erect phallus of a god might portend, I investigated the ancient Egyptian myth of Osiris.

Osiris suffered many misfortunes, not least the loss of his penis. This was swallowed by a Nile perch, or some say carp, in any event Osiris was unable to produce seed, yet he did have a son with his wife Isis. The boy was conceived miraculously *after Osiris himself had died.* This son was deified and called Horus. He was a sun god.

Horus takes many forms, but he is regularly depicted with a falcon's head. One eye of the falcon represents the sun and the other the moon. This suggests that the ancient Egyptians noticed these two 'eyes in the sky' are the same size. It is certainly a coincidence to find two spheres apparently randomly flying around, but when viewed from a third random point appearing to be the same size. A freak of perspective, but none the less a freak on Earth. The fact that the moon never turns its other face to us may also have struck the ancient astronomers as strange, indeed it is strange that the rotation and revolution of the moon take the same time.

All the Pharaohs were of the line of Horus, thus they all descended directly from the heavenly father Osiris. There can be little doubt that the astronomically minded descendants of Osiris would therefore scrutinize his stellar anatomy very closely.

One thing they may have noticed is the three points of light most easily seen in the phallus of Osiris appear equidistant and in alignment; their relationship appears isosceles.

The Point of the Belt

Above the phallus/dagger, Orion's three Belt stars generate another isosceles triangle *(see Figure 27)*, but the line of three stars is very nearly straight, so the Belt itself takes the form of the brightest stellar pointer in the sky. Watching the precessional motion of Orion it becomes clear that his Belt provides a useful measure of the progress of time on the changing celestial sphere.

For the first time in recorded history, the Belt of Orion has now arrived at the celestial equator.

So now we have Orion reaching the high point on the celestial ladder, at the same time as Polaris (with which Orion is therefore linked), and just as Polaris reaches its culmination near 90°,[8] Orion's Belt arrives at its culmination, near 0° on the celestial equator (vertically above the Earth's equator). Looking for further geometry on the celestial sphere today, the eye of the giant Orion (the star Heka) now rests at +10°, the lower foot (the star Saiph) at −10° and the star Mintaka, at the tip of the Belt, points to 0°. These figures are rounded, but they show that the entire figure of Orion can be seen balanced at the Belt across the celestial equator in AD 2000. This balance has not occurred for about 25,000 years.

THE SOLSTICE SUN

The overall image achieved by speeding up precessional motion bears close relation to an animated film. The film I had been watching showed a clear correspondence between the rise of Polaris and the rise of Orion, but the lead role was played by the sun.

The solstice sun appears to run along the ecliptic just in time to perch on the raised limb of Orion whilst Polaris just reaches its seat over the Earth's pole, and Orion's phallus becomes erect, and the Belt reaches 0°, and the four bright stars in Auriga align to the summer solstice sun. The stars are strange tonight.

But perhaps the most intriguing aspect of this current image of the solstice sun perched on the raised limb of Orion is yet to be seen.

In AD 2000 the solstice sun, perched on the limb of Orion, crosses the galactic equator.

The galactic equator is the central marker for the Milky Way. This is the great mythological river dividing the heavens. The solstice sun is currently crossing 0° on the galactic sphere, an event which occurs only twice in the precessional cycle.

Although the introduction of a second astronomical grided sphere at this point might seem excessive, I believe it is important to put this concurrence of Orion, the ecliptic, the celestial equator and the galactic equator into a historical perspective.

The raised limb of Orion just reaches the galactic equator and across the Milky Way 'river' are four bright stars in a bolt straight line. One wonders whether this has any bearing on the recognition of Osiris as the god of the underworld, because he is forever trapped below the galactic equator (indeed, Osiris complained to his progenitor Atum about this plight). If these images from the past are used to create a picture today, Osiris is now carrying the solstice sun across the Milky Way, below the galactic equator, for the first time in 25,830 years.

To recap, the view of Orion today is entirely unique in precessional history. The figure of a great ancient god stands with an erect line of stars between his legs. His raised limb reaches up, colliding with the sun at the solstice whilst it transits the galactic equator and his Belt just reaches up to 0° on the celestial equator.

In the Belt the most northerly star is called Mintaka. The three figures below, taken from the *Grey Stel Star Atlas*, illustrate its close proximity to the celestial equator over the coming millennium:

Mintaka AD 2000	0.3° below the celestial equator.
Mintaka AD 2450	0.1° below the celestial equator.
Mintaka AD 2800	0.2° below the celestial equator.

Compared with:

Mintaka AD 15000	47° below the celestial equator.

Mintaka is now, to all intents and purposes, not moving on the meridian for about 1,000 years. It actually reaches the top of the precessional ladder near the middle of the next millennium, but the movement amounts to just a third of a degree between AD 2000 to AD 3000.

If you imagine these events as the mobilization of ancient gods, the relevance of this particular time in the precessional cycle may be intuited from mythology, not only the ancient Egyptian but also the Greek, because both are based on the celestial sphere and both appear to be rooted in the precessional motion of that sphere. For example, in Greek mythology Orion regained his sight by looking at the sun Helios, who returned it to him, then he died from the sting of the scorpion.

The great giant Orion has now raised his club to its greatest height in all history and consequently that club is now occulted by the summer solstice sun for the first time in over 25,000 years.

In the ancient Greek myth, Orion is killed because he represents a threat to animal welfare and future well-being on Earth. He is a bragger, he can't stop killing animals and boasting of his prowess on Earth. He is blinded, but regains his sight by observing the sun.

In Egyptian mythology, the celestial picture today is one in which the god Osiris, obscured by the glare of the solstice sun, goes unseen, carrying his divine son Horus across the great celestial divide and into the underworld. Images not unlike these are described in The Book of the Dead.

So, in the present sky, Osiris, god of the underworld, is joined by his son Horus, or Ra Herakty (the sun), on the day the sun reaches its highest point, whilst simultaneously crossing the galactic equator.

This concurrence is a remarkable astronomical event, but more remarkable still if you worship Orion, the sun and the pole star (and build monuments pointing at them). For the ancients, the significance of all the geometric events occurring on the celestial sphere in the period AD 2000–2100 would probably outshine everything else in precessional history, like a thousand Christmases rolled into one.

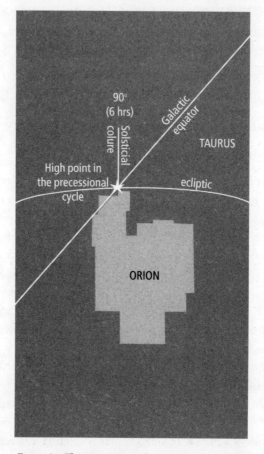

Figure 51: The concurrence above Orion in AD 2000

First and Last

The solstice sun will not cross the galactic equator again for another 12,900 years. This solar/galactic event last occurred at a 'mythical' point in human history called 'Zep Tepi', 'the First Time of Orion'. The First Time occurred when Orion/Osiris was at his lowest point on the Giza meridian. He is now at his height.[9]

Strangely, murals from ancient Egypt reflect this view of our own sky today. The point I have been trying to emphasize here is most clearly driven home by the ancient Egyptians themselves.

Figure 52: The figure controlling the passage of the sun is Horus. See how the sun takes a dramatic leap whilst passing over the Orion figure (Sahu).

Figure 52 shows the central portion of a famous ceiling mural from the temple of Seti I (1295–1186 BC). This celestial image is repeated elsewhere in Egyptian murals and it is well understood that the artwork does not represent the sky at the time it was completed.[10]

The picture shows a man with his raised arm creating a violent bend in a line passing above him. The line itself is the ecliptic – it defines the passage of the sun through the sky. Ra Herakty holds the rein of the sun and we can follow the passage of the sun over the raised limb of the man.

But something unnatural happens to the sun. The line of passage is radically changed by a great loop just as the sun reaches the high point on the raised limb of the figure. This is the point *currently occupied* by the sun at the summer solstice.

Is it simply coincidence that this high point of the sun occurs at the precise time in the precessional cycle when Polaris arrives over the Earth's pole and the sun crosses the galactic equator?

The Greeks also inherited mythology concerning the sun and the Milky Way. Some say the path of the sun was once the Milky Way itself, others that the sun deviates along the Milky Way, but the whole assembly confirms that the sun on the Milky Way is a portent in stellar lore.

Over the last few pages I have tried to outline certain events on the celestial sphere today.

I suggest our current sky would have been a great and awesome spectacle to the people of ancient Egypt. They worshipped Ra, Osiris and the pole star. Now their mythology is animate, the sky gods are on the move, Ra and Osiris are culminating together under Polaris. I think this synchronicity is occurring at the point in history the ancient Egyptians knew as 'the Eternal Return of Osiris'.

It seems to me that the ancients anticipated this high point in the precessional cycle of their god Osiris and their understanding of precessional motion allowed them to communicate through time by using the Great Pyramid as a vehicle and the starry sky as a record.

But if so, what have they tried to communicate?

✳ 5 ✳

THE MEASURE OF OSIRIS

*'Thus we had returned to
the true beginnings, in the
Neolithic Revolution. We
agreed that revolution was
essentially technological.'*[1]

So far we have seen the Great Pyramid synchronizing with an unusual number of bright stars. When the surrounding neighbouring stars are joined together they generate isosceles triangles without exception. We have also found a vertical alignment between the brightest star (Capella) and the highest mountain (Mt Katherine), coordinating with all 11 Great Pyramid spotlights. Then a precise isosceles triangle was discovered linking the summits of the highest points surrounding Mt Katherine and again at Giza and Mt Nezzi. Coupled with this astronomy and geography, certain associations exist between the mythology of ancient Egypt and the star patterns. There is, if you like, a mannerism in their communication. Great monuments require great architects and the best designers always speak through their work. The emphasis at Giza is on scale, on balance, on harmony, on equation, on a mirror. In fact the ancient window on the heavens is a mirror and that mirror now contains the brightest pole star in history.

These discoveries naturally led me to question the current view of the pyramids as tombs for dead Pharaohs, so I began searching for evidence confirming the burial of the three Pharaohs at Giza.

It was an extremely revealing search. After years of conventional schooling I had naturally assumed (along with most people) that Pharaohs were buried in pyramids. All these grandsons of Osiris were supposed to have built pyramids to contain their own mummified bodies. So where are these sons of the great god? Where are the Pharaohs Djoser, Sekhemket, Khaba, Sneferu, Khufu, Djedefre, Khafre and Menkaure? There is no decent physical evidence to demonstrate that any of them were ever buried in any pyramid – in fact not a single fingernail

71

from a single Pharaoh has ever been recovered from any ancient Egyptian pyramid!

However, the pyramids do all have empty 'burial chambers' and some even have an empty coffer still resting there. From this it has been deduced that the Pharaoh was once interred within and later his remains, and the splendours surrounding him, were stolen.

Indeed, most of the monuments were pillaged, but what did the robbers who broke into the Great Pyramid actually find?

'There was nothing whatever there, in the whole extent of the apartment from one end to another, nothing except an empty stone chest without a lid.'[2]

Within the Great Pyramid, Caliph Al Mamoun (whose men spent many weeks of hard toil cutting into the body of the building c.AD 820) reportedly found the ascending passage filled with carefully carved blocks of stone. Though the Caliph's account cannot necessarily be accepted as the truth, the other access to the Great Pyramid's upper chambers (the well shaft) was also filled with rubble and has only been cleared in recent history.

In the absence of direct physical evidence, perhaps there is another method of ascertaining whether Pharaohs were buried in pyramids. Surely the texts found within the later pyramids can confirm that Pharaohs were buried in these buildings?

In his book *Star Maps* (Octopus Books, 1979), Wm. R. Fix studies the texts in the pyramid of Unas, searching for clues to the events surrounding the Pharaoh's death. He suggests that the repetition of the following sentiment may have been misunderstood. The text on the chamber walls repeats:

'O Unas, thou art not gone dead,
thou art gone alive to sit on the throne of Osiris,
Re Atum does not give thee to Osiris,
He reckons not thy heart.'[3]

While Fix recognizes the historical assertion that Unas was indeed dead, and buried in this pyramid, he asks why he should require his presumably mummified remains to be surrounded by such an untimely lie?

Of course Unas may have been considered immortal in the first place and the text can be considered in either context, but above the words on the walls all the ceilings in the Unas pyramid are covered with hundreds of carefully rendered stars, and all the stars are resting on parallel lines.

The star = mountain = eternity symbolism is therefore manifest in the building most clearly in words and symbols. Coupled with this, the earliest symbols ever recovered from the interior of a pyramid were found inside the pyramid of Djoser, said to predate Giza. The ceiling of the 'burial chamber' here was carved with stars. Thus Djoser's pyramid, said to be the very earliest of the ancient Egyptian pyramids, was discovered with stars inside it, not Pharaohs.

Other evidence has led scholars such as Dr Kurt Mendelssohn to conclude:

'It is important for our own considerations to realize that there seem to have existed tombs with all the trappings of funeral monuments but containing no actual burial. Who or what was buried in these multiple tombs must remain a matter for conjecture.'[4]

(Egyptologists often complain that 'cranks' or 'pyramidiots' are responsible for comments such as these. I have therefore listed Dr Mendelssohn's academic credentials in the reference.)

Dr Mendelssohn also points out that 'There exist more large pyramids than Pharaohs who could have been buried in them.'

Certainly, the accepted chronology of the Pharaohs requires Sneferu, the father of Cheops, to have built three huge pyramids for his own burial. This does suggest a less than incisive logic in certain theorizing, either on his part or on the part of Egyptologists, not least because two of these pyramids are within shouting distance of each other. Indeed, the conventional chronology suggests that the sum total of stone moved in Sneferu's reign was far more substantial than at any other time in Pharaohnic history. Yet the layout of chambers within Sneferu's trio of pyramids is entirely individual and one 'burial chamber' required a 'ladder' to reach it. In order to excuse Sneferu's apparently incorrigible appetite for pyramids in which to be buried, Egyptologist Mark Lehner explains that the Pharoah probably finished one of his three pyramids as 'a cenotaph rather than a tomb'.[5] He also notes that 'The burial chamber in the satellite pyramid is far too small to have contained a human burial... It may instead have been for the ritual internment of a statue of the king.' Of course the statue must have been stolen.

A cenotaph! The ritual internment of a statue!

The whole picture is deeply confused. Dr Mendelssohn's research into these 'burials' led him to conclude: 'The main difficulty which Egyptologists face is the re-creation of the state of mind of human society 5000 years ago.'[6]

As for the pyramids themselves, they offer little evidence of burial. True, the body of a child was found in one, the body of a woman in another, and a few bones and viscera of unknown origin in a third, but other than this, the pyramids and their coffers have yielded little more than bull bones, a few broken jars and some petrified bats.

These discoveries (and disappointments) are outlined in what has been for many years the most respected book on the ancient pyramids, *The Pyramids of Egypt* (Pelican Books, 1949) by Dr I. E. S. Edwards. Dr Edwards is convinced from the outset that pyramids were used to bury Pharaohs. He also warns the impressionable reader against 'crank' theorists.

Entirely undaunted by the absence of evidence for his own theory, Dr Edwards describes the exploration of one pyramid after another – the Layer, the Bent, the Red, the seven small step pyramids – all with empty tombs, empty coffers or no interior at all. Finding an empty coffer, he tells us the Pharaoh's body 'must have been' placed in it. A moment of excitement occurs when the coffer in the pyramid of Sekhemket (*c.*2610 BC) is discovered to be intact:

> 'In spite of the unfinished condition of this pyramid, hopes were raised in the course of the excavation that it would contain the body of the king. Not only was the corridor sealed in three places ... but there was no trace of any tunnel by which robbers could have circumvented these obstacles. Most significant of all, however, seemed to be the fact that a closed sarcophagus, on which a wreath had been placed, was discovered in the burial chamber. This sarcophagus, carved from a single rectangular block of alabaster, was exceptional in one respect: instead of having the whole top as a lid, it had, at one end, a sliding panel... Some plaster which could be seen in the grooves suggested that the panel had not been moved since it was ceremonially closed at the time of the funeral. All these indications, however, proved deceptive: the sarcophagus when opened was found to be empty.'[7]

The shaft leading down to the empty coffer, however, once cleared of rubble, was found to be filled with 'twenty one gold bracelets, armlets, gold beads' and other items of jewellery.

Surely only the most tortured storyteller could invent a scenario in which robbers enter a pyramid, steal a Pharaoh's body, seal up the coffer again with wet plaster, leave piles of valuables in the exit tunnel, then fill the tunnel up with rubble before eloping with a bag of bones?

Surprisingly, this scenario occurs again, more than once. Another sealed and empty coffer was found under the pyramid of Cheops' son Djedefre:

'...the sarcophagus in the Unfinished Pyramid [was found] with its lid attached with mortar to the base, *but nevertheless empty*. It had been covered with a thick layer of clay and blocks of limestone had been laid around and above it for protection. [My emphasis.]'[8]

And so the search for a single morsel of Pharaohnic remains in a pyramid continues.

Perhaps we have yet to fully understand the process of royal burial in ancient Egypt. There are few clues from this remote period to help us, although Herodotus states quite firmly that the Pharaoh Khufu (Cheops) was 'buried elsewhere', not in the Great Pyramid. But on reflection, perhaps you should never take the word of an old historian.

Could it simply be that people from this period were in the habit of burying coffers in the pyramids with nobody in them? But what was the empty sarcophagus for, if not for human burial? Is it realistic to imagine an alternative scenario?

THREE PYRAMIDS

At Giza the Great Pyramid points to the stars of Orion, and the three main pyramids look like the stars of Orion, and Orion was the celestial image of the god Osiris. Given this perspective, the monuments on the Giza plateau were surely built in homage to Osiris in the first instance, with any connection with the Pharaohs being secondary to the overall design.

The most sensational recent archaeological discovery in the Valley of the Kings adds some weight to this argument. In 1997 a massive underground complex consisting of dozens of empty chambers was excavated in the Valley of the Kings. At the heart of the empty complex of bare chambers, a beautiful relief carving of Osiris was uncovered. Once again we see the importance of confined empty chambers in the architecture of ancient Egypt, but once again archaeologists have concluded that dead bodies must have occupied these empty chambers and subsequently been 'stolen'. Seldom if ever is the empty tomb chamber associated with the immortality of the god Osiris, though his image dominates the decoration of this newly found essentially empty structure, just as it dominates the Giza horizon. Is it not possible for us to imagine that certain empty spaces had great value in the religion of ancient Egypt? Surely the burial of a coffer with nobody in it *has* to be a symbolic gesture.

But why? What are these symbols saying?

At Giza, considering the whole plateau as a unit, there are three pyramids, each with a unique interior design, but in all Egypt only the Great Pyramid has two

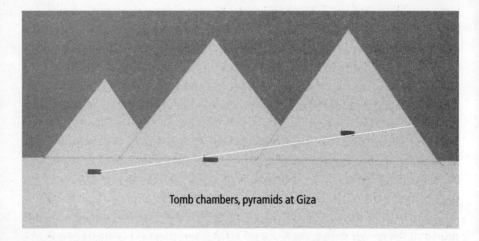

Tomb chambers, pyramids at Giza

Figure 53: The three pyramid profile

chambers situated so far above ground level. The middle pyramid at Giza has a burial chamber precisely at ground level and the third pyramid has a burial chamber
below ground level *(see Figure 53).*

Reading these symbols in the other direction, on the left there is a coffer below
the ground, in the middle there is a coffer at the ground level and finally on the
right there is a coffer above ground level (situated in the King's Chamber). So,
taken as a unit, the three pyramids illustrate the conveyance of the dead body in the
following way: the body rises from below ground in the south, reaches ground level
in the middle and ascends to Heaven in the north.

Whether this symbolic view has any credence or not, it is clear that the Great
Pyramid is actually suspending an empty coffer above ground level. Of all the pyramids, only the Great Pyramid has such a greatly elevated chamber and only the
Great Pyramid has miniature star shafts reaching into the heavens. In other words,
the King's Chamber is *in Heaven* with Osiris.

MYTH, SYMBOLS AND REALITY

Imagine you are living several thousand years in the future. You are an archaeologist, and you visit a long deserted and eroded part of the world called the Isle of
Wight, just off the southern coast of Britain.

On the island you are fortunate enough to discover the remains of an old stone
building created in the shape of a cross and from within the ruins you recover a

long-lost relic called the Bible, which tells the story of a man from God who was killed on a cross. Searching around the site, beneath some rubble you discover the worm-eaten remains of a large wooden cross!

With this discovery is it now wise for you to return home and declare to your colleagues that you have recovered the cross upon which Jesus Christ was crucified? Or should you consider the cross as a symbol of something, rather than a functional object?

Is it not time to consider that some of the pyramids' vacant coffers had no part in death but were in fact symbols designed to signify the eternal life of Osiris? After all, the ancient Egyptians were obsessed with eternal life and the Hollywood image of an empty coffin symbolizes the 'undead' state of Count Dracula even today.

Symbols of immortality were traditionally placed within or beneath a temple spire and the empty coffer, the deserted tomb, appears in every single one of the large Old Kingdom pyramids penetrated by Dr Edwards.

Nobody is dead. Osiris has defeated death. That was the faith of ancient Egypt.

Dealing with the Undead

So Osiris never really died as far as the ancient Egyptians were concerned, he lives to this day and beyond. He had a mortal form, but he became immortal. Yet how did he meet his mortal end?

Ancient myths tell us how the lord Osiris was tricked and murdered by his brother Set in a very unusual fashion. Set was jealous of Osiris, so he 'took the measure of Osiris' and built a special coffer to precisely agree with his brother's dimensions, then he tricked Osiris into lying down inside the carefully made coffer. Set and his cronies immediately slammed down the lid, sealed it up, took the coffer down to the Nile and threw it in.

It was a terrible way for Osiris to die. But all was not lost. The love, faith and divine powers of his wife Isis finally led to the recovery of the coffer, whereupon:

Osiris was released from the coffer that killed him. He left the coffer empty and became immortal.

Isn't it appropriate that the pyramids of Osiris should contain the symbol of his resurrection?

Moreover, the Great Pyramid itself reflects part of the image of Osiris in Heaven, as well as containing an empty coffer symbolizing the god's immortality. Has this pyramid therefore been waiting for 'the Eternal Return of Osiris' at Orion's high point?

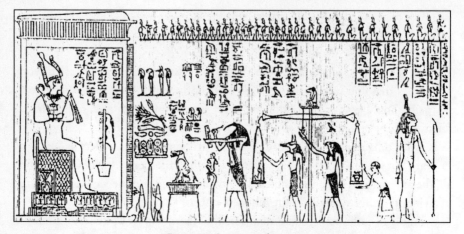

Figure 54: Osiris in judgement

In his immortalized form the god Osiris became the judge of the dead, but it is still far from clear when the judgement is supposed to take place.

Judging the Dead

An illustration from a New Kingdom papyrus shows Osiris watching a human heart being weighed against a feather *(see Figure 54)*. Osiris as judge of the dead uses the traditional balance to make his judgement and he always sits on a square throne in these scenes.

Osiris is in fact a very geometric god. His stars are ordered in right angles and isosceles triangles *(see Figure 55 for the right angle in Orion)*, while on the ground his temples are built from squares rising to the central apex of four isosceles walls.

I hope the edges of this argument are now pulling together. There are good reasons for recognizing the pyramids as symbols of eternal life and eternal light. They are stars and they are mountains, and they conform to the geometry of Osiris, and these stars appear to live forever.

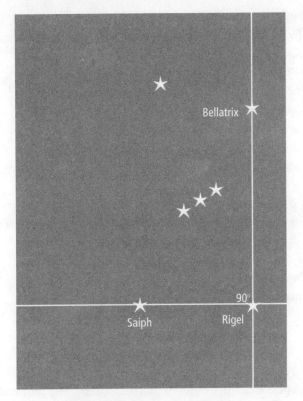

Figure 55: The right angle in Orion

STARRY CONSTELLATIONS

The earliest extant account of the night sky was written by the Greek Aratus, in a poem called *Phaenomena c.*250 BC. His work became renowned in Greece and later in Rome, and, as R. H. Allen explains,

> 'His poem is now apparently our sole source of knowledge as to the arrangement of the early constellations, and has been closely followed as an indispensable guide... His sphere, probably identical with that of Eudoxus of a century previous, accurately represents the heavens of about 2000–2200 BC.'[9]

Earlier, Eudoxus (*c.*350 BC) had written an astronomical work, now lost, called *The Mirror*. In the light of the mirror between stars and mountains, one has to wonder what Eudoxus had in mind when he chose that particular title.

It is said both Aratus and Eudoxus studied astronomy in Egypt. It was around the time of Eudoxus that the 12 zodiac signs were rendered at Denderah (in the Nile river kink).

Aratus says to his students of star lore, 'Look for signs upon signs.' He describes the sky as a beautiful tableau of surreal giants, kings, queens, birds, bears, lions, horses, dogs, goats, fish, serpents, a hare, a scorpion, a crab, a bull, a dragon, a sea monster, a boat, a stream – and just one isosceles triangle, the constellation Triangulum.

Aratus also advises, 'Look for *concurrence* of three,' a geometric term referring to the meeting of three lines.

Although Triangulum is the only geometric shape officially named in a sky full of figurative images, Aratus does describe another geometric shape in the constellation of Pegasus the winged horse: the Great Square. He also says that all the constellations he describes were created 'at once', 'in primordial time'. This suggests that Triangulum and the Great Square in Pegasus were also seen geometrically by our earliest ancestors.

CORNERS OF THE WORLD

The Great Square is a vast and magnificent constellation with four startlingly bright stars marking out the corners of an approximate square against a surprisingly dark background. I shortly realized that the square may offer a mirror image of the Earth's grid. I wondered if the celestial square and the terrestrial grid ever coincided. That is, does the square formed by the stars in Pegasus ever directly mirror the square formed by the parallels and meridians on Earth?

For various reasons the odds of such a match are very slim. The angle created between the horizontal (parallel) and the vertical (meridian) varies with latitude. Thus a 'square' matching the grid at the equator of the sphere will not match the grid at 60° north because the vertical lines (the meridians) are increasingly converging. Consequently the match of a stellar square with a terrestrial square is not only governed by the pitch of the Earth's axis matching the vertical, but also governed by the latitude on the Earth above which the square is located. Due to precessional motion, the whole grid is in constant motion.

I started the computer in order to discover if this great geometric giant in the sky ever harmonized with the Earth's grid. But I did not need the computer. The stars of the Great Square were not aligned to the meridian of the Earth in 2450 BC, or AD 1000, or AD 1500.

The stars in the Great Square of Pegasus are now beautifully aligned to both the meridian and the parallel of the Earth, stellar epoch AD 2000.

This is the first time in recorded history that the alignment of the Great Square has occurred in this way, and the stars are aligned over the Earth's parallel to an accuracy of one sixtieth of a degree and over the Earth's meridian to one quarter of a degree. This is a very fine alignment, reflected by these AD 2000 figures:

Alpha Pegasus	23 hrs 05 mins
Beta Pegasus	23 hrs 04 mins
Alpha Pegasus	15°12'
Gamma Pegasus	15°11'[10]

This geometry brought me straight from the ancient square throne of Osiris to the Great Square in the present day. I was extremely surprised to find three of the famous stars in the Great Square are now forming a right angle directly mirroring the grid on the Earth, but when I turned my attention to the fourth star in the square of Pegasus, I found this remarkable stellar geometry even more compelling:

Three of the four brilliant stars in the Great Square form an isosceles triangle.

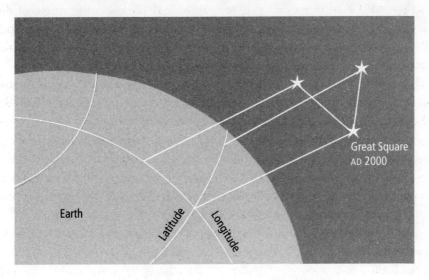

Figure 56: The Great Square aligned to the Earth's grid in AD 2000

It is unusual to find three random points forming a right angle, and equally unusual to build the square on a spherical grid, and also unlikely that three random points (only defined as a group by the chance of magnitude) will form an isosceles triangle. All these formations are only coincidence, but all these coincidences are happening at once, in epoch AD 2000, and that is the real coincidence.

The extraordinary geometric forms currently created by the brightest stars would definitely not be expected to occur repeatedly aligning to a single grid in a selection of random neighbouring points. This is itself a very important issue, but one that is extremely easy to prove for yourself.

I have just taken three identical coins out of my pocket and thrown them onto a few yards of carpet. The coins did not come to rest in an isosceles triangle. Try it for yourself, it is a simple yet scientific way of defining the odds of chance on your living-room carpet. If you turn up an isosceles triangle, see how many times you

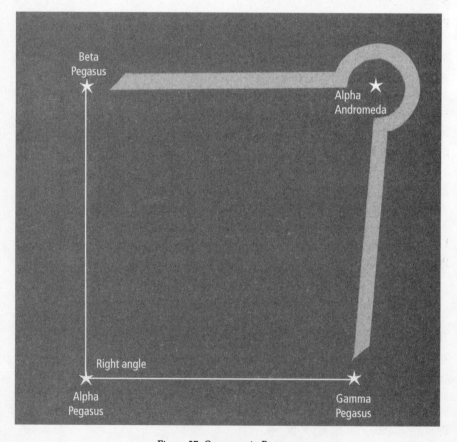

Figure 57: Geometry in Pegasus

can repeat it. The answer will very quickly reveal that three small random points spread over a large area seldom fall into an isosceles formation.

You may say, of course, the stellar triangles we are talking about are bound to occur because of the number of random shapes across the sky. None the less, from within this random pattern, the Great Pyramid repeatedly targets specific bright stars and in each case the neighbouring bright stars create an isosceles triangle. The fact that the three bright points are all neighbours (by virtue of magnitude), within the random pattern, confirms to me that the isosceles triangles have been 'picked out' with intent by the Giza architects, whose three pyramids reflect (by size) the magnitude and shape of the three stars in Orion's Belt.

The strange patterns forming on the celestial grid today led me closer to the visualization of the starry sky as a form of cosmic game of join the dots in which certain points created a certain understanding. But I was still some way from reading these patterns as one might read a text. I was far from understanding what was really being communicated from Giza. All I really knew at this stage was the Giza architects were certainly not 'Stone Age' in mind. I therefore tried to follow their code, adopting a strictly linear method.

I had followed the polar spotlight from the Great Pyramid today and found Polaris on target, so the next logical step was to follow the remaining pyramid spotlights onto the celestial sphere. Apart from Polaris, what else is the Great Pyramid pointing to today?

A BIG SHOCK

I started this AD 2000 research by following the vertical spotlight above the Great Pyramid. I was in for a big shock.

Vertically above Giza today is the apex of the constellation Triangulum!

Triangulum's apex has not passed over Giza before in recorded history, yet today its apex matches the apex of the Great Pyramid – and this 'sign upon sign' occurs in synchronization with Polaris passing over the pole, the solstice sun crossing the galactic equator, the phallus of Osiris standing erect while Osiris reaches his high point, four stars in Auriga aligning above the solstice sun and the Great Square of Pegasus aligning to the Earth's grid. Is there a notable pattern?

Figure 58: The apex of Triangulum now passes vertically over Giza

Earlier I used the analogy of a person walking up a street and repeatedly finding tennis balls organized in isosceles triangles. I said that at some point one is bound to register a pattern, but each person recognizes the pattern independently and indeed some people are too busy to notice it at all.

Whatever historians might say about the hunter gatherers in antiquity and whatever opinions may be agreed about the roots of human science, I went looking for a triangular sign in the sky above Giza in AD 2000 because the ancient symbols I was reading firmly directed me to this end. Polaris is on target. So, by taking an old directive, I followed the point of the Great Pyramid vertically upwards – and immediately found the only triangle named in the ancient sky passing directly above the Great Pyramid summit, apex to apex by vertical alignment for the first time in history.

Furthermore, the transit of the star Alpha Triangulum (Rasalmothallah) over Giza synchronizes incredibly precisely with the transit of Polaris over the pole of the Earth:

a. Polaris transits the pole most closely in AD 2100.
b. Alpha Triangulum transits the Great Pyramid most closely in AD 2080.

This is a difference of 20 years in a precessional cycle of 25,830 years. The match held out against the horizon earlier would have to be split yet again to define this difference. To all intents and purposes the above two alignments are simultaneous. Alpha Triangulum passes over the apex of the Great Pyramid as Polaris passes over the pole of the Earth.

The combination of these two alignments alone, in a single stellar epoch, should alert our attention to the ancient wisdom being displayed by these pyramid designers and their manner of symbolic communication. Their timing is immaculate, their science is our science. The world's most sophisticated antique pyramid on the ground now points vertically up to the only antique triangle in the sky (and the triangle therefore points down to the pyramid). The two antique symbols match up at the dawn of the new millennium. The equation once created between the Earth and the sky under Thuban is reproduced once again at Giza, but this time under Polaris.

THE TRAIL OF TRIANGULUM

I knew in my own mind when I discovered the alignment of Triangulum over Giza synchronizing with the culmination of Polaris that the Giza designers had foreseen this moment. Having directed attention to isosceles triangles repeatedly in 2450 BC they now direct attention to the perfect synchronization between their most singular pyramid and the single isosceles constellation, Triangulum. This I see as a 'way with words' and the words are like our own. They are simple linear symbols communicating across the abyss of history.

I looked further at Triangulum and discovered that to arrive over Giza in AD 2000, the Alpha star had left the celestial equator in 10,450 BC, moving north. This was 'the First Time of Osiris'. The journey of Triangulum from the celestial equator to the thirtieth parallel over Giza runs precisely concurrently with the journey of Orion from the bottom to the top of the precessional ladder (see Figure 60). Did the ancients mean to draw our attention to this precessional synchronization?

During the First Time of Osiris, a time reflected by the ground geometry at Giza,[11] the triangle in Triangulum lay on one side, perfectly aligned along the celestial equator at 0°. But now, at the precessional culmination of Osiris, the triangle passes over Giza.

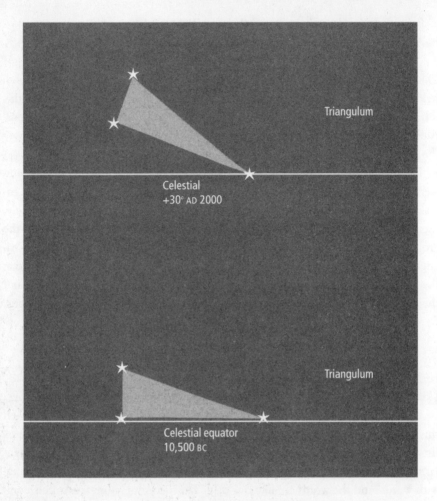

Figure 59: The rise of Triangulum

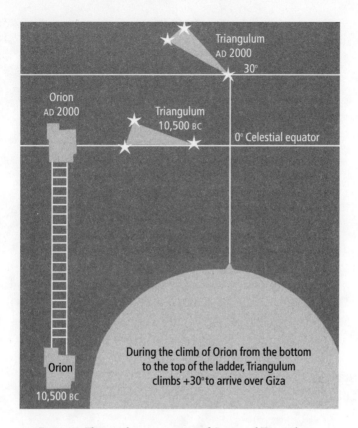

Figure 60: The simultaneous motion of Orion and Triangulum

The ancient window on the heavens is opening, once again revealing a triangle joining the stars, but now it is opening to the sky in AD 2000. Is there possibly more reason than we can imagine for worshipping a pole star, and was that unimaginable reason hermetically sealed in stone for the future?

✳ 6 ✳

LINES FROM THE PAST

'First people will deny a thing;
then they will belittle it; then
they will decide that it had
been known long ago.' [1]

It was now time to embark on a journey I will never forget. I had found a triangle over the Great Pyramid, a brilliant star over the pole, a square aligned to the Earth's grid, a line of four stars aligned to the solstice sun and the phallus of the Pharaohs' reported progenitor aligned to the meridian. These events are all current on the day I write and I was naturally concerned to define all the other pyramid spotlights on the celestial sphere in the present epoch.

But I began by looking once again at the polar spotlights.

HAMLET'S MILL

All the pyramids of the Old Kingdom have a shaft oriented to the polar region in the sky. This is one axis of the 'mill wheel' of the heavens and the arrival of a brilliant star at this point suggests that the heavenly axis is 'heating up'. In *Hamlet's Mill*, Giorgio de Santillana and Hertha von Deschend recover an abundance of evidence confirming the ancient preoccupation with this axis on the celestial sphere and its association with a predicted Earth shift. Their case is brilliantly constructed, drawing on a fantastic mixture of antique sources to reveal that almost identical rituals permeated the globe at some time in pre-literate history. They conclude our ancestors possessed an incredible knowledge of astronomy and the pitch of the Earth's precessing axis in space is inexorably linked to a cataclysmic Earth shift.

The pole of the Earth is at once the *axis mundi*, the 'mother mountain', the 'tree of Eden', the 'eternal mill wheel' or any number of staffs, sceptres and staves depicted in antique artwork. A celestial undercurrent runs through mythology right around the globe. Myths and fables from the Russian steppes to central Mali come into accord. It seems that in antiquity people's minds were 'wrapped in symbols', but now:

'Orientalists have lost all contact with astronomical imagination, or even the fundamentals of astronomy. When we find something which savours undeniably of astronomical lore, they find a way to label it under "pre-logical thought" or the like.'[2]

These contrasting views of ancient history readily reflect the difficulty of the subject we are about to deal with.

In *Hamlet's Mill*, after an exhaustive study concerning the transfer of astronomical information through the vehicle of myth, the question is posed:

'How and why does it always happen that this Mill, the peg of which is Polaris, has to be wrecked or unhinged? Once the archaic mind had grasped the forever enduring rotation, what caused it to think that the axle jumps out of the hole? What memory of catastrophic events has created this story of destruction?

...Nor is there any doubt that far antiquity was already aware of the shifting pole star.'[3]

We have already seen how two pyramid spotlights create a target shape around the pole *(see Figure 45, p.56)*. By following the two spotlights today I discovered that not only is Polaris currently within the bull's eye of the target, but also:

The star Yildun is now spotlighted on the outer circle of the target.

Remember Yildun fell into a Great Pyramid spotlight in 2450 BC? What a remarkable coincidence – the same star falls into a pyramid spotlight once again today.

In 2450 BC, Yildun was spotlighted by the south face angle of the Great Pyramid, then all the grid lines on the celestial sphere changed and all co-ordination was lost. No brilliant star has shone over the pole since then. But now, as Polaris reaches the central target and Triangulum passes overhead, Yildun falls back into alignment with another pyramid spotlight, this time the angle of the descending passage!

We saw earlier that by simply casting the dark blanket over the celestial pole I found the four brightest stars within the target area defined by the Great Pyramid today. These are Polaris, Yildun and the two next brightest stars. Three stars form an isosceles triangle with Polaris contained in the triangle *(see Figure 29)*.

This is the picture from Giza AD 2000, but the symbols are identical to those of 2450 BC, only this time the target is Polaris. Thus Triangulum above the pyramid today is duplicated by the same motif in the brightest three brightest stars, on target, surrounding Polaris.

Unfortunately the triangle around Polaris is not easy to see in light-polluted sky. However this coincidence led me further to believe the Giza architects were attempting to define a form of language in the stars, to register a pattern to travel through the millennia to reach us today at the culmination of Osiris.

The difficulty I have describing these triangles would be easily surpassed by the difficulty of trying to explain why they are all there in the first place. Indeed, the idea of trying to explain geometry between stars seems absurd. We are all well aware that the stars are random points of light, thrown together in a particular perspective by our swirling Milky Way Galaxy. Like so much chocolate, the random result is squared up for our convenience, in this case into sky charts. And from this microscopic planet suspended in the voids of the galaxy we create our personal grid on the chaotic Milky Way surrounding us.

But is the result really chaotic?

The pyramid builders seemed to be drawing attention to geometric patterns, but the patterns are in the present day night sky.

THE TIME MACHINE

Perhaps the real hurdle in this logic is history itself. That is to say, the problem with recognizing this fabulous intelligence from prehistory is bound up with the present day perception of history itself. So far, the archaeological evidence we possess has failed to convince the academic community that highly sophisticated people lived at any time in prehistory. But why do we feel so assured? Is it because of the proof we hold, or is it the lack of proof?

So far in this research I had done little more than follow a series of lines from the Great Pyramid up into the sky. The lines are simple and straight – and were certainly synchronized with the sky around 2450 BC under Thuban. If it is acceptable to recognize the Great Pyramid as a star pointer in 2450 BC, why not at another date when the brightest of all the pole stars appears over the pole?

Yet archaeologists and historians generally agree that nobody in prehistory had the facility to measure the precessional motion of stars, indeed many say precession wasn't recognized until Hipparchus in 150 BC. The feeling that we already know our past, and know it so well, allows little room for the hypothesis that precessional astronomy and ancient wisdom were thrown together on the Giza plateau in prehistory.

This clash of principles has been creating sparks for a long time, in fact since the ridiculing of Sir Norman Lockyer. To put the difference between the two camps most crudely, one side finds evidence of Atlantis or a similar advanced civilization and the other side does not. One side sees antiquity full of grisly cave men, the other, sophisticated astronomers. Archaeology from these remote times yields only the husk of evidence. Some say this husk once contained a beautiful butterfly, but others see no evidence of its flight.

So I cannot pursue the present day alignments of the Great Pyramid without challenging dogma in many camps, but on the other hand I have the feeling I am reading ancient lines which are defined as clearly as the lines on this page.

Let us see whether there is any more evidence to support the hypothesis that the Great Pyramid was wilfully aligned to the stars under Triangulum in the present day.

RIGEL RISING

I decided to follow the spotlight up the north face of the Great Pyramid into the present day night sky. I defined the parallel pinpointed by the pyramid's north face and then checked for the brightest star currently located on that parallel.

It was a tremendous shock. I remember shouting something, I couldn't believe it:

Rigel, the brightest star in the Orion constellation, is now aligned to the Great Pyramid north face with an accuracy of one fifteenth of a degree.

One fifteenth of a degree is less than the width of a matchstick held out at arm's length against the sky. It is one part in 5,450 on the Giza meridian. It is a tiny fraction.

So in AD 2000 the Great Pyramid points to the brightest star in the whole Orion constellation, the seventh brightest star in the heavens! This is the third brilliant star in Orion pinpointed by the Great Pyramid and this alignment is happening now, every day, along with the alignment to the Polaris triangle and to Triangulum overhead.

The alignment of Rigel to within one fifteenth of a degree is truly fantastic. Looking at the mobile sky grid over the past 12,000 years, Rigel has been travelling in a northerly direction up the precessional ladder. Its rise can be imagined if we 'fast forward' the precessional motion of the Earth. Rigel climbs and climbs and

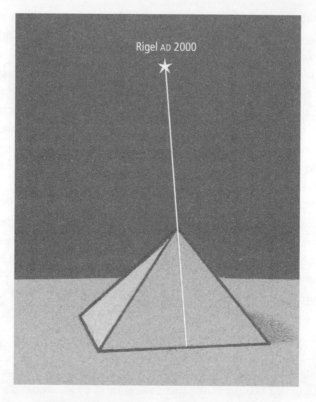

Figure 61: Rigel aligned to the Great Pyramid AD 2000

climbs up the meridian ladder, a total of 47°, reaching the top rung today. Its dramatic northerly shift now ceases and the star rests at its high point in the sky over Giza, indeed over the entire northern hemisphere of the Earth. As Rigel reaches this precessional peak it falls into alignment with the north face of the Great Pyramid, a position which it will retain for about 1,000 years. Rigel will move less than one third of a degree on one narrow parallel of the celestial sphere for the coming millennium, before sliding once again 47° to the south. The north face of the Great Pyramid spotlights precisely this one third of a degree on the meridian over Giza.

Naturally only one meridian angle from the ground at Giza can be used to specify this particular point on the meridian in the sky. That angle is defined by the pyramid's north face very precisely.

To co-ordinate the Great Pyramid with Rigel concurrently with Polaris transiting the pole and Triangulum transiting the summit you simply could not do better than this:

a. Polaris reaches the highest point in 2100 AD.
b. Alpha Triangulum creates a perfect vertical with the Great Pyramid 2080 AD.
c. Rigel becomes precisely aligned to the Great Pyramid's north face in 2080 AD.

Given a span of 25,830 years, these three alignments are really defined together. The distance travelled by a star on the celestial grid over 20 years is entirely unobservable to the naked eye. These precessional measures are extremely fine and they should, I believe, be recognized as alignments synchronized with immense precision by a sophisticated people in the past.

The building creating these extraordinarily fine measures on the celestial sphere today is itself aligned to the meridian of the Earth with near perfection. The tolerances of the building were given earlier *(see p.7)* and I asked at the time why any building needed to be so precise. I believe these three star alignments, created with such accuracy today, emphasize the true and extremely exact astronomical character of this building, and the high intelligence of those who designed it.

Given that these alignments occur under the brightest close transit pole star in history, I saw nothing less than a profoundly advanced intellect behind this stunning synchronicity.

SIGNS TO LOOK OUT FOR

With an alignment to Rigel to add to the earlier Orion alignments of Bellatrix and Alnitak, the ancient 'language' was becoming clearer still.

I looked at the star atlas plates once more, but I really found it hard to believe what I saw. I tried again and again. There was no doubt about it:

The stars Rigel, Bellatrix and Alnitak form an isosceles triangle.

The regular creation of stellar isosceles triangles has, in a sense, acted as a form of confirmation that lines are being correctly followed. I had therefore started looking for this characteristic isosceles triangle around Rigel. What I had not expected was that the three brilliant stars in Orion picked out by the Great Pyramid would join together to form the very isosceles triangle I was looking for. It is what I call 'a time-lapse triangle' because its three corners are highlighted in two specific epochs, two stars in stellar epoch 2450 BC and the third in stellar epoch AD 2000 *(see Figure 62)*, both epochs being characterized by the presence of a bright star at the pole. It is an extremely clever, precise and magical work of art.

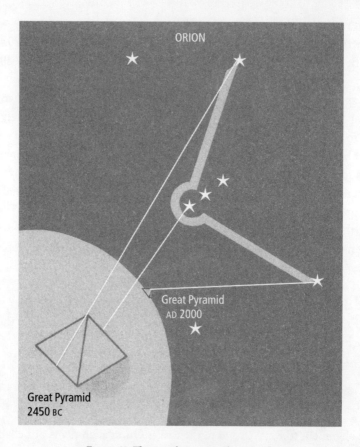

Figure 62: The time-lapse isosceles triangle

The Great Pyramid is really a sophisticated stellar device co-ordinated to the celestial sphere in two stellar epochs defined by the two brightest close transit pole stars in history. Here we can see the profound intelligence behind the system.

The effect is such that the north face of the Great Pyramid takes the measure of Osiris, from the shoulder Bellatrix in 2450 BC under one pole star to the toe Rigel under the next pole star in AD 2100. The measure is visible today, and if you visit the Giza plateau on a clear winter's night and stand at the entrance to the Great Pyramid, you may look up to see Rigel perched at the apex. The star will appear to land on the top of the pyramid every time the Earth turns for about the next 1,000 years.

Rigel is normally depicted as a raised foot, so the precessional climb of Orion is complete when his raised foot rests on the pyramid apex. It is quite beautiful to watch the mythology of the sky liaising with ancient architecture in this fashion. (I will discuss the mythology of Orion's foot later.)

Orion as seen looking up the north face
of the Great Pyramid in AD 2000

Figure 63: The precessional climb of Orion

By now I felt fully assured that I had cracked some form of symbolic code. The fabulously accurate alignment to Rigel, coupled with all the other notable events in the sky, left me in no doubt that a form of symbolic language is to this day contained in and demonstrated by the Great Pyramid.

What I find so compelling about the pyramid designers' work is their unbelievable accuracy. When Gerald Hawkin worked on decoding Stonehenge he was using tolerances of one degree, or sometimes more, on a single alignment.[4] In contrast, the measures between Rigel and Triangulum are co-ordinated to a fiftieth of a degree (in AD 2080), coinciding precisely with the moment Polaris reaches culmination after a 25,800-year absence.

If geometry was ever beautifully worked, it has been crafted to perfection at Giza. These are staggeringly fine lines.

MAN AND MEASURE

I naturally continued to follow the remaining pyramid spotlights in AD 2000 and these discoveries will be described shortly. But with the recognition of the isosceles triangle between three aligned stars in Orion my research took another turn.

The time-lapse triangle between Rigel, Bellatrix and Alnitak was a revelation in more ways than one. I had already found a series of right angles drawn between the Orion stars and had already noted the isosceles triangle of Orion's Belt. So I investigated the geometry of Orion further.

I found that not only is there a time-lapse triangle, but also:

Orion's Belt forms an isosceles triangle with Rigel.

These triangles can all be seen so clearly with the naked eye it is easy to overlook the geometry, but try throwing four pebbles on the ground to create two isosceles triangles as perfectly as this. You might need an eternity.

If the stars in the sky are but random points, then this geometry may be of passing interest. But I do not believe the ancient Egyptians visualized the brilliant stars as random points, I am quite certain they saw just the reverse. And is that

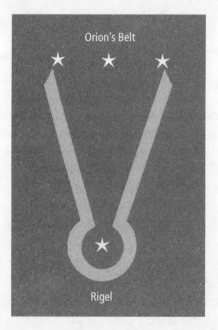

Figure 64: Rigel and the Belt isosceles triangle

why they have cleverly pointed to the three corners of an isosceles triangle in the Orion constellation?

They saw order, they saw strict geometry, they saw a form of Osiris unobserved today. They are passing on a religious vision: a god exists, with power over the stars. Surely the unusual geometry between the Orion stars suggests exactly this?

I had proved to my own satisfaction that three isosceles triangles and a series of right angles are not normal in a chance distribution of seven points. Of course the chance is there, but it is against the odds, and perhaps this is why the Orion constellation has attracted so much religious attention in the distant past.

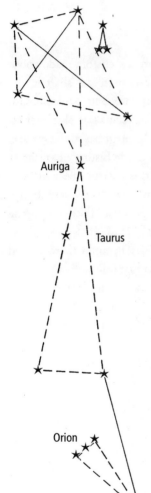

THE DUAT

The starry sky surrounding Osiris was called 'the Duat' by the ancient Egyptians. I decided to investigate the Duat more fully, casting the dark blanket over the Duat stars to reveal only the brightest points of light.

Nature certainly seems very organized in this particular area of the heavens *(see Figure 65)*. The brightest stars are joined by a series of isosceles triangles. If the worshippers of Osiris and the pyramid designers were looking at this geometry we may have an important insight into a scientific structure supporting their religious beliefs.

I can find no other record of this geometry between stars, no reference to a perfect right angle in Orion or to an isosceles triangle. Did you notice this geometry before? If not, the idea of a legominism makes some sense. This information concerning the geometry in the brightest Duat stars has been transferred through history by the pointers of the Great Pyramid.

Figure 65: The triangles above Orion, featuring only the brightest stars

It is also strange that the pole star and the computer technology to recognize the alignments of the Great Pyramid should arrive at the same time.

Coupled with this, the technology employed to accurately define the angle of the pyramid shafts has only been developed in the past decade.

It was time to continue the search and follow another spotlight from the Great Pyramid today.

UPUAUT

In 1994 German robotics engineer Rudolph Gantenbrink's custom-made robot 'Upuaut' climbed 200 feet up the Queen's Chamber southern star shaft in the Great Pyramid, recording a video *en route*. Guided by remote control from below, it finally reached an obstruction. The eight-inch square star shaft was blocked by a carefully crafted door (or slab) with two metal pins fixed like handles to the surface.

This is without doubt one of the most unusual finds in the history of archaeology, yet no archaeologist has found the need to accept this ancient invitation and turn the handles. Unfortunately the man and the robot who made this very strange discovery have been banned from continuing the investigation and penetrating the door itself.

And with the discovery of the little door in the Great Pyramid there arrived something that was not mentioned in the flurry of media that followed.

The door discovered by Rudolph Gantenbrink's robot was unlike any other ever found anywhere in the history of archaeology. It is entirely unique. We are told it remains closed. But whilst this inertia persists, the sky beyond the door is always wide open.

In order to find what the mysterious shaft ultimately leads to, the robot's journey can be imagined continuing on the same straight line through the little door and onto the celestial sphere beyond.

The robot travels along the spotlight beam, reaching the celestial sphere nearly 21° below the celestial equator. Today there are two bright stars in the spotlight projected from this mysteriously blocked shaft.

The two brightest stars aligned to this pyramid star shaft today are side by side in the constellation Lepus, directly beneath the feet of Orion.

These two stars are located on the same parallel (within one tenth of a degree) and are the brightest stars on the specified parallel. Consequently, when they are joined together they create a straight line under Orion/Osiris, a line which naturally mirrors the parallel of the Earth beneath.

The god Osiris is thereby underlined by the Great Pyramid only when he reaches his culmination in the precessional cycle. It is a literal language.

These two Lepus stars in the pyramid spotlight today have a single bright neighbour, the brightest star in Lepus, Arneb, or Alpha Lepus.

Taking the two stars in the pyramid spotlight and joining them to their neighbour Alpha Lepus creates yet another isosceles triangle.

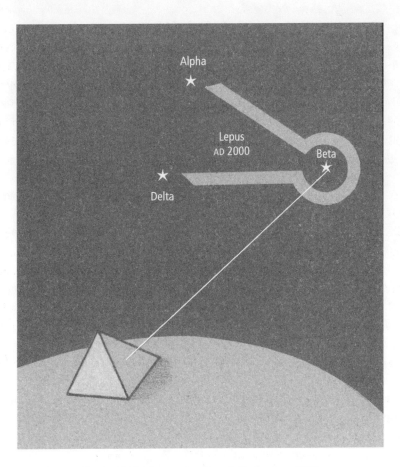

Figure 66: The Lepus triangle and alignment AD 2000

The unusual pattern of triangles I had discovered in the alignment sequence of 2450 BC was now being cleverly repeated in AD 2000.

A pattern of alignments is undeniably occurring once again. Today, just as in 2450 BC, bright stars are synchronized by the pyramid spotlights and once again they form isosceles triangles when the dark blanket is cast over them. With each new spotlight there appears to be further confirmation of stellar geometry falling into alignment with the Earth's grid: the isosceles triangle in Lepus rests on the celestial parallel, while the phallus, the four Auriga stars and the Great Square all rest on the meridian. Why is this alignment of bright stars to the Earth's grid so persistent in AD 2000?

GOING UP

I continued the intriguing search with the next spotlight on the south side of the pyramid, following the angle of the ascending passage onto the celestial sphere today. This angle locates only one bright star in stellar epoch AD 2000, a star called Alpha Columba. Alpha Columba lies directly beneath the two stars spotlighted in Lepus.

This was an unlikely chance, but the next discovery was stranger still:

The two stars spotlighted in Lepus and the star Alpha Columba form yet another isosceles triangle.

It is truly phenomenal.

Two consecutive alignments in AD 2000 unmistakably locate three stars and these three stars form an isosceles triangle aligned to the meridian.
The isosceles triangle points due south in the sky.

These AD 2000 alignments on the south side of the Great Pyramid now occur every time the Earth turns.

The full list of AD 2000 alignments to the Great Pyramid discovered so far is as follows:

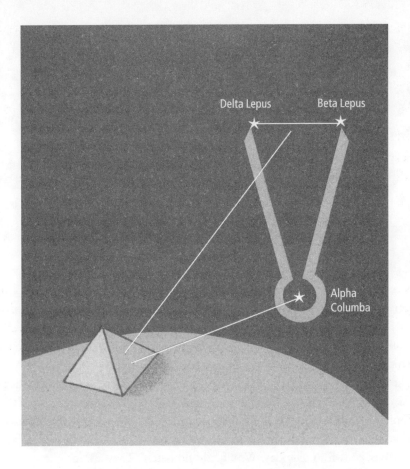

Figure 67: The double alignment forming an isosceles triangle in AD 2000

Alpha Triangulum	The apex of Triangulum
Alpha Ursa Minor (Polaris)	The pole star
Delta Ursa Minor (Yildun)	At the apex of an isosceles triangle around the pole star
Beta Orionis (Rigel)	At the apex of an isosceles triangle with Orion's Belt at the base (also isosceles with Alnitak and Bellatrix)
Beta and Delta Lepus	At the base of an isosceles triangle with Alpha Columba at the apex
Alpha Columba	At the apex of the isosceles triangle with Beta and Delta Lepus

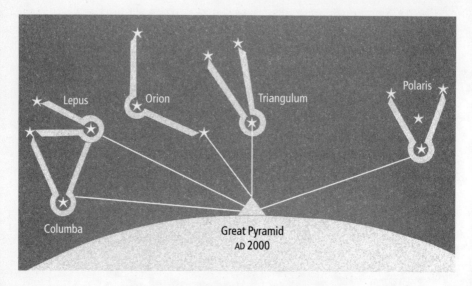

Figure 68

Looking at the illustration it is hard to imagine such continuity occurring by chance when the pointers themselves have such a triangular source.

The two stars in Lepus, Alpha Columba and Rigel are in the same vertical slice of the sky, thus this single section (a Decan) of the Duat has become the focus of three pyramid spotlights in AD 2000.

I can't help thinking that these pyramid designers tried extremely hard to make themselves known to us today. Who could do better? They ask for our attention. But are we ready to receive their communication?

I continued my research with the remaining pyramid angles.

I moved on to another south-facing spotlight from the Great Pyramid. The southern shaft leaving the King's Chamber describes an angle of 45°. The shaft meets the sky spotlighting the meridian 15° below the celestial equator. On this parallel in the sky today, a small but precise isosceles triangle of stars can be found:[5]

This small isosceles triangle symbolizes the ears of the hare Lepus, running directly beneath Orion's feet.

So the 45° shaft locates a well loved little isosceles triangle of stars yet again in the Duat, and in precisely the same slice of the sky as the other three spotlights from the pyramid's south face.

The starry sky is forever turning and therefore logic dictates that one would definitely not expect to locate stars in a single small vertical slice of the celestial sphere repeatedly with four random pointers. Despite this, there is now an isosceles triangle in the ears of Lepus to add to the other isosceles triangles developed earlier. But that is not the full story. There is something more to be said about this isosceles triangle in the ears of Lepus:

> *The isosceles triangle in the ears of Lepus is now nearly aligned over the Earth's meridian.*
> *Following this meridian north locates the star Rigel.*

I had now detailed the alignments of four consecutive stellar spotlights on the south side of the pyramid in AD 2000 and in each of the four cases I had identified an alignment to an isosceles triangle of stars *(see Figure 69)*.

All these alignments are in place today, on a small area of the celestial sphere in the immediate vicinity of Orion. This is a remarkable fact because clearly a random

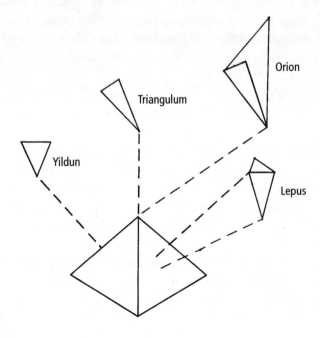

Figure 69

selection of parallels should produce a selection of stars spread equally haphazardly across the celestial sphere. Two isosceles triangles are found connecting bright stars in Lepus, a third between Lepus and Alpha Columba, a fourth joining Rigel, Alnitak and Bellatrix in Orion, a fifth with Triangulum and a sixth around Polaris. It's a clear pattern.

My problem was, if I was to continue to discover the same geometric form in every one of the Great Pyramid spotlights in the present day, was I in some sense obliged to acknowledge these alignments as intentional?

There is a danger that the whole concept of the brightest stars being organized geometrically is, in a way, unacceptable. There is the further danger that the concept of a sophisticated intelligence in antiquity is also unacceptable. Despite this, the Great Pyramid is extremely clinical, very clear and precise. It identifies geometry among the brightest stars right now, very accurately. Today we are all very familiar with following straight lines across a page in order to communicate, but we are less familiar with following straight lines into the sky. But the procedures are essentially identical and information can be conveyed in either manner.

I wondered whether the Giza designers were pointing at geometry between the stars not realizing that a paradigm shift would occur in the future. Are we out of step with our ancestors' vision of the Earth and sky? Did they believe their gods organized the stars geometrically and did they see these geometric shapes so clearly they never doubted their Creator? If so, there has definitely been a substantial shift away from this view, a shift now very hard to reconcile.

DUE SOUTH

There is one more pyramid spotlight pointing to the southern sky at Giza today. This spotlight defines the most southerly point on the horizon. All the stars appearing here are 60° below the celestial equator. This is the point where the constellation Crux currently rises. (As already noted, this is the most brilliant cluster of stars in the sky.)

Crux actually straddles the −60° celestial parallel today and consequently the cross in the constellation appears to stand upright due south across the Giza horizon, actually balancing half above and half below the horizon every day *(see Figure 70 and Appendix IV)*.

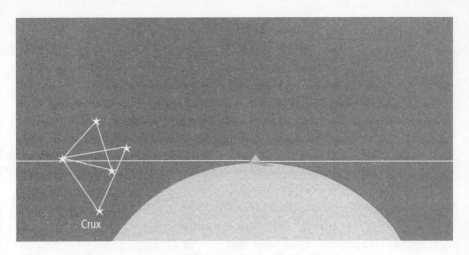

Figure 70: Crux on the Giza horizon AD 2000

Crux was also aligned on the south side of the pyramid in 2450 BC, but at this earlier date it was spotlighted by the ascending passage.

With the discovery of Crux on the Giza horizon in AD 2000, a series of duplicated alignments has now emerged, as if the signs were designed to agree:

Yildun	aligned 2450 BC and AD 2000
Crux	aligned 2450 BC and AD 2000
A pole star	aligned 2450 BC and AD 2000
Orion stars	aligned 2450 BC and AD 2000

To synchronize stars in this way is a fabulous achievement. There is no mechanical reason why a duplicate alignment with Crux and Yildun should arise in two separate pole star epochs – no reason other than by design.

The motion of all the stars on the meridian is dictated by precession and during the interval between 2450 BC and AD 2000 each star appears to move independently in relation to the grid. Yildun, for example, has climbed about 19° up the meridian ladder during this time, while Crux has climbed down the ladder by about 26°, yet despite the independent motion of each, both Yildun and Crux appear in synchronized alignment in the same two stellar epochs signposted by a bright pole star.

The monument speaks. It is a shockingly sophisticated vehicle of communication. It carries a phenomenal message.

✳ 7 ✳

SIGNS UPON SIGNS

*'...and I tried to show that
through all the immense
developments, the 'Mirror
of Being' is always the
object of true science...'*[1]

I tried viewing all the Great Pyramid alignments in the present day as a form of
script and it seems the most emphatic accent is repeatedly placed on the brilliant
stars of Orion. At each stage, in trying to translate these symbols, the figure of
Orion is ever present.

GALACTIC LINES

We live in what astronomers call 'the Orion arm' of the Milky Way Galaxy. The
galaxy also has a north pole and a south pole, just like the terrestrial and celestial
spheres.

Viewed from the Earth, the single line defined by the galactic equator appears
within the Milky Way, a brilliant band of light across the sky.

In the earliest records the Milky Way was a mythical river of stars nourishing the
imagination of many ancient astronomers. In his *Phaenomena* Aratus describes it as
follows:

'If ever on a clear night
when the dark goddess reveals
all of the stars to men in their glory
and not one is diminished by the midmonth moon
but each is a dagger of light in the gloom,
if ever on such a night

you see the awesome apparition
of the heavens asunder with a broad band of light,
or if someone standing beside you
points out a band of jewels in the sky:
that is what men call the Milky Way,
the Galaxy.'[2]

Osiris raises his arm to the Milky Way, just reaching up to the galactic equator (0°
on the galactic sphere). So I followed the line of the equator around the Milky Way
until I reached 300°. At this point on the galactic grid the stars in the constellation
Crux stand upright *aligned to the meridian of the galaxy.*[3]

In a simplified image, Osiris uses his raised limb to hold up the Milky Way like a
banner and from his elevated hand a great train of light is flexed across the sky. On
this silky strand a single brilliant cluster of jewels outshines all others. This is Crux,
sharing the line with Osiris, at 0° on the galactic equator (*see Figure 71*).

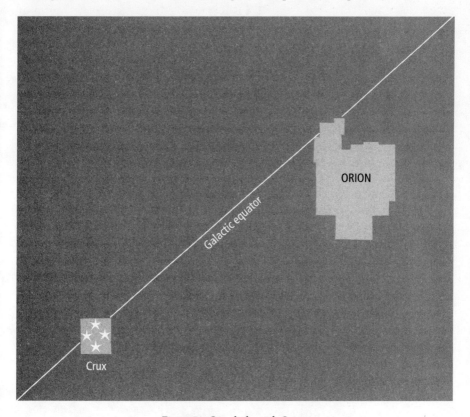

Figure 71: Crux links with Orion

If you follow the side of the Great Pyramid precisely to the southern horizon today, the linear link between Osiris and Crux is created once again, but this time across the land of Egypt.

The consequence of the link between Crux and Osiris in both stellar epochs is clear. If the lines are *read*, they draw attention to the galactic line between Osiris and Crux. This, in turn, leads to the realization that 90° of longitude separate them on the celestial sphere. And although alignments such as these appear against the odds of chance, they happen all the time in the sky today and the Great Pyramid points straight to a cluster of these anomalies.

In the preceding chapter I discussed all the star alignments on the south side of the Great Pyramid in the present day, but there is one important additional star to be considered.

LIBRA

Earlier we found the 45° spotlight from the King's Chamber locates the ears of Lepus, but I failed to mention that this alignment passes *between* the upper and

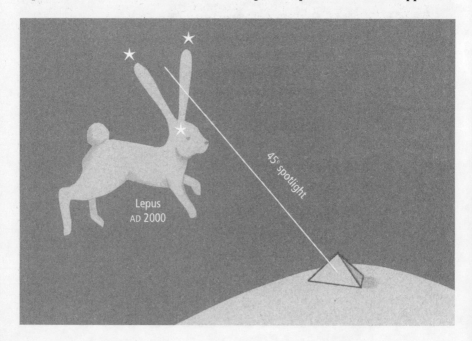

Figure 72: Forty-five degree spotlight on Lepus and on Libra

lower stars of the ears, as if through the triangle they create, and consequently this does not constitute a precise alignment to a single star.

There is, however, a bright star directly in the spotlight of the 45° star shaft today and this alignment from the King's Chamber is, I believe, the most important in the southern sky.

The brightest star directly spotlighted by the King's Chamber southern star shaft is in Libra. It is called Zubenelakrab (or Zubenelhakrabi). This is not an unusually complicated name for a star (however it may seem), but it is an unusual alignment for a number of reasons.

The three brightest stars in Libra form an isosceles triangle – or do they? On closer inspection the Alpha star at the apex of the scales of Libra is slightly misplaced and consequently the isosceles is imperfect. But the displaced Alpha star rests in the path of the sun, as if balanced on the ecliptic *(see Figure 73)*.

The passage of the sun through Libra is slightly unusual because it maintains an isosceles relationship with the two balances throughout most of its passage.

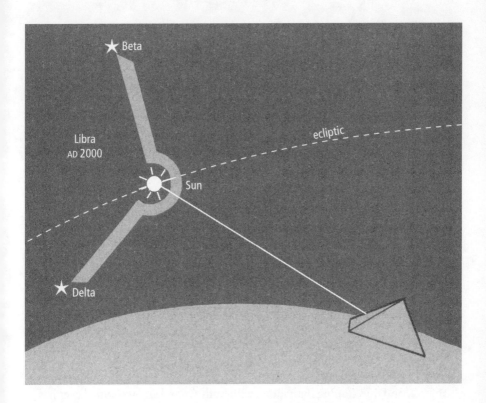

Figure 73: The brightest stars in Libra and the ecliptic

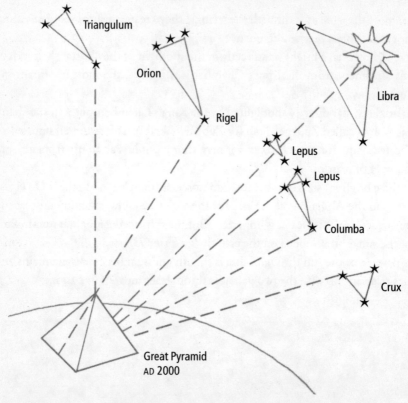

Figure 74: The spotlight on the sun in Libra and other spotlights to triangles, AD 2000

As the sun passes through Libra in AD 2000 it falls into the spotlight from the 45° star shaft, and as the alignment occurs, *the sun appears at the apex of the Libra scales, nearly occulting the Alpha star.*[4] At this time the sun itself creates a perfect isosceles triangle with the two bright stars in the balances *(see Figure 74).*

Earlier we saw the image of Osiris sitting in judgement yet only today we see the spotlight from his pyramid pinpointing the sun in Libra, the scales of justice.

It is a very powerful symbolic image and for an additional reason: by a chance of at least 4,000 to one[5] the stars in the two balances in Libra are different colours. One is red and one is green! The astronomer Michael E. Bakich explains how unusual this is:

'Beta Libra is the only star visible with the unaided eye which has a decidedly green tint. This is disputed by many observers, but many years of observing this star and questioning individuals with both trained and untrained eyes has convinced this writer of the validity of the above statement.'[6]

110

It is a striking image: the Great Pyramid bisecting the vertical at an angle of 45° and locating an isosceles triangle in Libra with the sun at the apex balancing two opposite colours.

I had now completed the star alignments currently occurring on the south side of the Great Pyramid *(see Figure 74)*. I was naturally curious to discover if similar star alignments would be discovered on the north side of the Great Pyramid in AD 2000.

THE FIERY DRAGON

The northern sky is dominated by Draco, a massive snake of 15 notable stars in a lazy looping line. Observers familiar with this constellation can more easily read the northern sky in general. The head of the dragon reaches Hercules, then the dragon coils back to meet Cephus (the King of Ethiopia). He twists again over Boötes (Orion's brother, the Ploughman), then with another great coil divides the Great Bear from the Little Bear, before finally the tip of his tail entwines the Little Bear and reaches up towards Polaris.

In 2450 BC we found two stars in Draco spotlighted by the Great Pyramid.

In AD 2000, there are two more!

The south face of the Great Pyramid now spotlights Delta Draco in one coil of the dragon and the lower (Queen's) chamber star shaft spotlights the star at the very tip of Draco's tail.[7]

Figure 75 shows the four stars in Draco aligned by the Great Pyramid in the stellar epochs AD 2000 and 2450 BC. The most extraordinary thing now happens:

Joining three of these aligned stars together creates a massive isosceles triangle.

So the geometry pinpointed in the northern sky today is coupled with exactly the same geometry on the south side of the pyramid. Indeed, exactly the same process of alignment identifies the isosceles triangles in Orion, those in Lepus, in Columba and in Crux, and in Triangulum overhead.

The more I looked, the more beautiful the artistry of these brilliant pyramid designers appeared. First they located the eye of the dragon, then they located the extreme point in one of the great coils, then the extreme point in the second great coil and then the extreme point of the tail itself.

111

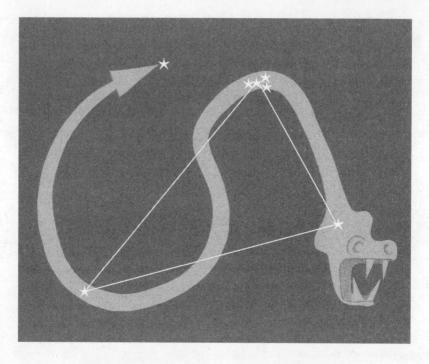

Figure 75: The four aligned dragon stars in AD 2000 and 2450 BC

Thus the four most extreme points on the dragon's body as we know it today are spot-lighted in every single case.

Ultimately Polaris (the extended tail of the dragon?) is the beacon light shining out over all these alignments. *All these northern and southern pyramid alignments are synchronized with the arrival of Polaris.*[8]

These alignments clearly identify the work of highly sophisticated astronomers who used the immutable language of geometry to carry their observations through history. They wanted to communicate. They have been scientific, analytical and clever. It is only the perception of a relentlessly primitive ancient history that prevents the fruition of this realization today.

By the time all the present day pyramid alignments had been plotted I realized the full enormity of what had been achieved. *(The total present day picture is simplified in symbols in Figure 76.)*

Still I was no nearer to understanding exactly what was being communicated. I had to establish a motive for the work.

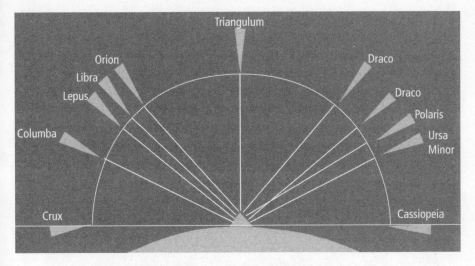

Figure 76: All the present day pyramid alignments

Looking for further clues in Egyptian mythology, I found that the god Osiris travels on 'the boat of a million years', according to *The Book of the Dead*. He is therefore still at sea, rising and falling on the precessional wave, and will continue his voyage for eternity.

But according to *The Book of the Dead* the deceased is afforded a spiritual journey to Heaven *at an unspecified time*. I remembered that all the Pharaohs expected to travel to the stars after death and began wondering if the transport of their souls was due to take place at a specific time, perhaps long after their death, and at a certain interval in the precessional journey of Orion. Were the Pharaohs mummified in order to preserve their bodies because the anticipated 'Eternal Return of Osiris' was such a long way in the future? Could the Great Pyramid be a marker in time defining the 'opening of the mouth' of the heavens to the deceased, or, if you like, the time when 'the dead shall be raised'?

The Egyptian belief in an entry into heaven was far from unique. The same belief prevailed across the ancient world, notably with the pyramid-building Mayans.

The Mayan people not only believed in the entry into heaven, they specified the entry point. They believed there was a gate into heaven, a 'star gate'. When I discovered the location of this gate I was once again surprised by a coincidence:

The Mayan star gate is located precisely where the solstice sun is found today, on the raised limb of Orion.

113

The same star gate is referred to as a 'change station' by J. L. E. Dreyer,⁹ who says that it is found 'between Gemini and Taurus'. This is precisely the location of the solstice sun in the present epoch.

It was also said by the ancient Egyptians that 'the human race was created when the sun was here'.¹⁰

More recently the archaeo-astronomer Adrian Gilbert has found a long straight shaft in the hills of the Commagene (a small state on the Upper Euphrates) which he likens to the star shafts of the Great Pyramid. Having first found this shaft aligning to the sun on the forepaw of Leo, he continued his research to find a second timed shaft alignment:

'To my amazement it turned out to be the very day on which the sun would stand directly above the outstretched right arm of Orion.'¹¹

The reverence for this area of the sky over many thousands of years of history and over many thousands of miles of territory leads me to wonder at the significance of the solstice sun arriving at this particular point in the heavens precisely when Polaris transits the pole.

We are told that Polaris is an omen of global shift and have seen the ancient Egyptian murals depicting the sun taking a violent leap when it arrives on the raised limb of Orion (see Figure 52). Whatever it is, the collective view suggests that *something* sensational happens when the brightest star reaches culmination over the pole. Polaris is, if you like, the full stop in the precessional sentence.

Running in tandem with these observations, the ancients may have believed the embarkation date for the anticipated celestial journey was dictated by a particular configuration of stars. The extended waiting period prior to departure would help to explain why the present alignments of the Great Pyramid are happening as the sun, at its extreme height, is held in the hand of Orion. The idea that a god or gods return to Earth at regular intervals is a very old one. Their arrival is said to be heralded by 'signs' in the heavens.

We are certainly now witness to the Great Pyramid identifying a series of signs mapped out between the most brilliant stars forming geometric patterns aligned to our own Earth's grid, including the erect phallus of an ancient stellar god, and all under Polaris, the brightest point of light ever to appear over the top of the world.

According to R. T. Rundle Clark, the Egyptian Creator god Atum is 'the arbiter of destiny perched on the world pole'.¹² But he also writes, 'Atum is essentially invisible.'

Is he correct or does the light of Atum now become visible with the arrival of Polaris?

✳ 8 ✳

SNAKES AND LADDERS

'The problem of numbers
remains to perplex us, and
from it all of metaphysics
was born.'[1]

To progress with the research I continued to follow lines, but with a variation: one of the lines was not straight. This was the buckled backbone of the dragon in the sky.

The head of Draco in the northern sky appears opposite Orion. Consequently, as Orion reaches his highest point in the precessional cycle today, the head of Draco reaches its lowest point. By spotlighting one constellation at its lowest point and another at its highest point the pyramid builders shout loud and clear about their very precise understanding of the precessional motion of the Earth.

It could be said that Orion and Draco are on a celestial seesaw, and one hinge point on the plank is the pole of the precessional axis, i.e. the pole of the ecliptic. The two constellations (specifically the eye of the dragon and the limb of Orion) are both resting on the meridian of the solstice sun at present. This meridian is called the solsticial colure and it joins the summer and winter solstice points, the current location of Orion and Scorpius.

I was enchanted by this image because a similar balance already exists in the mythology of the sky. It is well known that Orion was placed opposite the scorpion in order to preserve him from the fateful sting of the creature. But the head of the dragon is also in a sense 'opposite' Orion. As the precessional motion picture came to life I saw the dragon reaching down from its height in the northern sky, further and further down over the millennia of precession, until today its triangular head is as far south as it will ever be. It has reached an extreme point. It reaches its most southerly point just as Orion reaches his most northerly point, and just as the Great Pyramid fires two spotlights onto its snaking stellar form and one onto the brightest star in Orion.

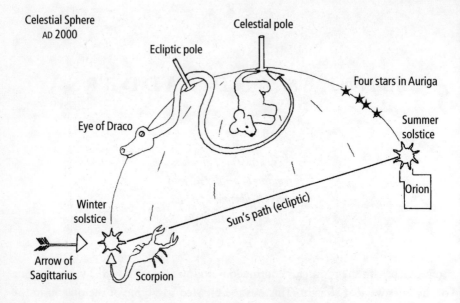

Figure 77: Draco and Orion balance

In the constellations of ancient Egypt the dragon stars are symbolized by a crocodile. The dragon and the crocodile are both primordial creatures, but they are also connected by their anatomy. They each have a series of triangles running down the full length of their backs, all the way to the tip of the tail. Obtuse as symbolism can be, I had been looking for this triangular feature. It was the antiquity of these creatures that caused me to wonder about the series of triangles in the sky gathered onto meridian lines by the Great Pyramid.

I went on to discover that these mythical celestial animals are dramatically reproduced in the real world. The image of the celestial dragon has actually been built on the surface of the Earth by the ancients, and its spine is made of stone.

THE EYE OF THE DRAGON

A series of doodles following the spotlights of the Great Pyramid today eventually led to a picture almost identical to Figure 78.

This shows how the Great Pyramid currently points to a meandering line in the sky and at the end of the line is an isosceles triangle of dominant stars. There is really no quantum leap to be found here, simply a series of straight lines pointing to a

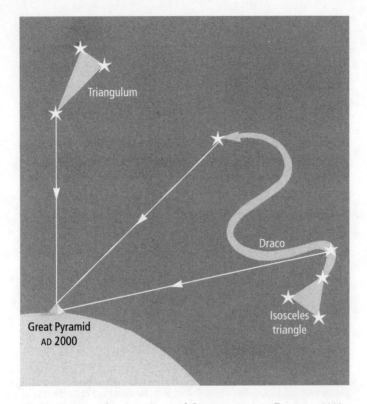

Figure 78: Triangulum over Giza and the two pointers to Draco, AD 2000

snaking line with an isosceles triangle at the end. It is one of the oldest games known in the world, the game of 'Snakes and Ladders'. A logical progression:

a. Up to the snake.
b. Along the snake.
c. Then down again.

Playing this game, we defined the location of Mt Katherine under Capella, so the following question arises naturally: does the triangle in Draco also co-ordinate with the Earth in AD 2000? Is it also pointing down, just like Triangulum?

I took the present day co-ordinates of the three brilliant stars in the dragon's head and transferred them to the Earth. There is a marked correspondence between the head of Draco on the celestial sphere in AD 2000 and the position of the British Isles on the terrestrial sphere. When the dragon is brought down to Earth, the head sits neatly over these islands *(see Figure 79)*.

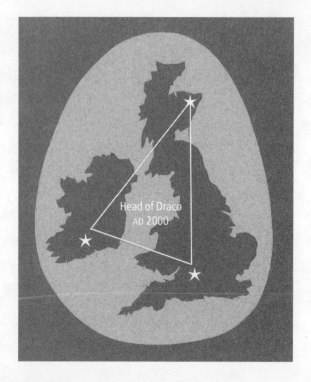

Figure 79: Draco over the Republic of Ireland and the British Isles

Being struck by a perceived visual duplication between the star map and the Earth map, I investigated the precise parallels of the three brilliant stars in the head of Draco. I was about to discover something that still astonishes me to this day.

First I followed the star at the apex of this stellar triangle, very accurately defining the vertical transit of the star over the British Isles, stellar epoch AD 2000.

The star now passes vertically over Ben Nevis, the highest point in Britain.

Now I had seen it all.

In 2450 BC I had found a brilliant triangle over Giza. I had transferred the stars of the triangle to the Earth and located the highest mountain in Egypt. Now, following the lines from Giza directly to an isosceles triangle of stars and down to Earth once more, I had located the highest mountain in the British Isles.

You may sense my incredulity at finding this star/mountain alignment today. And chance is not really the issue. The process is the same today under Polaris as it was in 2450 BC under Thuban: the Great Pyramid provides a linear progression, and

The brightest stars in the Orion constellation.
© Roger Ressmeyer/Corbis

Stars appear to travel in parallel lines orbiting the celestial pole.
© Roger Ressmeyer/Corbis

The interior of the tomb of Seti I (*c.*1300 BC). The sky is symbolized on grid lines creating units of 10°.

© Werner Forman Archive

The Giza pyramids overlooking Cairo at the apex of the Nile Delta. The three large pyramids symbolize the stars of Orion's Belt.
© Yann Arthus-Bertrand/Corbis

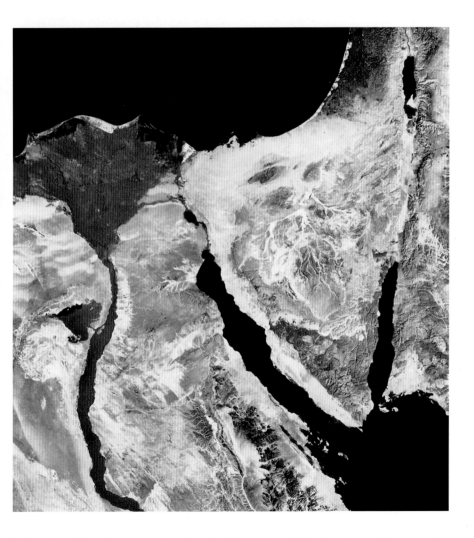

Infra-red satellite photograph showing the Nile Delta and Sinai peninsula. The apex of
the delta rests at 30° north.

© Earth Satellite Corporation/Science Photo Library

Silbury Hill in Wiltshire, the largest earth mound in Europe, concealing a stone
pyramid. The hill symbolizes the star Eltamin, the eye of the Dragon vertically overhead
in AD 2000.
© Cordaiy Photo Library/Corbis

Chinese pyramid. Over 100 pyramids have been recognized in China. The White
Pyramid is said to be the largest in the world.
© Hartwig Hausdorf

Monk's Mound at Cahokia, USA, 100 feet high with a base measuring approximately 980 × 780 feet. The star Vega currently passes vertically over the mound.
© Richard A. Cooke/Corbis

The pyramid fields near Xi'an in central China. Geometrically arranged mountains have been constructed across the globe.
© Hartwig Hausdorf

Parallel lines at Nazca creating the image of a humming bird.
© Yann Arthus-Bertrand/Corbis

An aerial view of the Avebury circle, 'The Dragon Ring'.
© Adam Woolfitt/Corbis

at the end of the line is an isosceles triangle of brilliant stars, and under the apex of the triangle is a 'high point'.

The accuracy of this present day vertical to Ben Nevis is within a tenth of a degree.[2] What I found so uncanny about this discovery is the fact that I was looking for a prodigious high point beneath these stars in the first place! But to immediately alight upon the very highest summit on an island the size of mainland Britain was a spectacular free fall.

Here we are in AD 2000 and the Great Pyramid is still speaking the same language as it did in 2450 BC: stars are mountains. I could hardly believe it, but there was far more to follow.

I looked beneath the second bright star in the head of Draco today.

The star passes vertically over Mt Brandon, the second highest point in the Irish Republic.

Mt Brandon is the most extreme westerly mountain in Eurasia, i.e. the highest point on the west of the continent overlooking the Atlantic. The alignment of Ben Nevis and Mt Brandon under two neighbouring brilliant stars today is wonderful. Both vertical alignments are accurate to one tenth of a degree.

This left me wondering even more about the nature of stars and mountains. Over a period of 24 hours these two high points pass beneath the two stars in Draco within a few minutes of each other, consequently to an observer on either mountain the zenith of the two stars would appear to be simultaneous to the naked eye today.

It is a very strange feature of nature finding two great mountains and two brilliant neighbouring stars so closely matched, but the triangle had yet to be completed, the brightest star in the dragon had yet to be brought down to Earth.

The third star in this brilliant triangle of stars is the very brightest of all the stars in the constellation Draco. It is called Eltanim, it is the sixty-sixth brightest star in the sky and it represents the eye of the dragon.

I followed the passage of Eltanim with England passing under the star. Would one really expect a third random stellar point to connect with a third extreme high point in Britain?

Eltanim now passes vertically over Silbury Hill, a concealed stone pyramid, the largest earth mound in Europe (see plate 6).

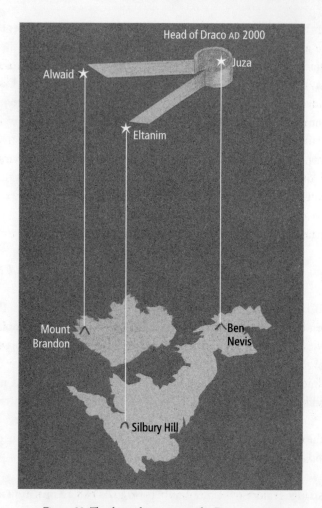

Figure 80: The three alignments under Draco, AD 2000

It is highly unlikely that Silbury Hill achieves this stellar distinction by accident, because we arrived at this stone pyramid covered with earth by following a linear progression from another stone pyramid, now resident under Triangulum.

All three vertical alignments beneath the head of Draco *(see Figure 80)* are accurate to one tenth of a degree in stellar epoch AD 2000.

The three stars in the head of Draco now pass over:

a. The most westerly mountain in Eurasia.
b. The highest point in Britain.
c. The largest ancient earth mound in Europe.

There appears to be a very clever method of communication here. The three Draco stars provide a perfect example of the stellar geometry pinpointed by the Giza designers so persistently under Thuban. Every day at present, within the space of half an hour, each brilliant star in the head of Draco passes over a prodigious high point as listed above.

These international pyramid builders surely knew the Earth in intimate detail – they demonstrated as much when Capella passed over Mt Katherine and the pyramid lit up with 11 alignments. It has done the same again today, carrying information through time and establishing a global heritage.

Silbury Hill at Avebury is a star symbol, just like the pyramids at Giza. This symbolism is alive once again under the eye of the dragon.

But there are yet more connections between Silbury Hill and Draco.

THE NAME OF THE DRAGON

Avebury must be one of the most beautiful ancient sites in the world. It is known today, as it has been throughout history, as 'The Dragon Ring' *(see plate 11)*.[3] The celestial name and the terrestrial name are the same, they mirror each other, they are balanced, indeed they are identical.

What is proof but an equation of symbols?

CELESTIAL DRAGON = TERRESTRIAL DRAGON

ELTANIM PARALLEL = SILBURY HILL PARALLEL

THE DRAGON'S STARS = THE DRAGON'S IMAGE ON THE GROUND

In Avebury church there is an antique stone font carved in the eleventh century. A dragon is seen wrapped around the font and a bishop is pointing to the eye of this dragon with his crosier. Some say the bishop is poking out the eye of the dragon, but in any event the singular motif on the antique font in Avebury is a man pointing to the eye of a dragon!

As for the ancient British pyramid at Avebury, it is linked by a dragon to its counterpart on the Giza plateau. Both are found beneath a famous isosceles triangle of stars in AD 2000 and the line linking them is none other than the dragon or serpent in the sky, the logos of health and wisdom, the snake curling round the northern poles, the mythical rope turning the celestial churn.

The pyramid builders were symbolists in landscapes above and below, they were the ultimate landscape artists. They were brilliant, they were technicians, they measured the Earth and the sky and discovered a mirror in AD 2000, under Polaris.

I felt I had received the reward I had been seeking. I was now in touch with extremely sophisticated symbolists who were using a geometric language. The symbolic pun between the mountain and the star (both 'high points') was revealing itself numerically. This is a magical language, but it is based in the mathematics of the celestial and terrestrial spheres and is therefore undeniably sophisticated, however prehistoric.

I started to read more of the language. Silbury Hill is a concealed stone pyramid now passing vertically beneath the brighter eye of the dragon. The high point matching the star today is drawing our attention to the duplicate alignment of the neighbouring star to Ben Nevis. (The identical procedure led us from the Great Pyramid to the summit of Mt Katherine in 2450 BC under the last pole star.)

Looking at the topography around Ben Nevis, I cast the blanket over the highest mountains and noticed something familiar in the pattern as the highest neighbouring points emerged:

The highest neighbouring
points in Britain are isosceles.

Furthermore, one of these isosceles triangles is aligned to the Earth's parallel of latitude.

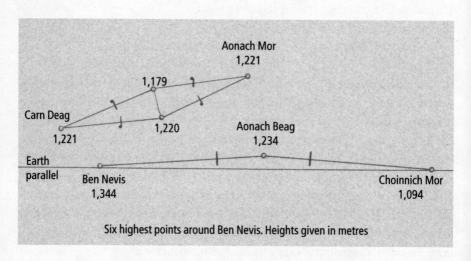

Six highest points around Ben Nevis. Heights given in metres

Figure 81: The highest neighbouring points in Britain

So the Great Pyramid directs our attention to the geometric arrangement of the highest points in Egypt and also in Britain. By building three mountains in an isosceles triangle aligned to the Earth's grid at Giza the architects could hardly have been more emphatic in demonstrating some understanding of this natural geometry.

When this research led us to the summit of Mt Katherine in 2450 BC we looked at the local topography and discovered that the high massifs adjacent to Mt Katherine produced an isosceles triangle aligned to the meridian. We then found isosceles triangles among the neighbours of Mt Nezzi overlooking Karnac and now once again at Ben Nevis.

I decided to look for the same form of symbolism in the topography surrounding Silbury Hill. I went looking for high points arranged in isosceles triangles at Avebury.

Silbury Hill and Avebury are placed equidistant from the local high point Woden Hill.

Remembering that at Giza the local high point creates an equilateral triangle with the pyramids, here at Avebury we can see the local high point creates an isosceles triangle with Avebury and Silbury Hill in the balances *(see Figure 82)*.

Dropping the magic blanket over the Avebury area, two massive hills are the first to appear, one called Milk Hill, the other called Tan Hill. These hills are the same height and are the highest points overlooking everything to the horizon and beyond *(see Figure 90)*. I joined them together on the map with the summit of Silbury Hill.[4]

These three high points form an isosceles triangle. The isosceles is perfectly formed between the three summits on the 1:50,000 scale Ordnance Survey map of the area. It is therefore safe to say that the three summits spread over three miles create an isosceles triangle accurate to a few yards on the ground.

As well as Silbury Hill, Milk Hill and Tan Hill forming an isosceles triangle, the summit of Woden Hill shares the meridian with Milk Hill.

I am trying to establish that natural topography was an integral part of this ancient yet highly sophisticated geomancy. I have arrived at Silbury Hill, transported by the brightest star in the dragon, and here on the ground, against the odds, I have found the same familiar shape yet again, an isosceles triangle between the highest points.

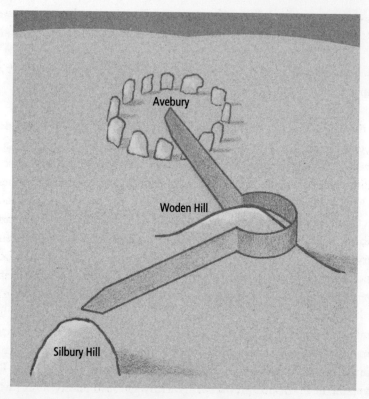

Figure 82: The balance at Avebury

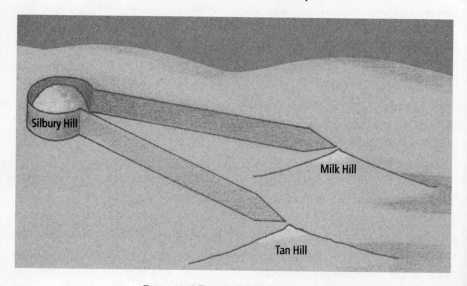

Figure 83: Silbury Hill isosceles triangle

A match is now taking place. The sky image is mirroring the Earth image, high point to high point, mountain to star; as above, so below; a mirror of triangles.

I was once again intrigued by the topography of this area. Using a 1:50,000 scale Ordnance Survey map I established this strange fact:

The three highest points looking east from Silbury Hill form an equilateral triangle over the ground.

According to the Ordnance Survey Map the equilateral triangle created by these three high points is accurate to about 100 yards over many miles. I doubt any logic would suggest that three random neighbouring points should create an equilateral triangle by chance, twice. But the chance has occurred once on the Giza plateau and here again at Avebury. At both sites the ancients constructed their own high points and at both sites the topography reveals an equilateral triangle of three neighbouring high points.

The 'language' I keep referring to can be found in the very features of the landscape. It is surely no accident that Woden Hill and Silbury Hill are also the same height, thereby mirroring the duplicate relationship between Tan Hill and Milk Hill. The man-made hill is mimicking the natural terrain, a balance once again.

There is a code which relates 'high points' geometrically. The Great Pyramid points to this code by spotlighting triangles between high points in the sky using a triangular high point on the ground. But now the emphasis shifts. The stellar pointers reflect a *global* picture and there are now duplicate symbols at Giza and at Avebury. Radiocarbon dating for the Great Pyramid suggests it was constructed (or reconstructed) around 3000 BC. The Avebury circle is believed to be of similar antiquity. Once again I say these builders have done everything in their global power to attract attention to the stellar and terrestrial points mirroring each other under the new pole star. What the ancient Egyptian and the ancient British builders achieved was a record for the future, something to be considered now, an egg that hatches under the light of Polaris.

I now investigated the topography of Avebury and nearby Stonehenge in some detail in order to discover more about this geometric language of high points.

The two sites are about 17 miles apart and so closely aligned on the meridian of the Earth that they are listed in *The Times World Atlas* as follows:

Avebury longitude	1.51 west
Stonehenge longitude	1.51 west

On close inspection the eastern extreme of Silbury Hill falls directly on the meridi-an of the western extremity of the Avebury circle, a neat little geometry (identical to Sneferu's arrangement of the Red and the Bent pyramids at Dashur).

The land between Avebury and Stonehenge is dominated by a big undulating carpet of grassland called the Marlborough Downs. On the ridge overlooking Ave-bury, the second and third highest points are about eight miles apart. Both high points feature a massive antique earthwork. These earthworks (called Rybury Camp and Martinsell Hill Fort) are perfectly aligned to the parallel of the globe by their extremities, but more striking still, they create an isosceles triangle with the stone circle at Avebury *(see Figure 84)*.

Using the same two earthworks on the Earth parallel, an isosceles triangle now finds Stonehenge *(see Figure 85)*.

Notice how the apex of this isosceles triangle is pointing towards Stonehenge, locating the area where the River Avon makes a very pronounced kink. From this particular point the ancient builders at Stonehenge created two straight parallel lines on the ground stretching for at least one-and-a-half miles. The lines are still visible today and have been called the Cursus. Following these wonderful old geo-metric lines across the English countryside brings you straight to Glastonbury Tor – the most revered mystical high point in England.

So the geometric language I have been referring to in the sky can be plainly seen on the downs of England. The land is carved into lines and circles. Monuments are

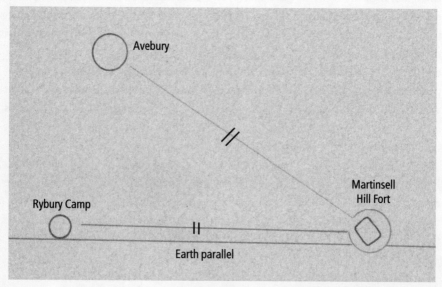

Figure 84: The earthworks and the isosceles triangle including Avebury

aligned to the meridian in England just as they are at Giza. All along there has been this signature, this common tongue, this play with signs, this geometry. And here, under the eye of Stonehenge, a straight line is defined passing the circle and leading directly to Glastonbury Tor.

The beautiful play with topography is in fact spread across the mainland of Britain. The ancient masters of geography demonstrate their talents in this simple manner:

a. Following the Earth parallel due west of Stonehenge leads directly to Dunkery Beacon, the highest point overlooking Exmoor.
b. Following the Earth parallel due east of Stonehenge leads directly to Leith Hill overlooking south-east England.
c. Following the meridian due north of Stonehenge leads directly to the Peak (also called High Peak and Kinder Scout) in the Midlands. Looking south from the Peak, there is no higher point in the country.

The Peak is so closely aligned to Stonehenge and Avebury that the figures in *The Times World Atlas* match as follows:

Avebury longitude	1°51' west
Stonehenge longitude	1°51' west
The Peak longitude	1°51' west

And from the same source:

Dunkery Beacon latitude	51°11' north
Stonehenge latitude	51°11' north
Leith Hill latitude	51°11' north

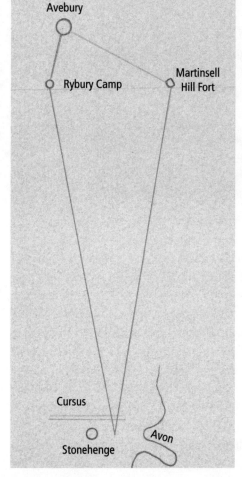

Figure 85: The isosceles to Stonehenge

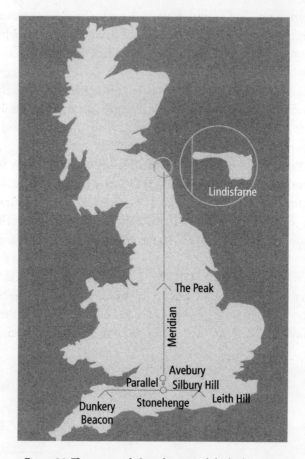

Figure 86: The cross with Stonehenge and the high points

There is a linear language here. These geographical alignments are once again concerned with defining the meridian of the Earth in relation to high points.

The facility of these ancient builders is remarkable. We find more of the same code revealed with the stellar alignment of Stonehenge discussed later. But before returning to Giza, I followed the meridian of Stonehenge northwards directly over the Sanctuary at Avebury, up to the Peak and onwards, up to the coast. Here I found the precise meridian of Avebury defined by the extreme fingertip of Lindisfarne Island. To look at it another way, if you proceed precisely due south from the fingertip of Lindisfarne you will pass the Peak, Avebury, Silbury Hill and Stonehenge (the same play already noted with the Red Sea fingertip.)

Surely this single meridian line falling from a famous fingertip of holy land absolutely precisely defining Avebury 200 miles away demonstrates exactly the

point about 'extremes' made earlier. If you catch a boat following this same meridian still further north from Lindisfarne you will arrive at the apex of Britain's most
pronounced isosceles triangle of land at Peterhead *(see Figure 86)*.

There is yet another feature in the old English landscape that is linked in an isosceles formation. The Cerne Giant stands indelicately above the peaceful countryside
even today. He is a naked man carved in the turf at an unknown date. His right arm
is raised, his penis is erect. Does this sound familiar?

Whatever the age of the Cerne Giant himself, nobody can ever know who first
marked the land here, or at Avebury, or at Stonehenge. But the land *was* marked
out long ago, and if you join the Cerne Giant with Glastonbury Tor and Stonehenge they create an isosceles triangle stretching 40 miles overland. The isosceles
formation includes Dunkery Beacon *(see Figure 87)*.

In his book *A View over Atlantis* John Michell described an ancient 'global web'.
He proclaimed that ancient sites around the world were part of one story, that 'a
great scientific instrument is sprawled over the entire surface of the globe'. Perhaps his intuitive grasp of this subject has yet to be fully recognized. He says:

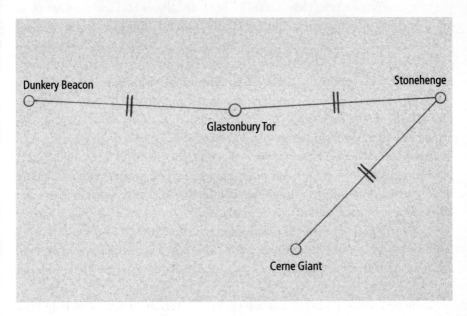

Figure 87: The Cerne Giant triangle

'No one knows how the world wide task was achieved, still less why. And this, of course is the ultimate question. If we knew why these people outside the range of written history devoted their entire skill and resources to the construction of a terrestrial pattern that measured both the Earth and the heavens, we would know the secret of their universal civilisation, a state which now seems hopelessly elusive.'[5]

The Cerne Giant, Glastonbury Tor, Dunkery Beacon, Stonehenge, the Peak, Lindisfarne, Peterhead, Silbury Hill, Leith Hill and Avebury, all these places are figured on a geometric web, and perhaps now as the dragon stars align vertically over the high points of Britain, we can more readily recognize the conviction driving these ancient builders. They had seen a form of God. They had recognized a parallel between the Earth and the sky. They made a record for the future, for a time when the brightest star in history shines over the top of the world, and they moved mountains to communicate this vision.

Pictures at an Exhibition

The artist Paul Klee once painted a picture called 'Taking a line for a walk'. Figure 88 shows how a line can be taken for a walk across the heavens from one bright star to the next, creating a strong clear linear link between Silbury Hill and the Giza pyramids. The line only becomes connected in this fashion during the lower culmination of Draco and the upper culmination of Orion. The link will be severed by precession. This co-ordination is very transient and the mirror of Draco stars is only now reflecting the mountains of the Earth. And at the end of the dragon's tail there lies Polaris, hovering over the north polar point of the world today, the focal point for all the meridians on Earth.

The prevailing conviction that the designers of Avebury and Stonehenge were 'hunter gatherers' or even 'early agrarians' appears unrealistic in light of the logical linear language they present across the countryside. Their profound understanding of astronomy and their precise meridian alignments are clear scientific signals from a pre-primitive global society.[6]

The Earth has obviously been measured in great detail at some time in prehistory – but I had yet to realize the full extent of this ancient understanding of Heaven and Earth as true twins.

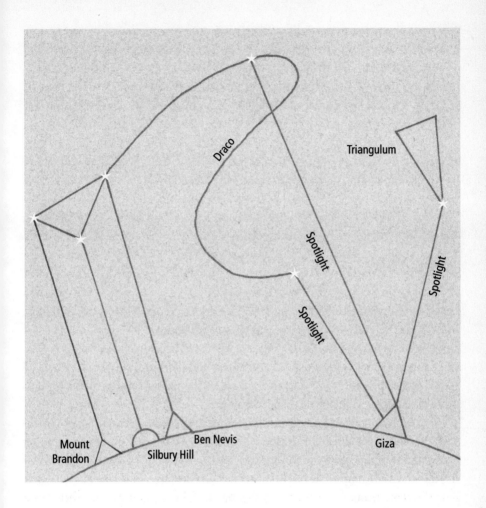

Figure 88: Taking a line for a walk

✳ 9 ✳

THE LAND OF TRIANGLES

'In fact, there was nothing
that could be called a "start",
least of all the intention to
explore the astronomical
nature of myth.' [1]

I decided to investigate further and see if I could find more evidence of this global web. I began by looking more closely at the constellations.

Between Draco and Scorpius two giant men are found in the sky. One is Hercules and the other is Ophiuchus. In the images described by Aratus, the heel of Hercules is resting (or stamping) on the head of the dragon and the heel of Ophiuchus is standing on the heart of the scorpion.

I shifted my attention from the stellar dragon to the scorpion lying more directly opposite Orion. As already mentioned, according to legend, the scorpion killed Orion and so it was placed as far away from him as possible.[2] I wanted to discover whether the star Antares, the brightest star in the scorpion, acted as a celestial marker in the same manner as Eltanim in the dragon. The connection was both linear and mythological. Antares is the fifteenth brightest star in the heavens, a beautiful red colour.

The logical question I asked myself was this: if the brightest star in the dragon yielded a vertical alignment to Avebury, would the brightest star in the scorpion also pass vertically above an ancient site today?

The method used to define the vertical alignment of a brilliant star over the Earth has already been described. It is a 'mirror' process in which the parallel occupied by the star on the celestial sphere is mirrored by the same parallel defined on the Earth below. I believe it is possible that the ancient expression 'as above, so below' has its origins in this process of transferring stars from their heavenly parallel down to their reciprocal parallel on Earth.

To find the overhead position of a star on modern maps is very straightforward. If the star is at 10° above the celestial equator it will pass over a parallel of land running right around the globe like a thin rubber band placed 10° above the Earth's equator.[3] Antares is about −26.5° below the celestial equator, so I investigated this parallel on the Earth.

EASTER ISLAND

Isolated, lonely and enigmatic Easter Island now passes beneath the star Antares.

Easter Island is a little delta-shaped lump of volcanic rock jutting out of the vastness of the Pacific Ocean 1,100 miles from Pitcairn Island and a similar distance from South America. It is one of the most remote areas of land on the planet. It covers only 45 square miles, yet spread across it are over 1,000 carved stone statues. The statues are called Moai and some are over 65 feet high, with one stone figure alone weighing 90 tons. The vast majority of the stones are worked in an identical sculptural style.

Easter Island is called 'the eye turned towards the sky',[4] but only a few of the giant statues here are looking skywards at Antares today. The vast majority are facing the sea. The statues have bland expressionless faces forever staring blankly at the formless ocean. They unanimously turn their gaze away from the small island they occupy, but why? What are these eyes turning away from? What great secret lies unseen behind them?

If the Moai statues on Easter Island were ever to turn their inert and stony bodies inland to gaze across their island they would see three great volcanoes dominating the now treeless terrain. It would be hard to find three more dominant isolated summits on the surface of the globe and I wondered why the Maoi statues so insistently turned their gaze away from these three volcanoes on their lonely island, preferring to gaze gauntly at the ocean.

Having found this remarkable group of figures below the star Antares I was bound to look at the topography in search of the isosceles triangle motif.

I joined the three volcanoes on Easter Island together, drawing a line from one summit across the map to the next summit and then to the third summit, the craggy lip of a volcano.

The three greatest summits on Easter Island form an isosceles triangle.

What an extraordinary observation. I went looking for an ancient site beneath a brilliant star today and I found one. Then I went looking for the triangular symbol between the highest points on the site and I immediately found an isosceles triangle.

I had found the same persistent code repeating itself three times. Once under Alpha Triangulum, locating Giza, a second time under Eltanim, locating Avebury, and now a third time under Antares, locating Easter Island.

It became clear to me that the ancient sites are now really synchronizing with the sky because Polaris has arrived.

Although I was looking for it, it was still a great shock to find another isosceles triangle of high points beneath a brilliant star. Isn't it odd to find the three prodigious points on Easter Island forming this special triangle when the high points neighbouring Avebury, and Ben Nevis, and Mt Katherine, and Mt Nezzi, and on the Giza plateau, all produce isosceles triangles also. One might conclude that three random points clearly create this type of geometry with great regularity, but such a conclusion is demonstrably incorrect. You can prove for yourself that three random points do not generally create an isosceles triangle. And so the enigma deepens.

The common yet unusual geometric topography at all these sites confers uniformity on the global web already mentioned. All these ancient stone monuments are concerned with a common geometry. At each location three high points mark out the corners of an isosceles or an equilateral triangle. Chance does not behave like this.

To those who are not irretrievably immersed in the current historical dogma it may be possible to see that Giza, Easter Island and Avebury appear to be synchronized by a subtle geographic and astronomical plan. And, yet more revealing, these sites are synchronized under the present day night sky. Indeed, we have only reached these sites via the brilliant stars now uniquely synchronized above them. I believe one sure reason for this synchronization is the arrival of our polar beacon Polaris. It is the presence of Polaris over the pole that triggers the pre-planned vertical alignment process uniquely at this time.

It seems that the monuments at Giza, Avebury and Easter Island were created as planetary markers by extremely advanced people who regarded the celestial and terrestrial spheres as geometric models of each other. This idea should not be an altogether unexpected one. There are innumerable written records from antiquity claiming that a mirror between Heaven and Earth exists. But these have more recently been dismissed as a lie, a fantasy or a pathetic mistake. The ancient written word was therefore insufficient to communicate the truth. But the truth was also set in stone.

Stars, pyramids, triangles, squares, circles and straight lines, these are the words in the language of the monument builders. Their genius was to graft immutable symbols on the surface of the globe. In this way their message could be passed on. The association of forms is at the root of all intellectual understanding, in fact our ability to equate and differentiate symbols is the cornerstone of all written language.

Obviously if the Avebury and Stonehenge builders were defining the meridians and parallels across the entire British countryside then their understanding of global geography was substantial. The same awareness of regional geography is displayed by the Giza designers with the relationship between Giza and Mt Katherine, the Nile Delta, the Valley of the Kings, the Red Sea fingertip, etc. At Easter Island exactly the same understanding of regional geography and topography is displayed. Either these craftsmen were all working to common guidelines, or the builders at each site simply happened by chance to build in these remote places entirely unaware that the geographic idiosyncrasies at each venue were identical and that bright stars would align vertically with these sites simultaneously in the distant future, precisely when Polaris transits the pole.

But even some of the celestial names are the same as the ancient sites beneath them:

a. Triangulum passes over the triangular pyramids.
b. Draco passes over the Dragon Ring.
c. Polaris passes over the polar point.

The Earth and the sky are arranged. The ancient message keeps repeating itself. It points to the highest summits in Egypt, in England and on Easter Island, suggesting they are not random, that they are part of a design. Who, one wonders, *could* design such a thing?

Archaeologists are in no dispute that Giza, Avebury and Easter Island are religious sites. The Creator made the Earth and the sky in mirror image, they are twins, they are Nut and Geb, they are dragon on dragon, triangle on triangle, they are 'signs upon signs', indeed they are just what Aratus told us to look out for.

Back at Easter Island, the dark gaunt figures see nothing but the formless ocean. They do not notice the unusual geometry of peaks behind them. These Moai figures are one of the most enigmatic ancient masterpieces on the planet. Are they perhaps caricatures of people today rather than yesterday? We may have failed to recognize the geometry of the Earth. We may feel secure in the knowledge that the topography of the planet is created by essentially chaotic forces within. Are we Moai, or can we turn to witness the order appearing in the chaos of volcanoes on Easter Island?

Leaving the volcanoes of Easter Island, I decided to look systematically at the brightest stars in the sky today. I was becoming increasingly convinced that other ancient sites around the world may now more fully reveal their common heritage and their allegiance to the night sky under Polaris. I started the research with our brightest star, the sun.

RA, RA

We saw earlier that when the sun passes into Libra it falls into alignment with the 45° spotlight from the Great Pyramid. This alignment occurs when the sun is located at −15°05 on the celestial sphere.

The ancient site of Nazca is located at −15° on the terrestrial sphere.

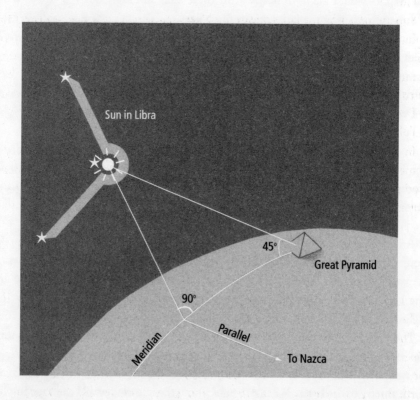

Figure 89: The alignment to the sun and the Libra isosceles from the Great Pyramid, AD 2000

On the few days of the year when the sun on the meridian is targeted by the 45° star shaft it shines vertically down on the plains of Nazca. In short, to arrive at Nazca from Giza requires a linear journey straight to the celestial sphere at 45° and a vertical drop from that parallel.

The Nazca plains are an expansive flat and arid land in the foothills of the Andes. The area is lonely and still. In times gone by it was used as a huge drawing board upon which signs, symbols and animal figures were inscribed by people who systematically cleared large quantities of small stones in long lines *(see plate 10)*. This fantastic artwork covers a huge area of the barren Nazca plains, but cannot be observed at ground level because of the great size of the figures. From the air, however, the Nazcan art has fantastic appeal. Once again, here is a vast artistic project laid out across the land yet invisible to, or hidden from, the native observer at ground level. (This is another feature common to the majority of ancient monuments. The geometry is usually invisible unless you take an overhead view, i.e. look at a map.)

Superimposed on the animal forms at Nazca, great geometric figures dissect the plain. These geometric shapes are created with ruler-straight lines; many are several miles long and many form acutely pointed isosceles shapes. The most recent research at Nazca has determined that these ancient geometric lines are often oriented to the highest points on the horizon. Indeed, the flat plain of Nazca is studded with a series of raised mounds or earthworks upon which many of the ancient straight lines rest or converge.

In the present stellar epoch, the sun passes overhead at Nazca on the same day it aligns to the 45° shaft in the Great Pyramid. Naturally I wondered if the pyramid spotlight was once again defining bright stars related to the topography of the globe. Were the stars of Libra in some way related to the Earth?

MAPS AND MOUNTAINS

The Libra stars currently pass over the Andes every day, so I began to study the highest points in this, the longest chain of mountains in the world.

The vast ranges of the Andes are hinged on Lake Titicaca in the elbow of South America. Overlooking this huge lake is Mt Illampu, one of the great mountains of the world. Mt Illampu is reportedly over 23,000 feet and consequently if you travel north through the continent of America from its summit, you will find no higher point on the entire continent. (Mt Illampu is 3,000 feet higher than the highest point in North America, Mt McKinley.)[6]

Maps are generally agreed that Mt Illampu or Mt Sajama are the highest points in Bolivia, though encyclopaedias disagree on this point. But the precise location of the apex of Mt Illampu has proved very hard to define. It does not appear precisely placed on the Navigation Chart and atlases vary by several minutes of degree regarding this location.

Maps of the Andes do vary considerably – the heights and the names of the highest points change with nearly every map – however, they generally agree that Mt Illampu is 15°51' south of the equator.

The brilliant star Alpha Libra now passes over Mt Illampu, a vertical alignment of star and mountain accurate to a tenth of a degree.

Once again, the brightest star in a constellation is passing over a prodigious summit.

It is true that the mountains much further south on the South American continent do rise above the height of Mt Illampu. But Mt Illampu appears certainly the highest point overlooking the northern half of South America and all of North America. It is therefore very strange once again to go looking for a high point beneath a brilliant star and fall to this particular prodigious peak under Alpha Libra. So where is Beta Libra today?

The chain of the Andes snakes away from Mt Illampu heading north and the peaks reduce in size. But as the chain continues into northern Peru, once again a small cluster of peaks rises to over 20,000 feet. The greatest of these peaks is called Mt Hauscaran. At 22,205 feet it is the highest summit in Peru.

The star Beta Libra passes over Mt Hauscaran, a vertical alignment accurate to one third part of a degree.[7]

I had gone looking for great mountains beneath the brightest stars in Libra, and this is what I had found:

1. Mount Illampu now passes under Alpha Libra.
2. Mount Hauscaran now passes under Beta Libra.

These predominant mountains of South America are over 700 miles apart, yet their locations are defined by the two brightest Libra stars today.

And there is further confirmation that ancient monument builders in South America were aware of this extraordinary mirror of stars and mountains:

138

The site of the Nazca Plain is at the apex of an isosceles triangle joining Mt Hauscaran and Mt Illampu.

If you compare Figures 89–90 and 91, the language of stars and triangles, and mountains and triangles, and mountains and stars, can clearly be seen.

People familiar with Bolivian mountains may well be asking why I have failed to include Mt Ancohuma or Mt Sajama. Indeed, one or two maps do suggest that Mt Ancohuma and Sajama are taller than Mt Illampu, but, more alarming still, some co-ordinates suggest that two mountains are in the same place. *The Times World Atlas* comprehensive edition gives co-ordinates for the great mountains of the world, but these co-ordinates do vary a little from those of the Operational Navigation Charts. Owing to 'Relief Data Unreliable' being printed over Mt Illampu and

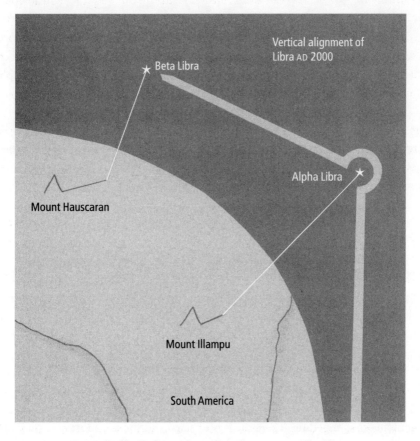

Figure 90: The duplicate alignments of mountains under Libra

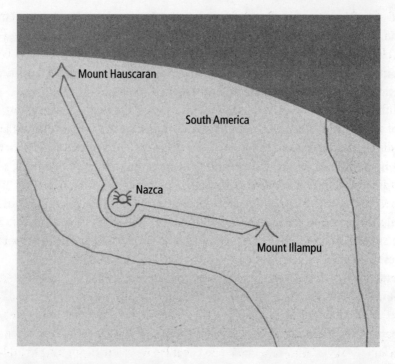

Figure 91: The isosceles triangle between Mt Illampu, Nazca and Mt Hauscaran

Mt Ancohuma on the navigation chart, I checked *The Times World Atlas* to discover the reported whereabouts of these two illusive peaks:

Mt Ancohuma 15°54' north		68°30' west
Mt Illampu 15°51' north		68°30' west

The atlas suggests these mountains are aligned on the Earth's meridian.

Wherever these mountains are precisely, they are the highest points overlooking Lake Titicaca and they have a third huge neighbour, Mt Illimani. This towering peak also features in the star mirror.

A SIDEWAYS LOOK

Before continuing with this search I would like to explain why I find these vertical alignments so compelling. There are lots of stars, and there are lots of mountains, and there are also lots of ancient sites. But if we now look back at the three 'high

point' alignments over the British Isles created under the triangular head of Draco
we can make a judgement about the alignment of Ben Nevis, Mt Brandon and Silbury Hill and compare these South American alignments under the Libra isosceles.
Both groups of stars form an isosceles triangle and both triangles align vertically
with extreme high points on the Earth today.

With these observations in South America, is it not extremely strange to find the
Draco stars locating the highest point in Britain and then to find the brightest Libra
stars doing exactly the same thing with the highest points in Bolivia and Peru – and
more revealing still to find the seventh wonder of the ancient world firing spotlights at both these constellations today?

There are lots of mountains, but these are exclusive peaks in every case: Ben
Nevis is the highest point in Britain, Mt Hauscaran is the highest point in Peru and
some say Mt Illampu is the highest point in Bolivia. Thus the sky defines the location of the highest mountains under an isosceles triangle of bright stars.

I only looked beneath the brightest stars in Draco and Libra because the Great
Pyramid is pointing to them on this day. These stars really are passing over the high
points on Earth now. The geography is firmly beneath our feet and fully visible on
our sophisticated maps, yet from the depths of antiquity, a pattern between the
Earth and the sky is being described. The Great Pyramid is now pointing to brilliant
stars passing over high points which are so predominant in the landscape that the
star = mountain formula now appears unmistakably on the face of the Earth.

At this stage I knew I had cracked a code, but I was running ahead of myself and
I had failed to look beneath the brightest star in the heavens.

ISIS

The star Sirius, symbol of the goddess Isis, is over 16° south of the celestial equator
at present and passes mainly above the oceans. However, like the stars of Libra,
Sirius also passes over the centre of South America and across the Andes.

As the Earth slowly turns, the parallel of Sirius on the celestial sphere can be
used to trace a fine line across central South America (the same process adopted
with Draco and Libra). I followed the line of Sirius over the Earth today.

And again I was astonished by what I found.

Sirius passes over Tiahuanaco.

Once again the alignment is accurate to one tenth of a degree.

Tiahuanaco is a massive enigma. Lying near the southern shore of Lake Titicaca, it is one of the largest ancient sites in the world. Its architecture is monumental, but its cultural roots are nowhere to be found. Although archaeologists suggest the site was inhabited for 2,000 years, no evidence of writing has been discovered here. The site is described by the *Reader's Digest* as follows:

'Its stones bear witness to a colossal style of building, square and rigid, which expresses itself in mathematically ordered and forbidding walls.'[8]

Huge statues were carved here by a race of people whose origins remain mysterious. The glyphs on the statues are unlike any others. Certain of the worked stones are 16 feet wide and 26 feet long, yet there is little oxygen in this high and remote place, and the stones were transported from quarries 40 and 100 miles away![9]

Tiahuanaco is home to the famous single stone doorway called the Gate of the Sun, but perhaps more importantly there is also a large pyramid on this remote site, known as the Akapana pyramid.

Sirius, the brightest star in the heavens, now passes over Tiahuanaco, aligning vertically with the Akapana pyramid'.[10]

Once again I had found an ancient site very precisely located beneath a brilliant star. But the astronomical alignment of Sirius and Tiahuanaco today is all the more enigmatic because Sirius is noted for its proper motion.[11] To calculate an alignment such as this several thousand years in advance would have required very sophisticated astronomical knowledge, including an understanding of precession and the proper motion of stars, as well as an exceptional familiarity with the world's geography. All these calculations would require sophistication akin to our own.

But I went looking for an ancient site to act as a present day marker for the sun in Libra and I found Nazca. I went looking for an ancient site to act as a present day marker for Sirius and I found Tiahuanaco.

How many such large and famous ancient sites are there in South America? How easy would it be to locate another site such as Tiahuanaco or Nazca? Isn't it remarkable to have located both these important sites precisely by the vertical alignments of the sun in Libra and of Sirius today?

With the next discovery, the situation became even clearer:

Sirius passes over Mt Illimani.

I mentioned earlier that Mt Illimani is the third prodigious summit overlooking Lake Titicaca. The parallel of Tiahuanaco is so closely matched with the parallel of the mountain that Sirius passes over both the mountain and the pyramid! So Sirius is also twinned with a high consort mountain on the ground, just like all the other stars.

It is a striking truth that Sirius, Alpha Libra and Beta Libra are all located vertically above the highest points in the northern Andes every day at present, but once again, this fantastic star and mountain co-ordination only happens under Polaris.

The article about Tiahuanaco quoted above ends with this question: 'Will we ever discover who these people, lost in the mist of age-old oblivion, really were?'

Perhaps we will never know, but we do recognize that as the sun passes vertically over Nazca, the brightest star in the night-time sky passes vertically over Tiahuanaco, the brightest star in the dragon passes over Avebury, the brightest star in Scorpius passes over Easter Island, the Alpha star in Triangulum passes over Giza and Polaris passes over the pole, all in one day, today. Can you see the pattern I see?

A LEGACY

The symbolic language adopted by the ancient monument builders across the globe becomes increasingly clear in South America. The topography in the area of Tiahuanaco is, once again, alarmingly geometric. Here again the builders were using geographic 'points' to create geometry and in the rarefied atmosphere of these high mountains their ability to do this is truly awe-inspiring.

Lake Titicaca is a large body of water overlooked by a line of dramatic high points to the east. The cluster of summits overlooking the lake (including Mt Illampu and Mt Illimani) are the highest group of mountains in South America. There are higher individual points in the south, but the group of summits overlooking Lake Titicaca is the highest range in all the Americas.

In order to discuss the topography in this area, imagine the magic blanket stretched evenly above all the Andes north of the Tropic of Capricorn. Now the blanket is released and falls uniformly over the mountains.

The first mountain to penetrate the blanket is naturally the highest point in this area, Mt Illampu or Mt Sajama. The second mountain to penetrate the blanket is the second highest point, etc. (Mt Illampu and Mt Ancohuma are so close together

I have included them as one point in this discussion.) These points can be joined by a line over Lake Titicaca *(see Figure 92)*. The line passes directly over Tiahuanaco.

Now the same blanket descends further to include the next high point and this pulls the geometry of the highest points into focus.

There is now a right angle between two high points, with the site of Tiahuanaco marking the right-angled corner at the southern tip of Lake Titicaca. I believe this geometry was intentional because we have seen it in Egypt and Britain already. It extends across the country here in the most spectacular fashion.

Two of the high points on the blanket also create another right angle *(see Figure 94)*, this time with Nazca.

And now imagine a much smaller blanket falling gently over the southern tip of Lake Titicaca. As it descends over the site of Tiahuanaco four predominant peaks penetrate its surface *(see Figure 95)*. These four points create two very accurate isosceles triangles. Indeed, Tiahuanaco is contained within the isosceles.

By what force of nature do the four highest points around Tiahuanaco

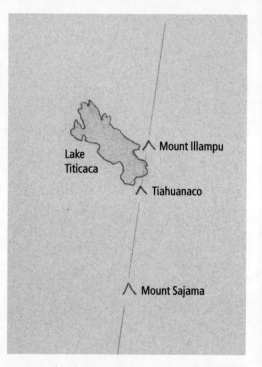

Figure 92: The alignment of Tiahuanaco

Figure 93: The three highest points and Tiahuanaco

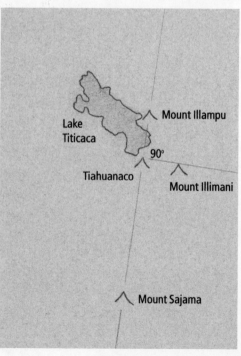

144

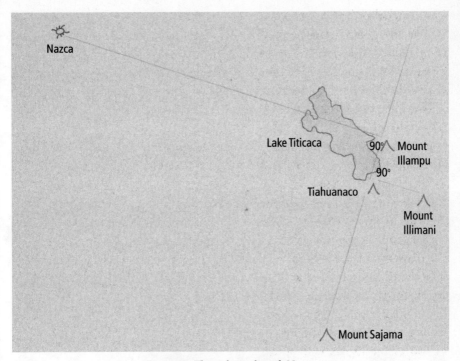

Figure 94: The right angle with Nazca

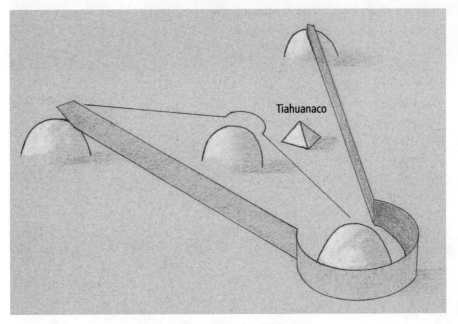

Figure 95: The topography of Tiahuanaco

create two isosceles triangles? Is it the same force that finds an equilateral triangle of high points adjacent to Avebury and an isosceles triangle of high points dominating Easter Island? And is it an awareness of this force that is spelled out at Giza? Surely all these monuments are monuments in common? They carry the same signature. They communicate the same understanding of astronomy and topography. This understanding arrived long ago. Look now at what occurs at Tiahuanaco:

The arrow figure generated by the high points surrounding Tiahuanaco crosses the meridian at exactly 45°!

We have seen this triangular arrow motif before. The lines described by this 45°-aligned triangle are related in a number of ways, as I hope to demonstrate. I believe the ancient monument builders defined the topography on Earth precisely and left us emphatic evidence of this. They found this enigmatic arrow of high points located at the southern tip of Lake Titicaca and used the 45° line to define the site of Cuzco, the capital of the Inca Empire.

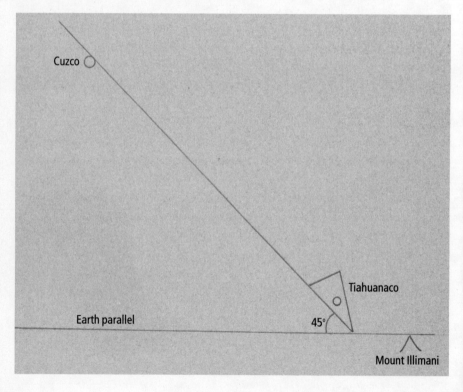

Figure 96: The 45° angle to Cuzco

146

The 45° line locating Cuzco from Tiahuanaco, coupled with the 90° angle locating Nazca, tied in with the geometric relationship of local high points, clearly infers that the people responsible for marking these sites on Earth were all privy to the same profound wisdom concerning the Earth and sky, a knowledge we have yet to fully uncover and understand.

Before leaving the mountains of South America I discovered that one star in the isosceles triangle formed by the ears of Lepus passes vertically over the site of Machu Pichu today.[12] (The ears of Lepus are spotlighted by the 45° shaft from the Great Pyramid, as discussed earlier.)

The odds of all these alignments occurring by chance are extremely small. Four high points, isolated at random, plucked from the Earth, are unlikely to form two isosceles triangles, much less ones at precisely 45° to the Earth's parallel. (The two largest pyramids on the Giza plateau are also aligned with each other at 45° to the Earth's grid.) This angle at Tiahuanaco is so exact when measured on the Operational Navigation Chart that I cannot fault it. Neither can I fault the isosceles forming this arrow – the three points surrounding Tiahuanaco on the chart are perfectly isosceles to the compass point.

Geometry is rather like language, it is a universal tongue. In Figures 97 and 98 I have only begun to unravel the complex geometric web co-ordinating the sites and mountains of South America, but I believe these simple illustrations go some way to demonstrating that ancient wisdom was not an illusion. It is the corresponding relationship with the brightest stars in the sky that gives the game away. These ancient sites were planned, either by some untapped psychic power (remote viewing, for example), or by using maps. The high points illustrated in Figure 98 are the highest summits on this part of the globe.

It is hard to believe that geometry such as this should occur by chance. These are, after all, the highest mountains and the greatest ancient sites in South America, and they are undeniably geometrically related to each other and to the celestial sphere. It is a fabulous work of art.

And the message is the same once again: there is a mirror between the Heaven and the Earth. That mirror is now creating a near perfect reflection over South America and over England, over Giza and over Easter Island. The reflection is perhaps too vast to contemplate, but none the less is very real and very mathematically precise.

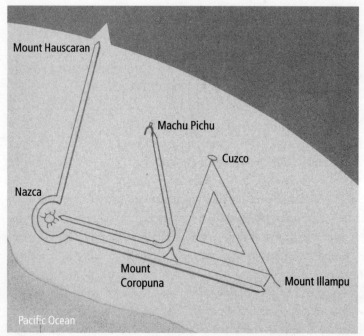

Figure 97: An appraisal of the Nazca, Tiahuanaco, Cuzco and Machu Pichu geometry with the highest points

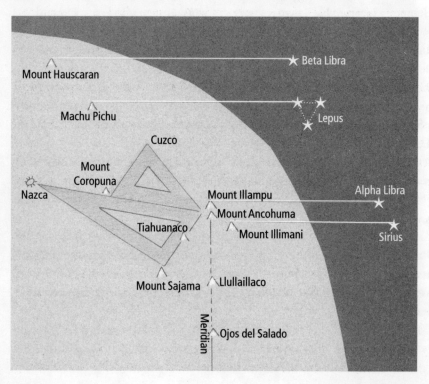

Figure 98: Star/mountain alignments over South America, AD 2000

* IO *

A TEST OF TIME

*'The effort of sorting out and
identifying the only presences
which totally eluded the action
of our hands led to those pure
objects of contemplation, the
stars in their courses.'* [1]

'What exactly are you writing about?'

Young people definitely ask the most difficult questions and my teenage daughters Isla and Katy wanted to know about my work. I knew I had to summarize the whole subject in a single soundbite.

'I think the stars are related to the highest points on the Earth and I am trying to explain why,' I replied.

When the conversation had finished I wondered how a father could possibly tell his young daughters of this belief. Surely no one can say that there really is a relationship between the brightest stars in the sky and the highest points on the Earth? Was I actually telling my own daughter to believe this?

After a great deal of thought I concluded that the judgement does not rest in my hands. Either there is a vertical relationship between the highest points on Earth and the brightest stars in the sky or there is not. It is a question of fact, not conjecture, so I decided to confirm the truth one way or the other.

The exact locations of the highest points and the brightest stars are easy enough to define on maps and charts (Bolivia excepted), so let us compare the two. The theory 'star = mountain' can be readily put to the test using the parallels defined on our charts of the sky and maps of the Earth today.

I decided to take the seven brightest stars in the sky today and find out if I could truly justify the claim I had made to my daughters. According to accepted astronomy the seven brightest stars are simply random points and could appear anywhere

149

on the surface of the celestial sphere, but with a noted preference for the Milky Way. In turn, the highest summits on the planet are also deemed to be random points, subject to the stresses of the Earth, but definitely not subject to, or connected with, any forces in deep space, unless you hold an equally deep religious view. It would be strange indeed to find that the brightest stars have any clear accurate vertical relationship with the very highest summits on the Earth, whatever view you hold.

Having established that our brightest star, Sirius, passes over Tiahuanaco and also over Mt Illimani, I decided to start the investigation by taking the second and third brightest stars in the sky and locating their passage over the Earth today.

These stars are called Alpha Centaurus and Alpha Carina, and they are both found way down south on the celestial sphere. I saw that both stars currently spend most of their time passing over water, excepting one brief transit over land in both cases. However, the passage of these two brilliant stars reveals one star passing over the southern extremity of South America and the other star passing over the northern extremity of the Antarctic peninsula.

These are the second and third brightest stars in the entire sky and they certainly don't pass over any magnificent dominating mountains. However, these two stars do pass over the two *extreme points* of two continents, so before casting further judgement I went on to deal with the fourth and the fifth brightest stars in the sky. These are Arcturus and Vega.

Figure 99: The three brightest stars over America and Antarctica

I brought these two brilliant stars down to Earth in the manner already described, starting with Arcturus.

ARCTURUS

The brilliant star Arcturus, in Boötes, is the brightest on the northern hemisphere of the celestial sphere. Boötes is the brother of Orion and he also has a belt of three stars. Arcturus represents his left foot.

This brilliant star now passes over central Mexico every day. Here is an extremely mountainous region of the world, a high plateau with volcanic peaks dotted around like so many large pimples on the skin of the Earth. Although the mountains of Mexico are not as high as the Andes, they are higher than any points in the Sierra Nevadas or Rocky Mountains of North America. In a nutshell, these Mexican mountains are higher than any points to the north in America, all the way up to Alaska.

If you drop the magic blanket over this 70 per cent of Central and North America, the very first four points to appear on the surface all overlook Mexico City (see Figure 100). Many major historical sites are found here, including the famous Aztec site of Teotihuacán, and a second extraordinary site, Cholula, the location of the 'world's largest pyramid'.[2]

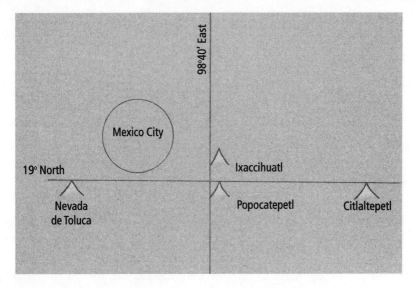

Figure 100: The highest mountains around Mexico City

151

See how the four highest points overlooking these sites are arranged on the blanket. By yet another strange fluke of nature these summits are aligned to the meridian and the parallel of the Earth. Once again I found it strange to see the world's prestigious mountains so well ordered on the terrestrial grid.

We can follow the passage of the Earth under the star Arcturus:

The brilliant star Arcturus now passes vertically over this line of Mexican mountains, accurate to one tenth of a degree, passing over the highest peak, the volcano Citlaltepetl, precisely!

So the brightest star in the northern hemisphere of the sky passes over the very highest summit on half of the American continent.

Chance is odd, but once again I had picked a random brilliant star out of the sky and found a prodigious peak, a world order summit, an indisputable giant among the great mountains of the world, directly beneath it. The line I was following around the globe fell so precisely over the summit of the volcano Citlaltepetl that I was captivated by the coincidence.

So far I had found that Sirius passes over Mt Illimani and Arcturus over Citlaltepetl, whilst the two other brightest stars in the sky pass over the most extreme points on two continents. The process appeared increasingly surreal, but these extreme points do match the stars today with great precision, *creating a mathematical equation.*

The research continued on a logical course. I went looking for an ancient site beneath the star Arcturus. I did not need another map.

Arcturus now passes very precisely over the largest pyramid in the world.

The largest ancient pyramid is located at Cholula. The volume of this monument is said to be greater than the Great Pyramid at Giza. It has a base area of 45 acres and a height of 210 feet.[3] Arcturus now passes vertically above it every day *(see Figure 101).*

Following Arcturus today led to the following discovery:

Mexico's greatest pyramid and Mexico's highest mountain share the same parallel of latitude. This is the reciprocal of the Arcturus parallel – but only at the time of Polaris.

I hope with this alignment to have established that the ancient pyramids are certainly intimately related to the highest points in their regional topography.

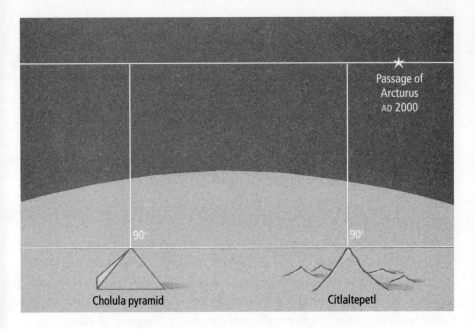

Figure 101: The vertical passage of Arcturus, AD 2000

Furthermore, these pyramids are now also related to the brightest points of light on the celestial sphere. The relationship is immediate and direct, it is a vertical relationship in AD 2000, and I believe the key to understanding this relationship is the recognition of the purposeful alignment of Alpha Triangulum over the Great Pyramid at Giza today.

TEOTIHUACÁN

One of the most famous ancient sites in this area of Mexico is just to the north of the Mexico City itself. It is called Teotihuacán and is home to three more pyramids. When compared like for like with the Giza pyramids, 'the area of each pyramid and the summit of each pyramid would almost exactly coincide'.[4]

In studying the Operational Navigation Chart of this area I was struck by another familiar pattern:

The highest three points adjacent to Teotihuacán form an isosceles triangle.

On the chart these three local high points are, once again, exactly isosceles.

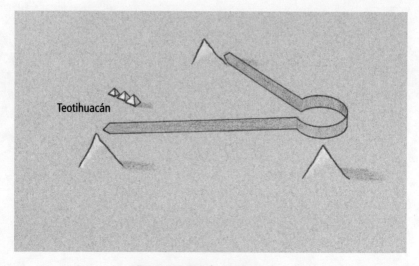

Figure 102: Teotihuacán isosceles

The navigation chart further establishes the common numerical language spoken by the Cholula pyramid and the pyramids of Teotihuacán and those at Giza. By raising an angle from the parallel at Cholula, measuring 51°51' to the north, the pyramids of Teotihuacán, some 50 miles away, are located on the line *(see Figure 103)*. This same angle, 51°51', is also the slope angle of the Great Pyramid. (Using precisely the same method and the same angle the circle of Avebury stones is located from the Avebury Sanctuary in England *(see Appendix II)*.)

I find it remarkable that two great sites of antiquity, and their pyramids, should now appear so precisely below Sirius and Arcturus. The fact that both sites include substantial pyramids lends considerable weight to the argument that the star = mountain = pyramid equation was recognized across the globe in ancient times.

But could I really expect to find the same thing happening yet again?

VEGA

I was bound to continue this illuminating search with the next brightest star, Vega. This is the second brightest star on the northern hemisphere of the celestial sphere and the fifth brightest in the sky.

Vega is the only brilliant star in the constellation Lyre, situated adjacent to the base of the Northern Cross, the swan Cygnus.

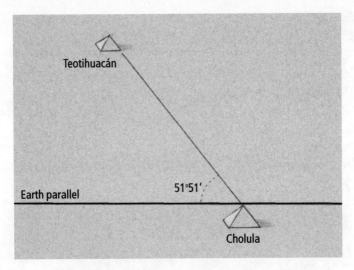

Figure 103: Teotihuacán and Cholula joined by an angle of 51°51'

I traced the parallel of Vega over the globe, just as I had done with Arcturus and all the other stars.

Vega now passes over Cahokia, 'the largest prehistoric settlement north of Mexico'.[5]

Cahokia, near St Louis in Illinois, right in the centre of the USA, is home to a group of ancient pyramid mounds.

The site consists of over 100 antique earth mounds overlooked by the enormous 'Monk's Mound', a flat-topped monument 100 feet high and approximately 980 × 780 feet at the base *(see plate 8)*. The mound was constructed from 250 million cubic feet of earth.[6] It is situated near St Louis in a dramatic kink in the Mississippi river due north of the river delta.

According to the site literature, 'It is the largest totally earthen prehistoric mound in the Western Hemisphere.'

Looking at the location of Cahokia in relation to the USA as a whole, I noticed that the site is located where the Mississippi makes a great loop and where three rivers converge on the meridian of the Mississippi Delta. The rivers are the Mississippi, the Missouri and the Illinois.

It is believed Cahokia was inhabited by hunter gatherers in antiquity, but the mounds were built much later, over a period of a couple of hundred years between AD 900 and AD 1150. The existing mounds may not, however, be the first markers to have appeared here.

This discovery confirms that notable stars in the sky today are now passing over the world's greatest pyramid sites:

a. The Great Pyramid under Alpha Triangulum (Rasalmothallah)
b. The Silbury pyramid under the brightest star in Draco (Eltanim)
c. The Akapana pyramid at Tiahuanaco under the brightest star in the sky (Sirius)
d. The largest pyramid in the world under the brightest northern hemisphere star (Arcturus)
e. Monk's Mound at Cahokia under the second brightest northern hemisphere star (Vega)

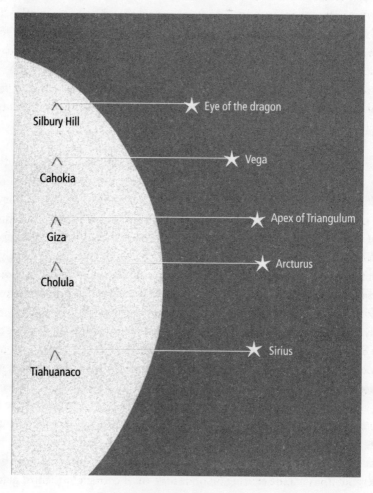

Figure 104: Pyramid parallels, AD 2000

It is a formidable list. For precessional motion to allow such a list to occur by chance strikes me as beyond the limits of reason, not least because Polaris arrives in tandem over the pole of the Earth. The brightest stars and the greatest pyramids are now very accurately synchronized for the first time in history, but the co-ordination of star and pyramid can only happen for a fleeting period of a few hundred years coinciding with the transit of Polaris over the pole, a time precisely defined by the vertical passage of Triangulum's apex over the apex of the Great Pyramid. The structure and planning are immensely clever.

With the alignment of Vega over Cahokia I concluded that these points on the Earth have been marked by ancient architects for a future purpose, yet I could only guess what that purpose may be. I was now certain that the site of Cahokia (like all the others) should be related to the local topography in some geometric manner and I wondered how this 'high point' geometry could be manifest in a relatively flat area such as Cahokia.

My search for this topographic geometry lead me down the meridian to the Mississippi Delta, but it was not until I followed the parallel of latitude to the west that I found the point I was looking for.

THE HEART OF THE BIG COUNTRY

In the centre of Colorado the Rocky Mountains rise to their greatest height. This world famous mountain range includes the highest points overlooking the heart of the USA.

By following the Earth's parallel from Cahokia I arrived at the highest points in the Rocky Mountains! The very highest mountain is Mt Elbert, the alignment of Cahokia and Mt Elbert on the Earth parallel falls within one third of a degree, but I nearly missed a crucial point.

Mt Elbert has a partner about 15 miles away (these are the two highest points in the Rockies), but if you draw a line between them and continue the straight line heading south, you arrive at the third highest point in the Rockies.

The three highest points in the Rocky Mountains rest on a straight line 60 miles long.

At this stage I realized the star Vega was passing over the two highest points in the Rockies, but on the line between the points the third corner of an isosceles triangle could be found. I had recovered a missing key.

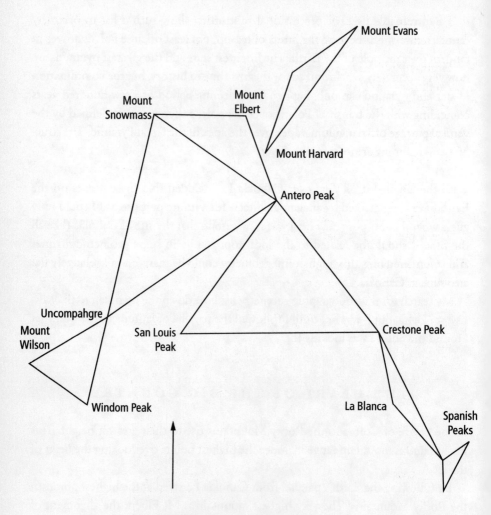

Figure 105: The pattern of isosceles triangles created by joining all the highest summits in Colorado (source: ONC G–19).

The star Vega was not only defining the highest mountains, it was also defining an isosceles triangle enclosing the highest land overlooking the heart of the USA.

STAR = MOUNTAIN = PYRAMID
Vega = Elbert = Cahokia

The formula has repeated itself once again, in the heart of the USA, in the heart of Mexico and in the heart of South America.

I had cracked the code. Three large pyramid sites are all but perfectly placed beneath three of the five brightest stars in the sky today:

Sirius = Mt Illimani = Akapana pyramid
Arcturus = Citlaltepetl = Cholula pyramid
Vega = Mt Elbert = Cahokia pyramid

And these three Alpha star alignments coincide with:

Alpha Triangulum over the Great Pyramid
The dragon's eye over the Silbury Hill pyramid
Antares over Easter Island
The Libran sun over Nazca
The Lepus ears over Machu Pichu

The ancient builders have ordered a bar code over the globe. Like all bar codes it is very linear, very direct and very precise *(see Figure 106)*.

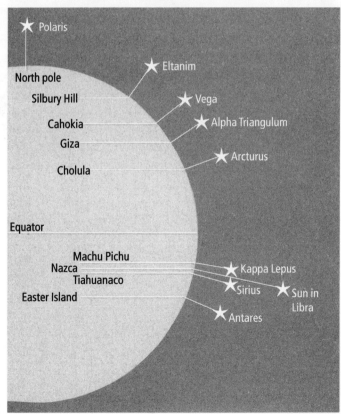

Figure 106:
A star mirror

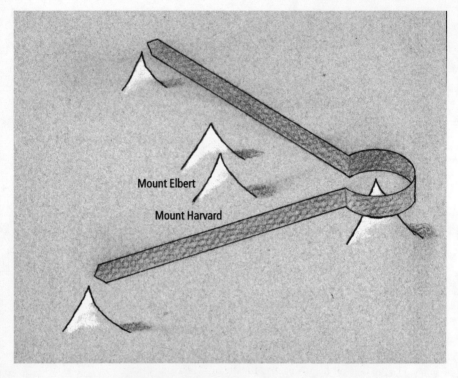

Figure 107: The highest points surrounding Mt Harvard and Mt Elbert
(source: ONC G–19)

I had established in my own mind that the ancient monument builders had built their own high points to attract attention to the mirror between bright stars and natural summits.

But they also illustrate a strange topographical feature of the Earth *(see Figure 108)*.

I continued to look for the very highest points in the Rocky Mountains, this time extending the blanket over the entire central range.

Each corner of the large isosceles triangle supports a second isosceles triangle and this is most clearly found with the highest points in the south-east area, where the process is duplicated *(see Figure 105)*.

I have clambered around some of the lower peaks in these magnificent and majestic Rocky Mountains; however, it never occurred to me that the highest ones could be organized geometrically. Why should it? Why should anyone believe the highest points on Earth are ordered into isosceles triangles? But it is not a question

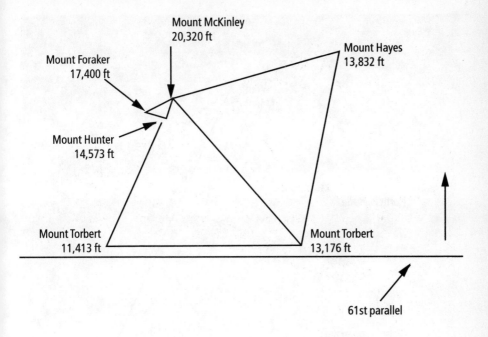

Figure 108: The highest points surrounding Mt McKinley (source: ONC D–11)

of belief. Geometry is a matter of measurement, of reality. I have worked for a few years on these maps, but I still find the concept almost impossible to grasp.

Let's wipe the slate clean and start afresh. Let's leave the Rocky Mountains and travel to the Sierra Nevadas, to the very highest point in these United States of America, and from this vast mountain we can stop and survey the surrounding land without prejudice.

MT WHITNEY

The Sierra Nevada is a spectacular mountain range overlooking California. It stretches over about 250 miles in a broad straight line with Lake Tahoe at the northern tip.

Mt Whitney is at the southern end of the range. It is the highest point in the USA (excluding Alaska), the highest point overlooking the body of American states and much of northern Mexico.

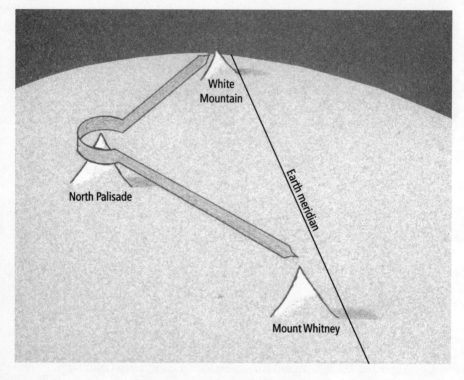

Figure 109: Rocky Mountain triangles

Once again I dropped the magic blanket. I located Mt Whitney and then let the blanket continue to fall, revealing the next two highest points.

The highest three points in the Sierra Nevadas form an isosceles triangle.

The ONC chart shows several summits for Mt Whitney. The corner of the isosceles triangle rests among them.

Again, although I was looking for this, it did seem strange to find an isosceles triangle appearing once more, this time composed of the highest group of points overlooking all these American states.

If you take a map of the south-western United States measuring over a metre square and you throw three grains of rice haphazardly onto it, would you expect to measure an exact isosceles triangle between the three grains of rice? The odds are seriously against you. But I have just taken that map[7] and located three precise points, linked only by their great elevation, and these three form an isosceles triangle accurate to the length of a grain of rice on this scale.

And the same isosceles geometry appears again if you drop the magic blanket over Mt McKinley, the highest point in North America (*see Figure 108*).

REVIEW

So far in this exercise we have considered the brightest five stars in the sky today. These stars pass vertically over the following places:

a. The highest group of mountains in central South America.
b. The highest group of mountains in Central America.
c. The highest group of mountains in central North America.
d. The southern extremity of South America.
e. The northern extremity of Antarctica.

The mountain alignments are so fine their accuracy cannot be illustrated on one map together due to the scale of this book. Was I right to tell my daughters about this?

But the issue raised by the above alignments has little to do with super-fine measuring – it is to do with the relationship between the extreme points in America and the brightest stars in the sky. The fact that there is a relationship appears very clearly *(see Figure 110)*.

Figure 110: The five brightest stars in the sky aligned over America, AD 2000

CAPELLA

I moved on to study the next brightest star, Capella, the sixth brightest star in the sky.

The passage of Capella over the United States is also interesting because it occupies the same parallel as Mt St Helens, accurate to one third of a degree. In fact precessional motion is now carrying Capella gradually towards the recently explosive summit of Mt St Helens.

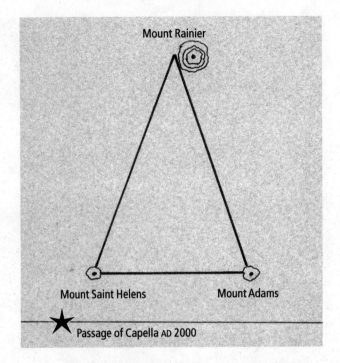

Figure 111: The triangle between Mt St Helens, Mt Adams and Mt Rainier,
aligned to the Earth's parallel (source: ONC G–19)

Mt St Helens is on the same parallel of latitude as its much taller neighbour, Mt Adams. Immediately north of these two mountains is Mt Rainier, the second highest mountain overlooking these combined American states.

Dropping the magic blanket over Mt Rainier immediately reveals a relationship between the first three points to appear *(see Figure 111)*. The geography of high points in the area of Mt Rainier is once again strangely oriented to the Earth's meridian and parallels. The three mountains form a far from perfect isosceles, but the form does align to the Earth's parallel, creating an arrowhead pointing north.

Following the arrow pointing to the north, the next three highest summits are found, once again, to be isosceles.

The highest peaks in this area produce a geometric pattern aligned to the Earth's grid *(see Figure 112)*.

165

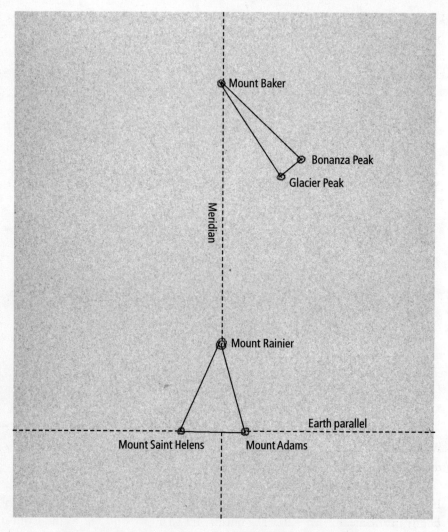

Figure 112: The highest points north of Mt Rainier (source: ONC G–19)

We have now considered Mt Elbert, Mt Whitney and Mt Rainier. At each venue we have located the highest neighbouring peaks and at each venue we have found an isosceles relationship between the peaks. It is worth pausing here to consider why the Giza architects built three isosceles mountains in an isosceles triangle.

But of course one might think that this proves nothing at all. Surely I am only showing that random points are consistently ordered into isosceles triangles? Yes, the neighbouring highest points on Earth do persistently create isosceles geometry when viewed in plan, but the crucial fact is that three small points spread over a large area at random very seldom create this special triangle. If we throw tennis balls onto a tennis court, or grains of rice onto a page, we do *not* repeatedly create isosceles geometry. How then does nature so manifestly repeatedly defeat the odds of chance?

The crux of the issue rests in the vision of Heaven and Earth as ordered, planned, a mirror, a divine creation. This is the vision of Nut and Geb, of the Earth and sky born as one but torn asunder, a mythological vision, a vision passed down with the pyramids.

Once, long ago, someone found proof of divine order, not in any fantasy, but in fact, on the real but geometrically ordered Earth. The desire to communicate was then truly immense.

RIGEL RISING

I had now considered the passage of the six brightest stars in the sky over the Earth today and it was time to move on to the seventh star.

Rigel, the seventh brightest star in the sky, is the brightest star in the Orion constellation. It also has a connection with the most extreme points on the American continent:

Rigel now passes over the most extreme easterly point of the Americas.

With Rigel so aligned in the sky today the seven brightest stars have now defined the following parallels on the Earth's surface:

1. The extreme northerly fingertip of Antarctica.
2. The extreme southerly tip of the Americas.
3. The extreme easterly tip of the Americas.
4. The highest group of mountains in South America.
5. The highest group of mountains in Central America.
6. The highest group of mountains in the Rocky Mountains.
7. Mt St Helens and Mt Adams, sharing the parallel beneath Mt Rainier.

Now I have to ask, how is it that these extreme points are so aligned in a chaotic universe? But I am not the first to ask this question.

The largest pyramid in the world is now also found vertically beneath one of these seven stars. And the Akapana pyramid at Tiahuanaco is found beneath Sirius.

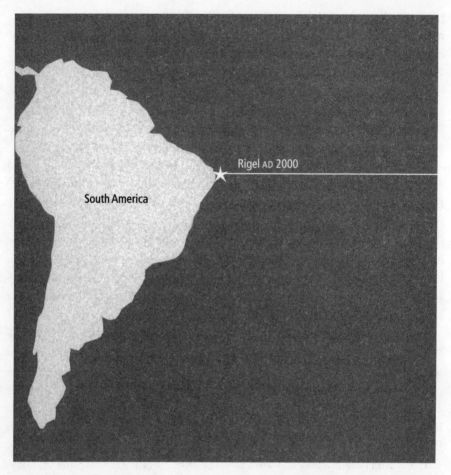

Figure 113: Rigel passing over the extreme easterly point of the Americas, AD 2000

And Cahokia is found beneath Vega. So the question has already been written, but the glyphs of the language are enormous and the page for the text is the surface of the Earth itself.

Just as John Michell wrote over 30 years ago, 'A great scientific instrument lies sprawled over the entire surface of the globe.'[8]

Now we can see some of the mechanism, and this 'scientific' instrument is very finely tuned indeed.

Before moving on I would like to insert the following anecdote because it helps to verify the case I am making concerning the geometry of the Earth. In this chapter I have spawned the idea that the highest points on the surface of the Earth are geometrically ordered. Such a hypothesis initially sounds totally outrageous. I am well aware of this. But contempt prior to investigation is invariably folly and it is clear that the subject of investigation is freely available on all good relief maps. With this in mind I was surprised late in this research to discover that China is perhaps home to the greatest of all the world's pyramids.

CHINA AND THE WHITE PYRAMID

At this stage I would like to discuss the stellar and terrestrial alignments of the pyramids in China, but unfortunately my current information is too sparse to do the subject justice. The Chinese pyramids may yet prove to be the largest in the world. One, the so-called 'White Pyramid', is said to be 984 feet tall and at even half this height it would surpass any other pyramid known on Earth. The little data I do have at present suggest that, like the pyramids at Giza, these Chinese pyramids are geometrically ordered and currently appear under Triangulum, in this case under the northern base, but this is speculation.

As for the location of the Chinese 'Pyramid Fields' *(see plate 9)* to the south of Xi'an in central China, when I first heard about the Chinese pyramids I ordered the Operational Navigation Chart of the surrounding area. The atlas had shown a particularly high point south-west of Xi'an in central China where I knew a number of the pyramids, including the White Pyramid, were located. But I needed a far better scale of map to define the high points precisely. I sent a fax to Stanford's in London[9] with an order for the relevant chart.

It was a strange experience waiting for the chart to arrive. During the two days that elapsed I realized I would open the map, place the dividers on the high point and *expect* to find an isosceles triangle with the two nearest neighbouring high points. During this wait I had time to reflect on what I was doing. The region of China I was looking forward to studying was completely unknown to me. None the less I was actually anticipating the topography before it came into view.

When the chart arrived I laid it across the desk. I found the high point overlooking Xi'an and then opened the dividers to the next high point, some 20 miles away. I swung the dividers in this manner and found the third highest summit.

The three points are isosceles, accurate to the width of a pinhead on the metre-square chart.

It was a very surreal experience. How could I have anticipated the precise topography of a region unknown to me if the pyramids themselves were not acting in a symbolic capacity, drawing attention to this persistent geometry on the surface of our planet?

So the White Pyramid lies beneath three great peaks forming an isosceles triangle which, like so many others, is very closely aligned to the Earth's parallel.

The pattern repeats itself once again, as if the ancient builders saw messages written on the very body of Gaia. It is clear then that pyramid builders around the world were working to a common code.[10]

Ultimately the pyramids illustrate the natural isosceles formation found repeatedly between the highest points on Earth. Thus they illustrate a form of divine geometry in which the Earth and the sky are intimately linked. The point is, they are not offering this isosceles geometry as a suggestion, they are *confirming* that the Earth itself is geometrically ordered. The conceptual leap is enormous, but before refuting this message, try making a close and patient study of the highest points around you. You may be surprised.

To learn more, I looked for this pervasive geometry elsewhere, in the art of the ancient Egyptians.

Figure 114 shows a familiar Egyptian pose – the head in profile, the shoulders face on and the legs back in profile again. (Do not try this at home.) The human body in the picture is turned unnaturally through 90° to achieve this position. The all-prevailing awareness of geometry in ancient Egypt is thus clearly expressed by their figurative as well as their architectural work. The geometric focus invariably rests at 'the extreme point' and the picture here, like hundreds of others, shows the traditional triangular apron reaching an extreme point at the belt of the man.

The pyramid points to the belt.

These are symbols, working through art, in order to communicate a far broader reality. So the triangle points to the belt, just like the Great Pyramid, and the celestial belt is another triangle. It is hard to overlook this geometry when it is so plainly outlined. The man and the maths are part of the same intimate yet universal form. We know nature involves geometry, but we don't necessarily anticipate such geometry between stars and mountains.

'Schwaller de Lubicz carefully measured seventy two of these aprons – almost all of them within the covered temple at Luxor – and found in every single case that the aprons were constructed according to precise mathematical considerations.'[11]

Figure 114: Man and triangle from ancient Egypt

Having now researched the vertical alignment of the seven brightest stars in the sky, I found something unexpected under the triangular apron.

✳ 11 ✳

MOVING HEAVEN

'It was clear to me for a long time that the origins of science had their deep roots in a particular myth, that of invariance.'[1]

When NASA scientists designed an interplanetary space vehicle ultimately destined for deep space, they realized that the craft, called Pioneer, would eventually fly out through the solar system, beyond the orbits of Neptune and Pluto, and into the void beyond. The realization that Earth was about to project something into deep space brought with it some sense of responsibility. The NASA scientists came to consider whether their little space probe would ever encounter 'intelligent life' elsewhere in the universe.

A team of scientists led by astronomer Carl Sagan tackled the problem head on when they decided to attach a message to the outside of the NASA vessel.

The Pioneer craft is now literally billions of miles away from us and some hope prevails that in the fullness of time NASA's winged messenger will catch the attention of an alien.

But designing the message was not easy. The problems arising from attempting to communicate with an unknown intelligence at an unknown time in the future are substantial. Can the alien see? Can it hear? How big is it? Etc. Trying to write a message to aliens is fraught with hazards. None the less Carl Sagan and his team finally created a design inscribed on a gold-plated plaque. The method of communication employed by NASA was the very best the world could expect.

The message now hurtling through deep space:

a. has no writing on it
b. is in code
c. is conveyed by geometry

d. employs angled straight lines in order to transfer information
e. angles the lines at specific stars
f. and couples all the angles and the stars together to create a message.

Does this sound familiar?

Ultimately decoding the NASA message permits the alien intelligence to determine the whereabouts of the planet Earth in space, *but 100 years ago nobody on Earth could possibly have decoded it*. We didn't have the astronomical knowledge. The stars used in the message are all pulsars and these were undiscovered in AD 1900. So only a race of astronomers as advanced as our own can decode the NASA message.

I wonder whether an intelligent alien in distant space will one day discover the plaque and eventually crack the code. I also wonder whether it will then be dismissed as nothing but a chance series of scratches on an enigmatic lump of metal. You see, I wonder whether this alien will think of itself as the most intelligent creature in the entire universe.

With this in mind, I turned again to the Great Pyramid at Giza. Historians have only recently agreed that the pyramid is pointing at the stars. The idea was ridiculed

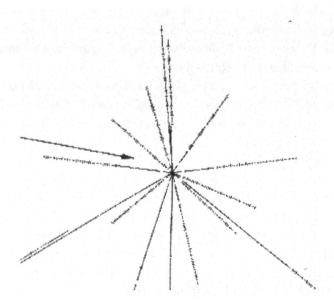

Figure 115: The NASA message

only 50 years ago by people devoid of astronomical knowledge and unable to accept that anything more radical than their preconceived notions could possibly arrive from the past. For these people the Great Pyramid shafts were considered to be for the purposes of ventilating the interior chambers of the pyramid, yet at least two of these shafts did not penetrate the interior chambers when they were built. The flaw in this logic has only recently been recognized and put to rights. It was, then, our earlier perceptions of the Great Pyramid that were primitive, not the monument itself.

Throughout this book I have claimed that a language of symbols exists at Giza and that a message is being passed on. Osiris is now standing aligned in the sky. His greatest star, Rigel, is now falling into alignment with the north face of the Great Pyramid whilst Alpha Triangulum passes vertically above it and Polaris transits the pole. These alignments are so closely synchronized with the culmination of Polaris that the synchronization itself speaks to us intelligently *(see Appendix I)*.

These lines at Giza are not random scratches, they are very cleverly contrived signals. The Great Pyramid points to the foot of Orion. The mountain is therefore under the heel of the god Osiris just as the dragon is under the heel of Hercules and the scorpion under the heel of Ophiuchus.

An international collection of myths attest to the fact that the arrival of Polaris is associated with something of great significance, though Polaris has now arrived over the Earth's pole at a time when the language of myth has all but lost its meaning in something akin to a 'tyranny of science'.[2]

However, from this point onwards, I am going to assume that the Giza site was designed to convey information using a linear language. I will not speculate about the origins of the designers, much less about the time that the Great Pyramid was designed, but I am acknowledging the intelligence of its designers and that the angles they defined were brilliantly conceived. In short, their monument carries information conveyed by linear geometry.

The message so far received from Giza has a very metaphysical flavour. The idea that Heaven and Earth co-exist in a form of esoteric embrace is not necessarily one resting easily with our modern perception of the universe. But surely this is what is interesting? The pyramid designers provoke us. They provide a demonstration. They show us quite clinically that the seven brightest stars on our celestial sphere do, in today's reality, pass over the highest mountains and the most extreme continental points. They have placed massive pyramids below three of these seven brilliant stars. The message therefore arrives with its own evidence; it is a form of proof.

AN ABERRATION

During a late-night review of the star alignments of the Great Pyramid, a glaring anomaly suddenly appeared over the face of the Giza plateau.

Stars and mountains are becoming vertically aligned in AD 2000. But if this message is truly perceived, then the three Giza pyramids *should* now appear vertically beneath the stars of Orion's Belt. They don't. The mirror is wrong. The Belt of Orion now reaches the celestial equator at 0° and due to precession the three Belt stars can travel no further north on the celestial sphere. Suddenly I saw the contradiction. The Belt stars can never pass vertically over Giza and create a true vertical reflection. So how do three pyramids at 30° north provide a mirror image of three stars over the equator at 0°?

I could not understand it. I had found Tiahuanaco under Sirius, I had found Cholula under Arcturus, I had found Cahokia under Vega, I had found Easter Island under Antares, Avebury under Draco, Nazca under the Libran sun, Machu Pichu under the Lepus ears, *but I would never find Giza under Orion's Belt*. The other pyramids around the world were reflecting the light of a consort star by vertical alignment – why not those at Giza?

Certainly the apex of Triangulum passes over Giza today, but the pyramids at Giza do not reflect the image of Triangulum, they reflect the image of Orion's Belt.

This seemingly intransigent problem was the greatest of all I encountered in this research. The Giza builders had broken their own pattern and I could not see why.

The more I thought about it, the more convinced I became that this anomaly existed for a reason. But what?

I studied the 30° displacement at Giza. The three pyramids are a visible duplication of the three stars of Orion's Belt and they should (indeed must) appear vertically under the three stars they reflect. Instead the Belt stars are 30° to the south. If you are looking for the star mirror, the Giza pyramids appear to be wrongly located on the Earth.

I realized that the daily circular motion of Polaris now creates a small dot on the celestial sphere centred about 30° above the Giza horizon and Orion's Belt is now 30° from the vertical at Giza. Was this at all relevant?

Finally, I took a mythological view. If the Egyptian Creator god Atum, who resides at the pole, were now to come down to Earth, he would require the pole to shift 30° in order to land on the 'Horizon of Khufu' at Giza. And I realized, in a silent moment working into the night, that if Atum did come down to Earth, and the Earth moved 30°, his son Osiris would be elevated vertically over the pyramids of Giza, a god above his temple. Indeed, the partnership between father and son is

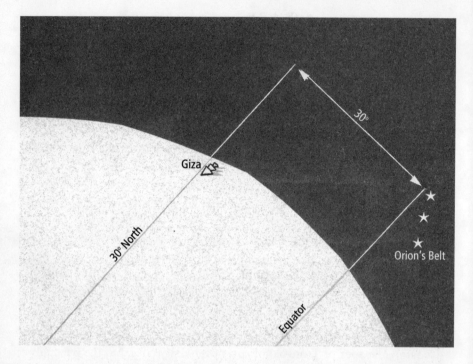

Figure 116: The 30° displacement of Orion's Belt over Giza

discovered in a right-angled relationship hinged at the apex of the Great Pyramid today, or at the centre of the Earth.

The answer to the insoluble problem was suddenly clear: the Earth itself must move in order for this divine partnership to be reconciled at Giza. The Earth must shift 30° to the south.

Alternatively, the Duat stars on the celestial sphere would have to move up uniformly 30° to the north.

In either event the stars would appear to fall from the sky.

All at once the Egyptian mural images depicting a shifting of the sun (see Figure 52, p.69), and the predicted cataclysmic Earth shift 'when the poles light up', coupled with the 'stars falling from the sky' in the Biblical reference to Armageddon, seemed immutably captured by the position of the three Giza pyramids 30° away from their consort stars today. And when the moment had passed, I realized that in trying to achieve the predicted direct vertical match at Giza I had fallen upon a dark secret.

The ancients defined the current location of Rigel so precisely that they surely knew that the Belt stars could only pass over Giza if the Earth shifts 30° to the

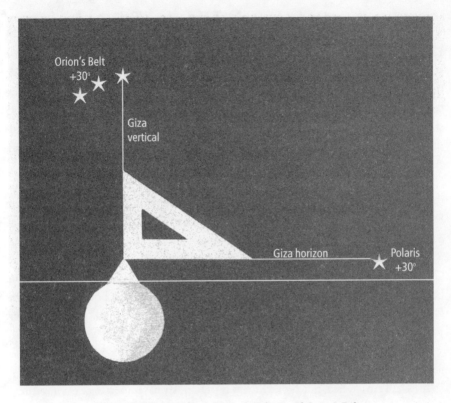

Figure 117: The right angle between Polaris and Orion's Belt

south. So they have drawn attention to the displacement of their three Giza pyramids at the culmination of Orion *for a reason.*

So far in this book I have attempted to illustrate a series of logical linear progressions. In fact I have done little more than follow the 11 straight lines described by the Great Pyramid and meandered with the starry dragon, assuming their direction to be a directive. But here something more esoteric and more difficult to describe came into the picture. Having followed these lines I developed the feeling I was reading an instruction or that the designers of the lines had consciously created a puzzle.

If the exclusion of the Giza pyramids from the star mirror was deliberately contrived, then the architecture at Giza intentionally encourages us to rectify this 30° displacement and produce a perfect mirror image over Giza. In order to bring Osiris over his temple we need to simulate the shifting of the Earth by 30° or the stars of Orion by 30°. I decided to do this.

OSIRIS ON THE EARTH

I simulated a 30° shift of the Duat stars over the Earth by simply adding 30° to the parallels of the Duat stars, so bringing the stars of Orion's Belt from 0° to +30°, directly over the Giza pyramids. (This is the shift on the celestial rather than the terrestrial sphere, but it is the equivalent of moving the landmass uniformly 30° to the south on the planet.) Shifting the stars in this manner I included the most brilliant beacons of light surrounding Orion in the Duat: Sirius, Procyon, Aldebaran, Alheka and Elnath.)

When I had isolated the stars of the Duat in their new location (+30°), using the same method as before, I brought all the brilliant stars down to the Earth. All the Duat stars thus received a new parallel over the Earth, which it appeared to me was a directive inferred by the global arrangement of pyramids.

I said earlier that I felt I had recognized 'an instruction' in the structure of the Great Pyramid itself. I am still uncertain as to the exact nature of this directive because it can be achieved in two different ways, but I did feel bound to bring the Giza pyramids under their consort stars in AD 2000 by one method or the other. I also noticed this passage from Graham Hancock:

'In the southern hemisphere, Hapgood's model shows the landmass that we now call Antarctica, much of which was previously at temperate or even warm latitudes, being shifted *in its entirety* inside the Antarctic circle. The overall movement is seen as having been in the region of 30°.'[3]

Once my simulation was achieved, I followed the passage of all the Duat stars over the Earth just as I had done with the seven brightest stars earlier.

This was the most incredible moment. I first traced the passage of the star Alnitak, the star symbolizing the Great Pyramid.

Alnitak +30° passes vertically over Mt Everest.

Imagine my position. I had gone out on a limb, following signs and symbols in an emerging esoteric language. I had found the vertical alignment of our seven brightest stars over the Americas and each time I had found an 'extreme point' beneath the stars. And now I had followed the strangely perceived directive, I had taken instructions from the pyramid at +30° and as soon as +30° was added to the star mirror I had immediately discovered the brilliant star Alnitak passing over the highest point on the planet with uncanny accuracy.

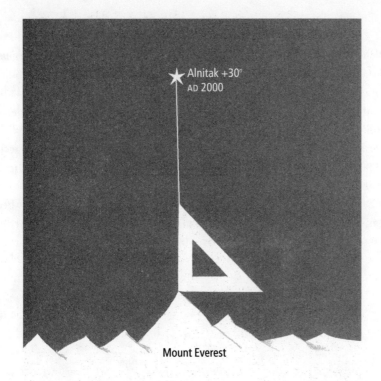

Figure 118: Alnitak +30° passes over Mt Everest

This was inescapable mathematical confirmation of the perceived directive. Alnitak was recognized by Robert Bauval as the single star in the sky representing the Great Pyramid, and now, only a few years after Bauval's discovery, I had found that by lifting Alnitak precisely 30° to the north, the star aligns vertically with Mt Everest with an accuracy of 0.1° in AD 2000.[4]

I was left with little to suggest that the directive I had envisaged was anything other than preconceived. Like the alien directed to Earth, I now had no doubt that the ancient code-maker was intelligent.

For those with a symbolic turn of mind, the observation that Triangulum points to +30° on the celestial sphere and −30° on the galactic sphere may help to distil the equation now being expressed by the 30° misplacement of Osiris and his pyramids. I use this example to attempt to convey the entire symbolic context within which this form of communication takes place. I may add that Boötes and Hercules both have belts with three stars resting around +30° on the celestial sphere today, and Boötes is Orion's brother, but I cannot say how this should be interpreted exactly.

To some degree I am attempting to say that certain symbolic language *cannot* be expressed in words, for if it could, there would be no need for it. But symbolism is none the less an extremely powerful force in the realms of communication and here I had anticipated the vertical alignment of a brilliant Duat star over an extreme point on the Earth *before* I made the calculation. And for this reason the resulting observation that Alnitak +30° now passes over Mt Everest with uncanny accuracy left me in no doubt that I had correctly interpreted a message committed to stone many thousands of years ago.

The depth of the message contained by the Giza pyramids was only now becoming clear. I decided to continue with this analysis, following the other Duat stars in the simulated 30° shift. With Alnitak over Mt Everest the whole spectacular picture was about to be revealed.

THERE IS A MIRROR

'But it was true science
after a fashion.' [1]

To find the true reflection of all the brilliant Duat stars, I decided to proceed in a systematic fashion. I would establish the vertical alignment of all the brilliant Duat stars raised by 30° and if this led me to the top of a great mountain I would investigate the topography of the region, just as I had done in America.

Having found Alnitak +30° passing over Mt Everest I was bound to cast the magic blanket over the highest points in the world.

Once again I was astonished.

The highest points surrounding Mt Everest also create isosceles geometry.

With this discovery I was beginning to entertain the dizzying idea that all the highest points of land on Earth are geometrically placed in isosceles relationships. Bearing in mind every other example so far discussed, one has to ask once again why this geometry is so persistent.

But this is an experiment with random points and so a massive contradiction looms up to greet us. Does chance always produce this pattern between neighbouring points? If so, are they truly random?

I studied the high points more closely.

The three highest neighbouring points, Dhaulagiri, Mt Everest and Kangchenjunga, are in a straight line.

(Kangchenjunga is the third highest point in the world.)

I was looking at this relationship when I realized that in the +30° simulation the star Alnilam in the centre of Orion's Belt was also passing over this region.

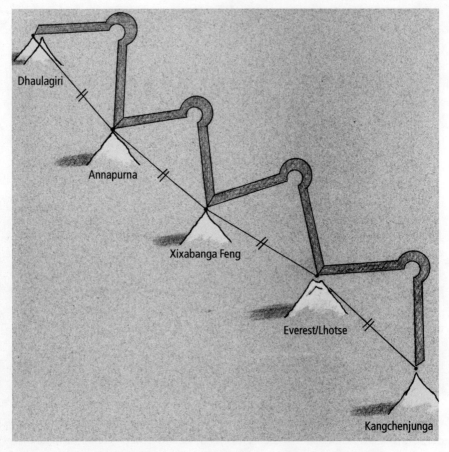

Figure 119: The highest mountain chain in the world (source: ONC H–9)

ALNILAM +30°

I followed the passage of Alnilam +30° as it passed over the Earth.

Alnilam +30° passes vertically over Dhaulagiri. This alignment is accurate to a tenth of a degree.

It is a truly remarkable combination: the three highest points are joined by a straight line and two of the Orion Belt stars +30° pass over two of the high points on the line. Once again this simulation can only take place at the precessional culmination of Orion.

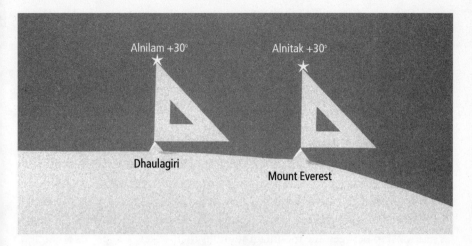

Figure 120: Alnitak and Alnilam +30°, AD 2000

Now the pattern was becoming clearer. The message from Giza takes the form of an instruction: +30°. This leads to the discovery of the co-ordination of Orion's Belt with two of the highest points on the Earth.

I realized that I needed to define all the parallels of all the brightest stars in the Duat in order to see the whole picture. It was like a game of join the dots, but each dot was precisely placed.

I had already been amazed by the strange alignments of the seven brightest stars vertically over the Americas, but now I was using a +30° code, something carefully defined by these strange architects, and something that would lead me to discover an unbelievably beautiful star mirror.

MINTAKA +30°

Having found two of the world's highest adjacent summits synchronized with two neighbouring stars in Orion's Belt, the search then continued with the third star in the Belt, Mintaka. I wondered whether Mintaka +30° would also co-ordinate with one of the highest points in the Himalayas.

Mintaka +30° passes vertically over Mt Kun Ka Shan.

This is the greatest Himalayan peak overlooking all lowland China. It is so singular and so huge that nothing across half the mainland of China compares in height. At

183

24,900 feet, it is by far the highest point at the eastern extreme of the Himalayas. There is simply no other point comparable to this great peak looking north or south or east over China. Even the local peaks are dwarfed thousands of feet below this great monolithic mountain.

The alignment between star and mountain is once again accurate to one tenth of a degree.

So the parallels of Mt Everest, Dhaulagiri and Kun Ka Shan provide the perfect mirror image of the parallels occupied by Orion's three Belt stars +30°. Extreme high points in every case! Accurate to a tenth of a degree in every case! Three times in a row, with each of the stars of Orion's Belt. What an extraordinary synchronicity.

The relationship between star and mountain is very strange, but so is the isosceles relationship between the mountain summits themselves. The points are so few, so small and so dispersed on this scale. Yet we have now found this isosceles relationship between the very highest points in the world.

If the few points in each case were truly chaotic then we could not predict their arrangement. But it seems an isosceles arrangement is *predictable*.

I decided to check this isosceles theory with the highest summits surrounding Kun Ka Shan. Once again I ordered the chart for this unknown region.

Dropping an imaginary blanket over 40,000 square miles around Mt Kun Ka Shan, I found the highest three points. First Mt Kun Ka Shan appears on the blanket, followed by the next two highest points.

These three summits form an isosceles triangle

In the case of this triangle, one side is very closely aligned to the Earth's meridian, in just the same manner as the triangle of high points overlooking Xi'an is closely aligned to the Earth's parallel, etc.

Either we are discovering here that the high points in China and elsewhere are not truly chaotic or we are discovering that a few random points are always related by isosceles geometry. In either event something has to give. Either the mountains are predictably arranged, or randomness itself is predictable on Earth. However, we already know that we ourselves are incapable of producing these triangles with random points.

I have deviated from the track we were following. To recap, we have discovered an accurate vertical alignment between Mt Everest and Alnitak +30°, an equally accurate alignment between Alnilam +30° and Mt Dhaulagiri, and then a third

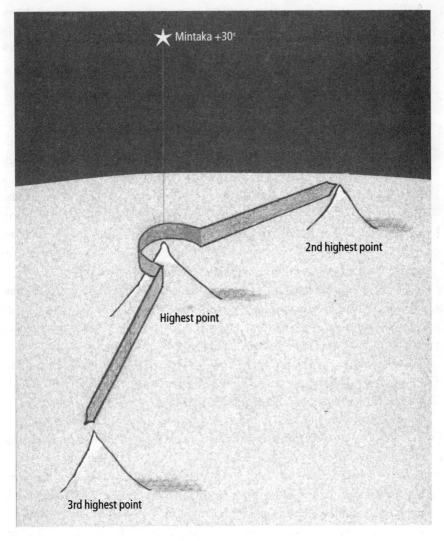

Figure 121: The isosceles around Mt Kun Ka Shan (source: ONC H–11)

equally accurate alignment between Mintaka +30° and Mt Kun Ka Shan *(see Figure 122).*

At each mountain site shown in Figure 122 the highest points form isosceles triangles. If we now remember the magic blanket dropping over Giza, the same configuration of three high points can be seen there. Thus the mountains at Giza are illustrating the world-wide phenomenon we are now discovering everywhere we look.

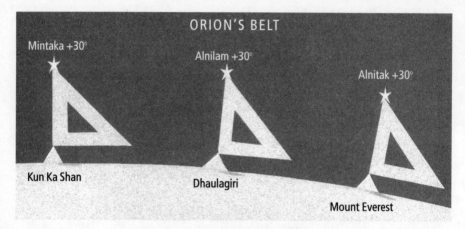

Figure 122: Orion's Belt +30° AD 2000, daily alignments

To find the same geometric order among the highest points in the world is a very strange thing, and I certainly find it very hard to digest. Nevertheless the mountains and stars were there before me. So I continued this research following the brightest star in the Duat.

How far could the +30° mirror extend?

SIRIUS +30°

I wondered what would happen to Sirius, the brightest star in the sky, if it were to be shifted from its perch over Tiahuanaco and Mt Illimani and raised 30°.

Both Sirius and Alnitak were spotlighted by the Great Pyramid in 2450 BC. Having found the highest point in the world under Alnitak +30°, I naturally wondered what might be found vertically beneath the brightest star in the sky +30°.

Once again I was electrified.

The star Sirius passes vertically over Mt Rasdajan, the highest point overlooking North Africa![2]

It was the most extraordinary discovery.

Like Alnitak +30° and Mt Everest, this measure also falls within 0.1°.

I had now found four alignments precisely picking out four of the highest locations on Earth! With a +30° shift, Alnitak, Alnilam, Mintaka and Sirius all fall into perfect alignment with fabulous world-dominating mountains.

I still found it hard to believe. To go looking for a high point under Orion's Belt and then to immediately find the world's greatest summit is a chance very hard to evaluate. To then take a second neighbouring bright star and immediately find one of the highest neighbouring points is a fabulous coincidence. But to then take a third and a fourth star and find one mountain overlooking half of China and the other overlooking half of Africa really is a miracle.

This perhaps explains my prolonged account about the decision to simulate a +30° shift in the first place. Earlier we saw Sirius, Arcturus and Vega aligning beautifully over three major mountains and three major pyramid sites in America. The mirror image is established by pyramids across the globe collectively today. But the message from Giza is deeper. The Giza designers have communicated the figure +30° by placing the three Giza pyramids out of alignment with their true consort stars. And the fabulous parallel created between the world's great mountains and these brilliant Duat stars has clearly been recorded in the past *because it requires a +30° shift to be recognized.*

I hope to have established that the +30° shift is not some fantastic fabrication I happened to invent in passing, but rather a message from ancient Egypt, elegantly laid out in the three Giza pyramids at 30° north.

I felt bound to labour this point because if the reader now recognizes why I have decided to shift the Duat stars by +30° the remaining data will bring home the reality reflected in the star mirror. It is a true reflection, there is a miraculous mirror image.

I had located Mt Rasdajan under Sirius so I decided to check the arrangement of the highest surrounding points, just as I had with all the other mountains located under brilliant stars. I took up the Operational Navigation Chart for the Ethiopian mountains including Mt Rasdajan.

So far there appears to be an inevitable isosceles relationship between the very highest points in every region of the globe. Would this relationship persist in Ethiopia, at the throne of the King of Ethiopia, Mt Rasdajan?

I found Mt Rasdajan and the second highest peak very close by. These twin peaks are the highest two points in North Africa:[3]

The twin peaks are aligned at 45° to the Earth's meridian.

On the chart, the 45° angle between Mt Rasdajan and its highest companion is *perfect*. Remember the perfect 45° arrow at Tiahuanaco and the 45° alignment of Giza's two largest pyramids?

187

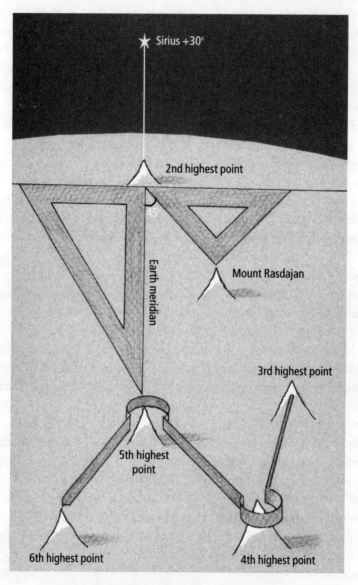

Figure 123: The Rasdajan triangles (source: ONC K–5)

I decided to spread the blanket to include the highest points in the 90,000 square miles surrounding Mt Rasdajan. The result was once again isosceles triangles and a line on the meridian *(see Figure 123)*.

A strange form of geometric truth is appearing. The highest mountain groups in the world create a seemingly endless series of isosceles triangles across the globe.

Certainly a few of these forms would be expected from chance, but why so many? Why this arrangement? After all, this doesn't happen to balls on a tennis court, so why does it happen with mountains?

At this stage I had only considered four brilliant stars in the Duat +30°, so I decided to continue the search.

PROCYON +30°

The brightest star stationed above Sirius in the Duat is the eighth brightest star on the celestial sphere. This is Procyon, so named because it precedes the Dog Star, Sirius. Procyon rises 'before the Dog' and it is said even experienced sailors sometimes confuse the two stars because Procyon is so brilliant.

If Procyon is shifted +30° with Sirius, Orion's Belt and the other Duat stars, it too passes over the Himalayas. It travels over the Kun Lun Shan mountain range and on towards K2, the second highest mountain in the world.

Procyon does not pass exactly over K2, but it does pass very close by (rather like Vega and Mt Elbert), so I decided to investigate this alignment more closely.

K2 is found on a ridge with a 26,470 foot peak at one end and K2 at the other. Working on the Operational Navigation Chart, I joined K2 with its companion on the ridge.

The angle between K2 and its companion is precisely 45°, just as it is with Mt Rasdajan and its companion.

I dropped the imaginary blanket over a 90,000 square mile area around K2.

Apart from the ridge, two more high points are the first to appear on the blanket. These points are the only other summits in the region above 26,000 feet. One is the massive Nanga Parbat, about 100 miles away, and the third great peak, called Disteghil, is about 75 miles away.

On the chart these two high points form a perfect isosceles triangle with K2.

And:

Procyon +30° passes absolutely precisely over one corner of this isosceles triangle, the summit of Nanga Parbat.

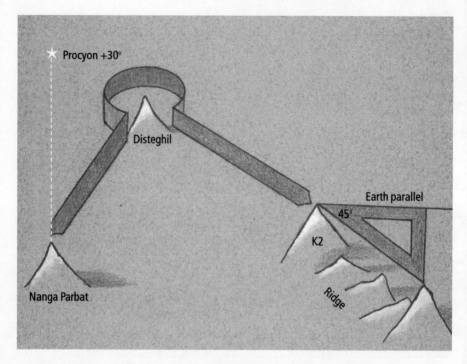

Figure 124: The Procyon alignment to Nanga Parbat (source: ONC G–7)

The alignment of Procyon +30° to Nanga Parbat is so precise I cannot split the two parallels on the chart. The fact that Nanga Parbat is the second highest point after K2 is an odd fluctuation, but then Nanga Parbat and K2 form an isosceles triangle with the third highest point, so Procyon +30° is vertically aligned to one corner of an isosceles triangle joining three of the world's greatest summits including K2. (Exactly the same applies to Vega passing vertically over the Rocky Mountains.)

'WHO WILL THEN EXPLAIN THE EXPLAINED?'

It seems that the three Giza pyramids were built at +30° as a sign. In order to interpret the sign it is necessary to recognize three things. First, that the three pyramids offer a mirror image of Orion's Belt. Second, that the mirror fails to work as it should when Polaris reaches culmination over the pole. Third, that the mirror can be corrected by shifting the stars on the celestial sphere uniformly 30° to the north.

When the sky or Earth shift is simulated, these are the resulting figures[4] reflecting the equation between stars and mountains today:

Alnitak +30°	28°00'
Mt Everest	28°00'
Alnilam +30°	28°45'
Mt Dhaulagiri	28°45'
Mintaka +30°	29°42'
Mt Kun Ka Shan	29°42'
Sirius +30°	13°25'
Mt Rasdajan	13°25'
Procyon +30°	35°13'
K2 triangle	35°13'

The mirror image between the highest points on Earth and some of the brightest stars +30° in the most brilliant area of the sky is undeniably visible in the numbers listed above. These figures are rounded by less than one tenth of one degree to create the equations.

It was time to move on and continue the search through the brilliant Duat +30°.

THE SEED OF OSIRIS

I mentioned earlier that I suspected the stars in the dagger of Orion symbolized the phallus of Osiris. I was keen to discover where the ejaculation point of the erect and culminating Orion is now reflected in this strange +30° mirror.

Having first shifted the Duat stars north by 30°, I once again brought the stars vertically down over the Earth.

I was stunned.

The star at the top of the erect phallus +30° passes vertically over Thebes and the Valley of the Kings, aligning perfectly vertically with Mt Nezzi.

This mountain and star alignment is also accurate to a tenth of a degree.

As mentioned earlier, Mt Nezzi is the singular high point overlooking the great temple of Karnac and the Valley of the Kings and Valley of the Queens, the remote valleys in the desert mountains where the Pharaohs were buried in great numbers. The Pharaohs have therefore placed their bodies under the seed point of the phallus of Osiris +30°, *but only when it is erect, as it is today, standing upright on the meridian.*

The great god Atum, the single Creator in the mythology of the Pharaohs, masturbated in order to create the universe. The sons of this god are now found under the seed point of Osiris, in the Valley of the Kings, as if immaculately sown into the fabric of the star and mountain mirror now translating itself across the globe.

How could the Pharaohs have chosen a more appropriate place to await the return of Osiris? They are now perfectly located in their own +30° equation. What an immense achievement this is. Precessional motion has now produced a synchronization that has never occurred before in history and can never occur again. The Pharaohs were anticipating this time, aware of their unique position on Earth, under Heaven as it is today.

There is good cause to suggest that the Pharaohs saw in the phallus the potential for regeneration, the promise of eternal life in 'the birthplace of stars',[5] the 'fish's mouth', the Orion nebula.

I continued by following the phallus stars, this time looking at the star at the base, or southern end of the phallus. This star +30° passes over Syene and the sacred Island of Elephantine at Aswan; the alignment is also accurate to a tenth of a degree. This is the site of one of the earliest known astronomical observatories in history.

It seems something very compelling is missing from our ancient history. Something here places the past and the present together, almost as if all history were no more than a cycle of events endlessly repeated, and once understood. And is the cycle now coming full circle once again? What did the Pharaohs anticipate? Why are they now so aligned under the sky? Why are the Duat stars so perfectly synchronized with the mountains on Earth?

Figure 125 shows the synchronization now occurring between the Duat stars and Egypt using +30° in the equation. This synchronization of the phallus occurs a few hours after all the other Duat star alignments over the Himalayas.

But the synchronization does not end there. I continued the investigation of these star and mountain parallels with the next brilliant Duat star, Bellatrix.

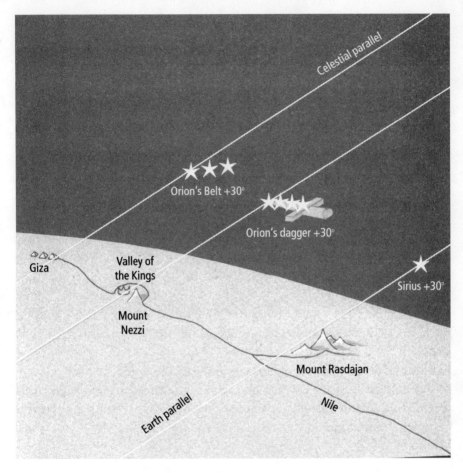

Figure 125: The phallus and the Belt over Egypt, including Sirius and Mt Rasdajan

BELLATRIX +30°

If you were asked to locate the two highest points overlooking the northern half of Asia, including all Russia, Kazakhstan and Mongolia, you could do no better than point to Mt Muztag and Mt Bukadaban Feng. These two mountains in China are the same height, but they mark the northern extreme of the Tibetan plateau, overlooking the entire great vista of northern Asia all the way to the Arctic Circle and the pole.

The star Bellatrix +30° passes over both these mountains. They are aligned on the Earth's parallel.

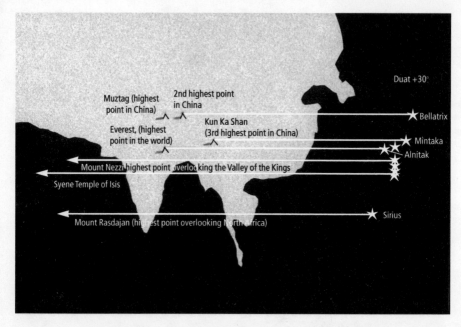

Figure 126: The passage of the Duat stars +30° over the Himalayas

This dual alignment is once again accurate to a tenth of a degree.

My shock at the synchronization of stars and mountains has never left me. The stars of the Duat +30° simply *are* co-ordinated with the highest points on Earth today. It is a numerical reality:

Alnitak +30°	28°00'
Mt Everest	28°00'
Alnilam +30°	28°45'
Mt Dhaulagiri	28°45'
Mintaka +30°	29°42'
Mt Kun Ka Shan	29°42'
Sirius +30°	13°25'
Mt Rasdajan	13°25'
Procyon +30°	35°13'
K2 triangle	35°13'

Top Dagger Star +30°	25°50'
Mt Nezzi	25°50'
Bellatrix +30°	36°40'
Mt Bukadaban Feng and Mt Muztag	36°40'

The stars listed above are self-selected in the sense that they are the most brilliant stars in a single holy area of the ancient sky. The mountains are, without doubt, among a select few mountains with the greatest vistas in the world. They include four of the most prodigious peaks in Asia and the highest point overlooking North Africa. To put it another way, there are certainly fewer than 15 comparable predominant points elsewhere in Asia or North Africa, yet these points all synchronize with the stars of the Duat +30° precisely today. It is a startling truth.

BETELGEUSE +30°

The mountain alignment search continued with the great red giant Betelgeuse. Betelgeuse is opposite Bellatrix, it represents the right shoulder of Orion and the second brightest star in the Orion constellation.

Adding precisely 30° to the parallel of Betelgeuse above the Earth today I followed the path of this brilliant Orion star over the turning globe.

Betelgeuse +30° passes vertically over Cilo Dagi.

The star/mountain alignment is once again accurate to a tenth of a degree.

Cilo Dagi is a singular great mountain in southern Turkey very close to the border with Syria and Iraq. It is the highest point in southern Turkey and overlooks all the mountains in Iran, Saudi Arabia, the Lebanon, Syria, Jordan, the Yemen, Oman and Egypt.

In other words, if you wished to define a singular high point with a clear vista extending over the Middle East you could not do better than point to this singular 13,100 foot summit. (Cilo Dagi, Mt Aragats and El Brus form an isosceles triangle.)

Whilst it is certainly true to suggest that a random selection of parallels will locate high points on the globe, it is equally untrue to suggest that a random selection should locate the very highest points on one or two continents with this fluency.

SAIPH +30°

Once again raising the Duat 30°, I traced the passage of Saiph, the lower foot of Orion, across the globe.

Saiph passes over a massive delta-shaped mountain group called Tibeski in the heart of the Sahara Desert. This massif covers about 30,000 square miles and dominates millions of square miles of the surrounding desert. The whole elevated area is overlooked by two peaks and a third, the highest, is found on a ridge. The geometry is far from definitive in this area because certain 'reported' high points of 11,100 feet appear where the contours at 8,000 feet make no allowance for such a peak.[6] However, Figure 132 shows the general configuration of high points on the Tibeski massif and also shows the passage of Saiph +30° over the area.

It is worth noting that this remote mountain seat dominating an enormous area of the Earth's surface only became known to the Western world in the twentieth century. Indeed, none of the maps we have been using were available 100 years ago and in the case of Tibeski the final resolution of all these high points appears unfortunately incomplete.

This alignment of a ninth brilliant Duat star over a predominant high point creating an isosceles triangle with a vista extending over the entire Sahara Desert tends

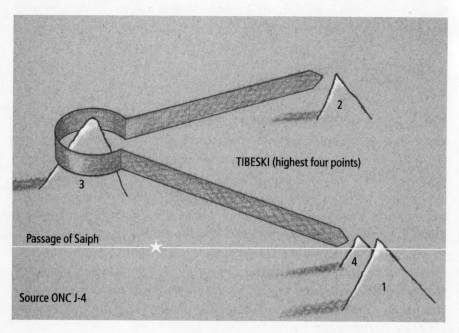

Figure 127: Tibeski

to underline the message already relayed by the other eight Duat star alignments discussed so far.

We have now created a list of mountains best described as the most predominant in Asia and North Africa. A geography professor could barely compile a better list.

a. *Mt Everest*, the highest point in the world and the highest southerly point in the Himalayas
b. *Nanga Parbat* and, via an isosceles triangle, K2, the second highest point in the world and the highest westerly point in the Himalayas
c. *Kun Ka Shan*, the highest point overlooking lowland China and the eastern Himalayas
d. *Mt Muztag* and *Mt Bukadaban Feng*, the highest points overlooking northern Asia from north of the Himalayas
e. *Mt Rasdajan*, overlooking North Africa
f. *Mt Cilo Dagi*, overlooking the Middle East
g. *Mt Tarso Ahon at Tibeski* overlooking the Sahara

One could hardly ask for a more specific list of the highest points in Asia and North Africa. Yet these summits appear like celestial markers under the brightest stars in the Duat +30° (rounding the figures by only a tenth of a degree). That is the overwhelming nature of this mirror.

THE EYE OF ORION

Perhaps the most intriguing alignment in this extraordinary reflection is found directly beneath the little triangle of stars defining what is often referred to as 'the eye of Orion'. These stars are not brilliant, but they can easily be seen in a clear night sky *(see plate 1)*.

Orion, depicted as a man in the sky, has stars forming two legs and two shoulders, but there is no bright star to be found where the head should appear. There is, however, a small triangle of stars where the head would be anticipated, and Heka, the brightest of this trio, is the one referred to as the eye of Orion.

In the mythology of ancient Greece the 'eye of Zeus' was Mount Olympus.[7] Mt Olympus is the highest point in Greece and by coincidence it lies close on the fortieth parallel, with a companion in Turkey, Mt Ararat. Thus any star passing over Mt Ararat (the mountain base is 40 miles in diameter) will also appear overhead from Mt Olympus.

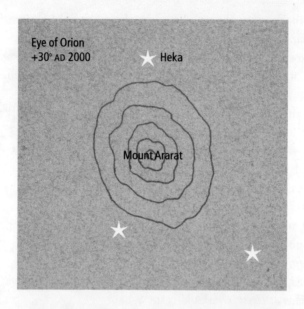

Figure 128: The eye of Orion +30° passing over Mt Ararat

When the Duat is raised 30°, the little triangle of stars in the head of Orion passes over Mt Ararat and the whole eye of Orion encircles the mountain summits.

The star mirror gets bigger:

Alnitak +30°	28°00'
Mt Everest	28°00'
Alnilam +30°	28°45'
Mt Dhaulagiri	28°45'
Mintaka +30°	29°42'
Mt Kun Ka Shan	29°42'
Sirius +30°	13°25'
Mt Rasdajan	13°25'
Procyon +30°	35°13'
K2 triangle	35°13'

Top Dagger Star +30°	25°50'
Mt Nezzi	25°50'
Bellatrix +30°	36°40'
Mt Bukadaban Feng	36°40'
Betelgeuse +30°	37°30'
Cilo Dagi	37°30'
Saiph	20°20'
Tarso Ahon	20°20'
Heka +30°	39°55'
Mt Ararat	39°55'

And the list continues.

ALDEBARAN +30°

I found a further alignment when I turned my attention to another brilliant Duat star, Aldebaran, the brightest star in Taurus. Aldebaran is the star commonly seen to represent the red eye of the bull looking down over Orion.

Aldebaran +30° passes over the highest plateau in the Alps.

Is it not strange once again to pick the brightest star in Taurus +30° and find it passing over the highest area of land in the Alps?

REVIEW

So the geometric order of the Earth and the sky I have been discussing throughout this book had already been observed long ago and cleverly marked for future observers. The mind is offered symbols in order to grasp the reality. Exactly like all great works of art Giza is the embodiment of an idea, something much bigger than itself. The Giza artists have illustrated their understanding of global geometry in the most refined manner. They already knew the highest points in the

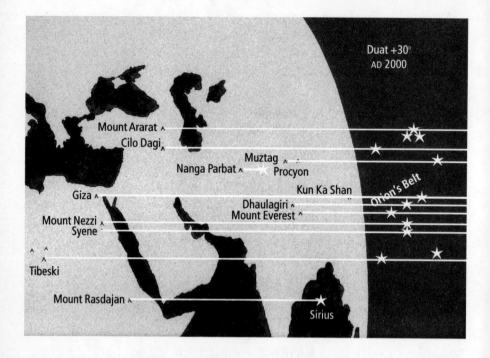

Figure 129: The Duat stars +30° passing over the Earth

world created isosceles triangles. They saw the work of gods on Earth and they made their humble imitation.

Thus the religious vision of the Earth and the sky as mirror images of each other appears to be based on a factual understanding reached in prehistory.

The gods and the mountains are forever inseparable. They have been bound together since Atum created 'the primordial mound'[8] and have reached out in a brotherly chain of giants straddling the globe from Kangchenjunga to Mt Meru. The medicine man has always 'gone to the mountain' just as Moses did. Jesus gave the Sermon on the Mount including the words 'on Earth as it is in Heaven'. Have we lost a truly scientific understanding of what these words really mean?

SEVENTH HEAVEN

In all the research described in this book I have relied upon a principle of *recognition by exclusion* or *recognition by extension*, but this is not an easy process to describe, other than by example.

A case did arise earlier when we looked at Aratus's list of constellations *(see p.80)*. In the list Triangulum is a most notable and exclusive constellation in one context, i.e. it is the only one of the 48 ancient constellations to be given a geometric title, rather than a figurative one. This is a process of identification akin to putting one red marble into a bag full of black ones.

This process of definition by exclusion is at the heart of the star mirror. It is the exclusivity of the high points on the blanket and the exclusivity of the stars in the Duat penetrating a similar blanket that attract our attention. In other words, when we look at the night sky we do not tend to look at all the dark patches, we are naturally attracted to the brightest lights, and these are, by a pun in definition, the most extreme points. Our most primitive methods of identification are bound up with this process of 'the biggest', 'the longest', 'the highest', 'the brightest', etc. We naturally measure from one extreme to the other. This natural human inclination towards defining the outer limit leads us back to the brightest star in Orion, Rigel.

RIGEL

We have seen already how Sirius passes over Mt Illimani at present, but how it passes vertically over Mt Rasdajan when the +30° code is applied.

Surely Rigel +30° should also pass over a magnificent mountain?

But the seventh star is different, it does not pass over such a mountain, it is unlike its neighbours in the Duat, it is excluded from the pattern. Indeed, Rigel changes the pattern.

Rigel +30° passes over the delta of the River Ganges and Brahmaputra.

So Rigel +30° reveals another facet in the star mirror and it is once again related to the phallus of Orion +30°.

As Rigel +30° passes from the Ganges/Brahmaputra Delta over India, it cuts a line across the subcontinent isolating the whole triangular peninsula of India to the south.

A fabulous correlation occurs in this passage over India because the presently vertical phallus of Orion aligns perfectly with the broadest river in India, the Brahmaputra, *along the self-same stretch where the Brahmaputra follows the Earth's meridian.*

The great Brahmaputra river runs from east to west on the parallel but then takes a right angle turn at 26° and flows from north to south, thus providing a direct meridian mirror for the vertical phallus. The upper end of the phallus in the sky aligns most noticeably with this right angle of water, which I believe is the broadest stretch of river in the world. This in turn draws attention to the kink in the Nile river, because both the kink in the Nile and the right angle in the Brahmaputra occur at 26° north, under the point of the phallus +30°.

When the phallus aligns to the Brahmaputra on the meridian a remarkable synchronicity occurs across the country. The mirror of Orion stars +30° briefly appears synchronized in seven places *in the same few minutes of time.*

The picture created is quite remarkable.

The phallus (dagger) stars align with the Brahmaputra river concurrently with Bellatrix passing over Mt Muztag, which is quite unlikely in itself, but within minutes of this strange dual synchronization, Sirius, Rigel, Saiph, Betelgeuse and Heka all pass over a separate body of water!

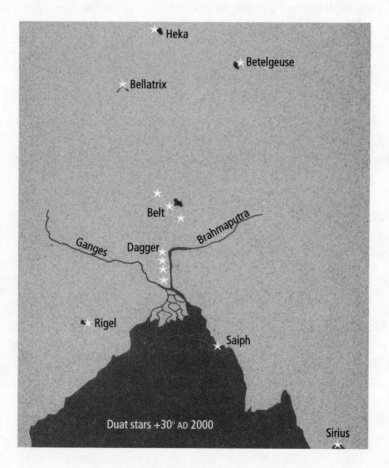

Figure 130: The Orion water image

So, the distinction of Rigel in the star mirror brings with it the same slightly esoteric but logical progression I attempted to follow earlier. Rigel +30° does not pass
over the highest mountain in the world, it passes over the mouths of the 'largest
river delta in the world',[9] thus providing another triangular extreme in the equation.

The Earth is then geometrically ordered and the features of the Earth are seen as
symbols in a divinely arranged universal masterpiece. Or, at least, are we now just
beginning to fathom the evidence sustaining this prehistoric belief?

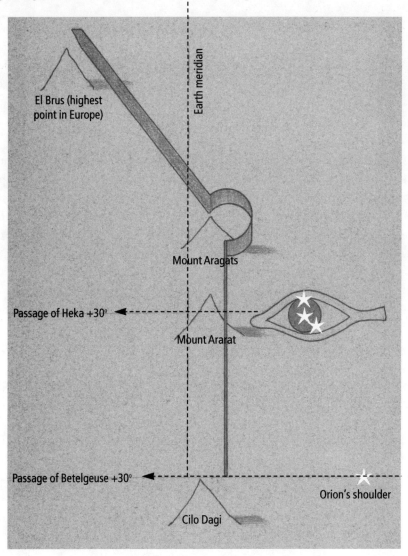

Figure 131: The eye (source: Bartholomew 1:1,000,000 Caucasus)

REFLECTIONS

'Had they deceived us,
Or deceived themselves,
the quiet-voiced elders,
Bequeathing us merely
a receipt for deceit?' [1]

At the beginning of this book I gave a brief account of purchasing a chart of central Australia. I said that before opening the map I first drew a shape on a piece of paper. When I joined the three highest points (Mt Ziel, Mt Woodroffe and Mt Edward) on the previously unopened map, I had already drawn the shape created by them. The shape was an isosceles triangle. It is so persistent I felt sure I would find it once again in Australia, and there it is, joining the three highest points in the central deserts. It may seem strange, almost ridiculous, to measure the Earth in this way with dividers, but I had learned this process from past masters.

And from the same wise source there came a signal. Their beacon at Giza is now alight once again, it has come to life, spotlighting the brilliant stars once more. Something from long ago is being reborn. The wisdom of the ancients is not a miscalculation, it is sharp and precise, it is tactical, refined, penetrating, symbolic and scientific. It is *real*. The reality is all before us – three high points in an isosceles triangle at Giza are reflected by three high points in a stellar triangle above, and the same triangle persists around the globe and in the sky.

The global nature of this legacy is realized in the pyramids aligned vertically under Vega, Arcturus and Sirius in the present day. Equally surprising is the realization that the brightest stars in the Duat are geometrically ordered, and once again, the main feature of this geometry is the isosceles triangle *(see Figure 62)*.

I said earlier that the ancient architects left 'a form of proof' and I will try to explain what I mean by this.

WHAT IS PROOF?

From the fathomless depths of space we receive the light of various stars. But each brilliant gem in the sky is nothing more than a historical record of where the particular star used to be and what the light shining from it once looked like. If every star in the whole galaxy surrounding our solar system had miraculously disappeared yesterday we would be none the wiser tomorrow. In this respect the night sky is but a record of history. We are told that astronomers have penetrated 15 billion years into this history, then it is 21 billion, and again perhaps only 12 billion. These times and distances are still uncertain.

If we can really see (or detect) something 15 billion years old in our own sky, and if we can also detect billions of galaxies like our own, it becomes almost impossible to imagine the size of whatever we are looking into. The concept of Nut and Geb, in the light of the universe as we know it today, makes absolutely no sense at all. It would seem to be a brazen conceit to suggest that this little Earth of ours could represent half the universe. But this is exactly what we are told to believe over and over again, in text after text, from ancient China to modern Islam.

The Koran, for example, states:

'Are the disbelievers unaware that the heaven and the Earth were one solid mass which we tore asunder?'[2]

And the same message comes from China:

'[The Kunlun mountain chain] is the backbone from which the other mountain chains proceed, and they form together a kind of terrestrial skeleton. The rivers form the veins and the arteries, and the mountains the bones of the living Earth. The whole is imagined to be so like the heavens that certain stars correspond to certain terrestrial spaces, and exercise rule over them. Kunlun rules the hills as the Pole star rules the stars.'[3]

There can be little doubt that these broadly based concepts have their roots in prehistory. And the universal concept of a divine bond between Earth and sky is beautifully expressed in the Bible, in Job 38:25–33:

'The waters are hid with a stone, and the face of the deep is frozen.
Canst thou bind the sweet influences of the Pleiades, or loose the bands
  of Orion?

Canst thou bring forth Mazzaroth[4] in his season? Or canst thou guide Arcturus
with his sons?

Knowest thou the ordinance of heaven? Canst thou set the domain thereof in
the Earth?'

The domain of Heaven on Earth; celestial becomes terrestrial. 'On Earth as it is in
Heaven.'

Surely this is exactly the sentiment expressed by the people who built Avebury,
Giza, Tiahuanaco, Teotihuacán, Nazca, Cholula, Machu Pichu, Cuzco, Easter Island,
Cahokia and the Chinese pyramid fields? And I hope I can now illustrate that pre-
cisely the same divine vision was shared by the people who built Stonehenge.

If you find the eye of Orion in the sky and follow his imagined gaze due north
there are two bright stars directly above his head. The stars are called Elnath and
Alheka, and they represent the twin horns of the bull Taurus.

I added 30° to these stars, just like all the other Duat stars.

Alheka +30° now passes vertically over Stonehenge.

The intelligence displayed by the people who devised this global scheme is illustrated to the full with this alignment. The star Alheka is situated on the same celestial
meridian as the head of the dragon which passes over Avebury, and when we join
Avebury and Stonehenge on Earth we find the two sites are on the same meridian
also. As soon as we realize this correspondence was intentional we are led along
straight lines into the ancient world of terrestrial symbolism.

By following the second star representing the horns of the bull we can immediately see this language at work.

The second star in the simulation passes vertically over the two extreme northerly points on mainland Britain. I studied the area for isosceles geometry and found
there are three extreme points on the northern mainland *and these three points form an
isosceles triangle.*[5] The points are Duncansby Head, Strathy Point and Cape Wrath.

Despite all this, I may have failed to convey to the reader that these isosceles relationships are truly a global phenomena. After all, the idea just sounds ridiculous,
and it sounded ridiculous to me as well. But I have found it is true, and somehow
the truth seems more important.

The tips of the bull's horns join together to form a straight line with Betelgeuse.
The upper horn tip forms an isosceles triangle with the shoulders of Orion.

The earlier explanation of a seesaw between Draco and Orion has now found its
use. The sites of Avebury and Stonehenge are communicating the same message as

that received from Giza. The precise location of Stonehenge is clearly integrated into the +30° code because the star passing over Stonehenge in the simulation is the first bright star to be found in the Duat directly above Orion's head! (The alignment once again is within a tenth of a degree.)

'A great scientific instrument lies sprawled over the entire surface of the globe. At some period, perhaps 4,000 years ago, almost every corner of the world was visited by a group of men who came with a particular task to accomplish.'[6]

These words of John Michell ring truer still. But as we move into the new millennium the sky itself is revealing the awesome truth of John Michell's much misunderstood vision. It was no illusion, although the academic community generally mistook it for one, but the writing was already on the wall. As Joseph Campbell said, 'The Geomancers' vision interprets the Earth in terms of the heavens. They saw the mountains as stars.'[7]

THE EYE OF THE DRAGON

Living in the West Country of England I often visit the ancient Avebury stones and the surrounding countryside. I once stood at Silbury Hill and watched the bright eye of the dragon passing overhead in the midnight sky at the summer solstice.

The research I have conducted for this book was completed over a period of about four years. As the work progressed the breadth of the enquiry broadened and I now find my desk and bookcases crammed with maps and charts from across the world. I had no idea at the outset that the investigation into the 11 meridian angles of the Great Pyramid would lead so far afield and I found myself poorly equipped for the task.

I believe the ancient pyramids, stone circles and mounds dotted around the planet are often unlikely to be the first monuments to mark these sites. If a piece of ground itself was once regarded as hallowed or sacred, no amount of investigation can determine exactly when this reverence first arose.

By strange coincidence in the present day certain areas of Wiltshire are becoming focal points for a form of vigil, perhaps similar to those inspired by the sky in times gone by. The land, most particularly in the areas around Avebury and Stonehenge, has become increasingly enigmatic over the past two decades. Every summer enormous geometric shapes appear in the fields around this area. Though initially believed to be the work of pranksters, the majority of these 'crop circles' have subsequently proven to be other than man-made. The 'downing' of crops generally creates a superbly constructed geometric figure created by the mass bending of crop stems. Over the past few years the geometric figures have become increasingly complex, creating defined geometric forms akin to the Fibonacci spiral.

The realization that these incredible features of the Wiltshire landscape are not all strange pranks was reached through a scientific analysis of the crop stem. It was revealed that in 'genuine' formations each downed stem had been subjected to a short burst of microwave radiation, leaving a detectable trace in the fields themselves. The effect was such that the *cells in the stem changed shape*, forcing a near 90° turn in the vertical direction of the crop in many cases.

Arriving early at an untouched 'downing' myself, it was very plain to see that the pattern in the crop was not made by people with paddles on their feet. The crop itself was not broken, all the cereal was intact, but each straight stem appeared to have grown around a corner. It is intriguing to be living in this part of the country, because these geometric shapes are now attracting people from around the world each summer.

The point I am trying to reach is that the countryside where the crops are now so regularly downed by this unusual process is the very land already marked by a prodigious array of ancient monuments including Avebury and Stonehenge. (This is, if you like, where the two star patterns meet, the true vertical over Avebury and the +30° vertical over Stonehenge.) One monument marks the lower culmination of Draco (Silbury Hill) and one marks the upper culmination of the bull's horn (Stonehenge). Once again it is a strange coincidence that the land here is being marked by an unknown force and it brings home the fact that it is impossible to date the location of any ancient site, because it is impossible to tell what visible feature may first have caused that site to be revered.

But now Stonehenge is found aligned under a bright Duat star +30° and this once again illustrates the precision employed by those who marked the site. The meridian of Stonehenge and the meridian of Avebury Sanctuary some 17 miles away are identical. The dragon takes off from the Sanctuary across the rolling countryside until its great stone spine arrives at Avebury circle *(see plate 11)*. If you raise an angle of precisely 51°51' from the parallel of the Sanctuary, the straight line takes you to the heart of the Avebury stone circle a mile or more away. The same angle, 51°51', is found on all four sides on the Great Pyramid at Giza.

Whilst insisting that the monument builders around the world were privy to extremely detailed data regarding the celestial and terrestrial spheres, I have been inferring throughout this book that charts, maps or similar highly technical facilities were available in the distant past. But there is so little evidence of this. Where are the charts, the compasses and all the machinery for travelling and mapping the planet?

Little has survived the passage of time, yet there are accurate maps of Antarctica predating Columbus. In his analysis of our most ancient maps Charles Hapgood makes this observation:

'The trigonometry of the projection (or rather its information on the size of the Earth) suggests the work of Alexandrian geographers, but the evident knowledge of longitude implies a people unknown to us.'[8]

In *Fingerprints of the Gods*, Graham Hancock investigates many of the monuments discussed in this book. After an exhilarating and exhaustive journey from one ancient site to the next, Hancock is left in no doubt that a highly advanced civilization preceded our own:

'Certain mysterious structures scattered around the world were built to preserve and transmit the knowledge of an advanced civilization of remote antiquity which was destroyed by a great upheaval.'[9]

For an alternative view, Dr Zahi Hawass, currently the Director of the Giza Plateau, said he is not averse to the idea of an older civilization in Egypt, but he complains, 'So far there has been no hard evidence to support the theory of a prior civilization.'[10]

But is it possible the evidence is harder than we think? Is it carried by *design* and is the 'trace' (measured in millions of tons) carefully crafted and placed? A hundred years ago Sir Norman Lockyer demonstrated that if you study an ancient civilization it is essential to follow the straight lines they described. Likewise today, it is quite certain that no intelligence will be discerned from Carl Sagan's NASA message if the imagined alien does not first follow his straight lines. So, when Egyptologists see no evidence of a prior civilization, is it only because they have not followed the point of the Great Pyramid straight into the sky?

If there was a highly advanced civilization, or group, on Earth in prehistory (as I believe there clearly was), then it is certainly possible that we ourselves have yet to understand the particular intellectual platform upon which they were situated. And it is not for us to make any presumption about where that platform may be found.

It seems a possible flaw lies in our own approach to the subject. We have assumed for a long time that the people who preceded us were never as wise as we are today; moreover, we have not approached the ancient monuments as vehicles of communication. A further problem is that archaeologists are unlikely to recognize an astronomical language, even if it is plainly written, because they are not generally conversant with astronomy. And without an understanding of precessional motion these phenomenal astronomical coincidences are unlikely to be correctly evaluated.

As Robert Bauval said regarding his own discoveries, 'I don't think coincidence is any longer an issue,' yet despite this expert insight, many in the Establishment passed off his great advance as 'serendipity'. But of course you have to be in a position to understand the nature of a coincidence in order to appraise the value of it in the first place. Science is little more than the observation and record of coincidence.

Having made this evaluation, I find it quite certain that the ancient monuments of the world are vehicles of communication and that they have something important to relate *en masse*. They are glyphs in language.

THE RIVER OF TEARS

I illustrated earlier how the figure of Orion now appears to have reached the top of the mountain in the sense that Rigel now aligns with the north face of the Great Pyramid. Rigel shares this position with Orion's neighbouring constellation the 'heavenly stream' Eridanus. So the image produced at Giza today is one in which the celestial stream spouts out of the top and babbles all the way down the western flank of the pyramid as Rigel passes over the meridian.

Eridanus issues from Orion's left foot, but with his raised arm he also reaches the other celestial stream, the Milky Way. So Orion becomes the single starry image in the sky joining the two heavenly streams. This bridge afforded by the Orion constellation may well be connected to the mythical story of Phaethon, the son of the sun Helios in Greek mythology.

Phaethon only discovered that he was the son of the sun in adolescence. He was then determined to take his father's chariot along the ecliptic. (The boat of Ra and the chariot of Helios are therefore similar vehicles.) Phaethon, however, was not fit to drive the chariot of the sun:

'The sight of the animals that constituted the signs of the Zodiac frightened him and he left his ordained path. He dropped too low and risked setting fire to the Earth; then he rose too high and the stars complained to Zeus. To

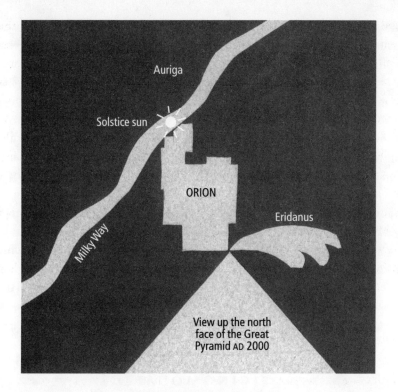

Figure 132: The heavenly stream

prevent a universal conflagration Zeus struck the boy down with his thunder-bolt and hurled him into the river Eridanus.'[11]

The raised limb of Orion now reaches the sun at its very highest point, and above the sun is the Charioteer, and in the constellation of the Charioteer are four notable stars in a straight line, all strung neatly along the solsticial colure today. Is it more than chance that through the dark and indistinct corridors of mythological history comes a myth describing an event almost identical to the image from Egypt in which the sun takes a violent turn?

Both myth and mural describe a god disturbing the sun. In the Greek it is Zeus casting the sun down from its highest path into the river Eridanus. In the sky the god in question is surely Orion, reaching the high point of the sun, on the ecliptic and on the Milky Way, with the solstice sun and the Chariot above, and Eridanus at his feet – precisely today's sky, but not the sky of 2,000 years ago.

In Plato's *Timaeus*, Solon is given the following advice regarding the legend of Phaethon:

'The truth behind it is in a deviation of the bodies that revolve in Heaven around the Earth, and a destruction, occurring at long intervals, of things on Earth by a great conflagration.'[12]

The same myth was interpreted as:

'The departure of the sun and planets from their former path and the enthroning of Eridanus, which together with Auriga was to take over the function of the Milky Way.'[13]

Earlier in this book we looked at the strange loop in the passage of the sun as it passed over the Orion figure in the ancient Egyptian mural *(see Figure 52)*. In these Greek accounts a similar event is described in which the sun and planets 'depart from their former path'. The movement described here could be caused by the Earth's axis shifting or it could be caused by a greatly accelerated continental drift – in either event a global calamity.

Meanwhile, the 'enthroning of Eridanus' may be related to the Age of Aquarius.

NOTICING AQUARIUS

The celestial stream Eridanus is said to be many things, including the Nile river, the Po and the Ganges river, but it is also described as the stream of water poured from the pitcher carried by Aquarius.

Eridanus crosses more parallels on the celestial sphere than any other constellation, but the source of the stream is undeniably the raised foot of Orion. Thus Orion and Aquarius are directly associated in star lore by their relationship with Eridanus.

Aratus, in the *Phaenomena*, describes Eridanus as 'under the feet of the gods, a river of tears that reaches at last the left foot of Orion'. A very similar image arises in the *Bhagavata Purana*:

'The river flowed over the great toe of Vishnu's left foot, which had previously, as he lifted it up, made a fissure in the shell of the mundane egg, and thus gave entrance to the heavenly stream.'[14]

(This picture of Vishnu is a perfectly traced image of Orion viewed by looking up the north face of the Great Pyramid today.)

So, with Eridanus, the celestial 'stream of tears', at his feet, Orion carries the solstice sun on his raised limb through the star gate and across the river of the Milky Way. At the same time:

The star Alpha Aquarius is crossing the celestial equator for the first time in recorded history.

To be precise, in tandem with all the other synchronized events discussed throughout this book, Alpha Aquarius will have crossed the celestial equator in the next 100 years. It is not quite there yet.

To give the full picture, the passage of Alpha Aquarius across the celestial equator coincides with the following events:

a. A mirror image appearing between the Great Square and the Earth's grid.

b. The arrival of Polaris over the north pole of the Earth.

c. The arrival of Orion's Belt at 0° (pointing along the 0° line to Alpha Aquarius).

d. The passage of the solstice sun across the galactic equator.

e. The passage of the solstice sun from Gemini into Taurus.

f. The passage of Alpha Triangulum vertically over Giza.

g. The passage of the four aligned stars in Auriga across the solsticial colure.

h. The passage of the winter solstice sun over the scorpion's sting.

i. The passage of Antares over Easter Island.

j. The passage of Draco's head over Silbury Hill, Ben Nevis and Mt Brandon.

k. The passage of the Libran sun over Nazca.

l. The passage of Alpha Libra over Mt Illampu.

m. The passage of Beta Libra over Mt Hauscaran.

n. The passage of Sirius over Mt Illimani and the Akapana pyramid.

o. The passage of Arcturus over Citlaltepetl and the Cholula pyramid.

p. The passage of Vega over the Rocky Mountains and the Cahokia mounds.

These events all coincide with arrival of Osiris at his precessional culmination, holding up the solstice sun.

At the same time the Great Pyramid spotlights now point us to:

a. *The sun* appearing at the apex of the balances in Libra.

b. *Polaris* over the top of the world.

c. *Rigel*, the brightest star in Orion, forming an isosceles triangle with Alnitak and Bellatrix.

d. *Alpha Triangulum*, at the pointed end of the only Triangle constellation.

e. *Crux*, the brightest small cluster of stars in the sky forming two overlapping isosceles triangles on the Giza horizon.

f. *Yildun*, the star at the apex of an isosceles triangle of the brightest three stars 'on target' surrounding Polaris.

g. *Draco*, the snaking dragon with an isosceles head passing over Silbury Hill, Ben Nevis and Mt Brandon.

h. *Lepus and Columba* with the isosceles triangle formed between Beta Lepus, Delta Lepus and Alpha Columba.

(The alignment of the Great Pyramid spotlights with these brilliant stars coincides with the events given in the earlier list.)

It seems clear then that the relationship between stars and mountains, between Heaven and Earth, has been noted in the past and has been magically frozen for millennia in the ancient monuments of the world, mysteriously coming to light under Polaris.

THE SHIFT

But we have also found that Giza provides a code, an Earth or sky shift of 30°.

And just as all the events listed earlier arise in a small window of history, so the alignments of the Duat stars +30° also occur uniquely at this time:

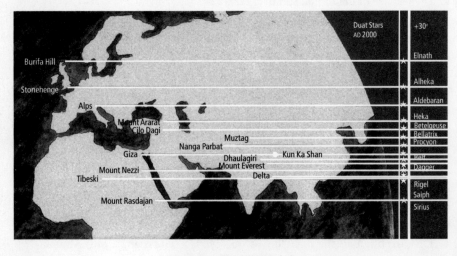

Figure 133: The full 30° shift

Alnitak +30°	28°00'
Mt Everest	28°00'
Alnilam +30°	28°45'
Mt Dhaulagiri	28°45'
Mintaka +30°	29°42'
Mt Kun Ka Shan	29°42'
Giza	
Sirius +30°	13°25'
Mt Rasdajan	13°25'
Procyon +30°	35°13'
K2 triangle	35°13'
Top Dagger Star +30°	25°50'
Mt Nezzi	25°50'
Bellatrix +30°	36°40'
Mt Bukadaban Feng and Mt Muztag	36°40'
Betelgeuse +30°	37°30'
Cilo Dagi	37°30'
Heka +30°	39°55'
Mt Ararat	39°55'
Saiph +30°	20°20'
Tibeski	20°20'
Aldebaran +30°	16°30'
Alpine plateau	16°30'
Alheka +30°	51°10'
Stonehenge	51°10'
Elnath +30°	58°40'
Burifa Hill	58°40'

Forgive the repetition of this list of rounded figures for the final time, but I am trying to emphasize that the relationship between the brightest stars and the highest
mountains is a very true reflection.

METAPHYSICS

My whole perspective was changed by these equations because I could no longer
imagine the Earth and the cosmos as products of careless fate. With this change I
glanced away from my current perspectives to those of distant history – and found
at every turn that men and woman long ago had spoken of the star mirror.

These, for example, are the words of a diviner living in the seventh century
before Christ:

> 'The signs on Earth as those in heaven give us signals. Sky and Earth both pro-
> duce portents; though appearing separately, they are not separate because sky
> and Earth are related.'[15]

It seems certain we once knew about the star mirror and yet lost that awareness.
Today, religious communities still refer to the 'kingdom of Heaven on Earth', but
has the true reflection long been overlooked?

I also discovered that in antiquity the pyramids of the Pharaohs were not said to
contain their bodies, but rather:

> '...the sciences of arithmetic and geometry, that they might retain the records
> for the benefit of those who could afterward comprehend them ... the posi-
> tion of the stars and their cycles.'[16]

What might the Pharaohs have made of 'the position of the stars'? Perhaps they
considered the geometric arrangement of all the bright stars in the Duat a sign,
something designed by their Creator in order to communicate directly with religious folk on Earth. If such a form of communication can be imagined, then
the juxtaposition of mind and star is altered, just as it may have been for the
Pharaohs.

It appears certain that in times gone by the star mirror was recognized as the
work of a universal Creator. Such a Creator is central to various writings, including
The Book of the Dead, the Bible, the Koran and Hindu texts. Yet despite all these wise
words and ancient teachings the prevailing twentieth-century inclination is to

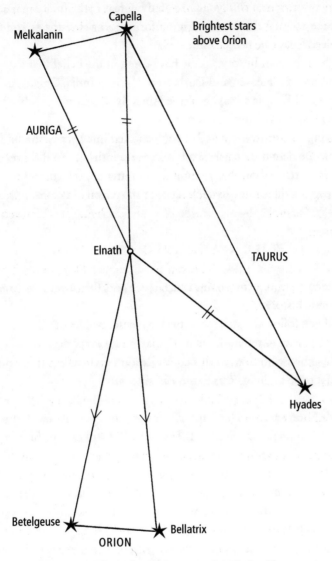

Figure 134: The six brightest stars on Orion's shoulders

regard these sentiments as somehow invalid. However, the mirror is a manifest fact and the ancients have left the proof of it.

The Earth and the stars are profoundly related by geometry. The two spheres do in fact have a common element in their appearance. The observation that the ancient world as a whole embraced a religious vision of a divine Creator who designed the Heaven and the Earth as twins lends further substantial weight to the idea that the stars were wilfully aligned to the Great Pyramid today for a purpose. That purpose was, I believe, to convey information about the star mirror to the future, indeed to us, the people under Polaris.

Throughout human history people have dwelt in the belief that a divine source created and ordered Heaven and Earth. Records from India, China, America, Australia, Africa and Eurasia all say the same thing. By disbelieving in this divine order it is we who become the freaks in history.

By denying the existence of highly sophisticated intelligence in our distant past we may also be denying ourselves a transient opportunity to discover something extremely important about the turning Earth. After all, the current heating at the poles was predicted long ago to coincide with the arrival of Polaris.

THE GALACTIC PYRAMID

I would like to make one final point which challenges the current wisdom regarding our pre-literate history.

Today, if you follow the straight vertical line described by the Great Pyramid into the sky, it will come to rest at the apex of Triangulum every day.

Nobody knows who defined this constellation or when, but the earliest written account of it once again appears in the *Phaenomena*:

'Beneath Andromeda still another sign is constructed, drawn with three sides; an isosceles triangle whose base, though scant, is still easy to find for its two stars outsparkle many another.'[17]

Looking closely at this definition of Triangulum by Aratus, and at the constellation itself, I noticed the brightest three stars do not actually form the isosceles triangle Aratus appears to describe.

The three brightest stars in Triangulum form a right-angled triangle, not an isosceles.

But the isosceles triangle referred to by Aratus does exist. If you follow his instructions carefully and take the two stars that 'outsparkle many others' (Alpha and Beta Triangulum), you will find these two stars do in fact form the base of an isosceles triangle. But at the apex of the triangle is the Andromeda Galaxy.

Andromeda is our brightest and biggest galactic neighbour. It is visible to the naked eye on a clear night in an unpolluted sky.

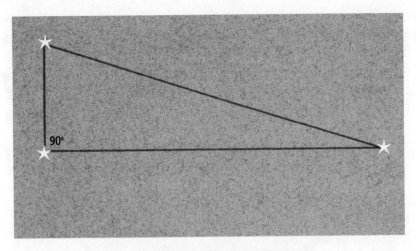

Figure 135: Triangulum, the three brightest stars

So we are directed from Giza to Triangulum and from Triangulum to the Andromeda Galaxy with elementary arrows. This does not necessarily infer the Giza builders came from the Andromeda Galaxy, but in light of all the other intelligence displayed it does firmly suggest that they understood some galactic astronomy.

Geometry is a great message maker. The rules of geometry will never change. Just as NASA demonstrated, if you wish to provide a universal signal of intelligence then geometry is a sure vehicle. And to fix this signal on Earth and in the stars is a wise method of preservation. So only one geometric figure is described in the ancient sky, defined as 'an isosceles triangle', even though the three stars are not isosceles, but more nearly a right angle.

Galactic astronomy was unknown to us only 100 years ago.

The maps we have used throughout this book were unprepared 100 years ago. The essential stellar computer programme was unknown 50 years ago. Could our ancestors have recognized a cyclical rise and fall in the progress of history?

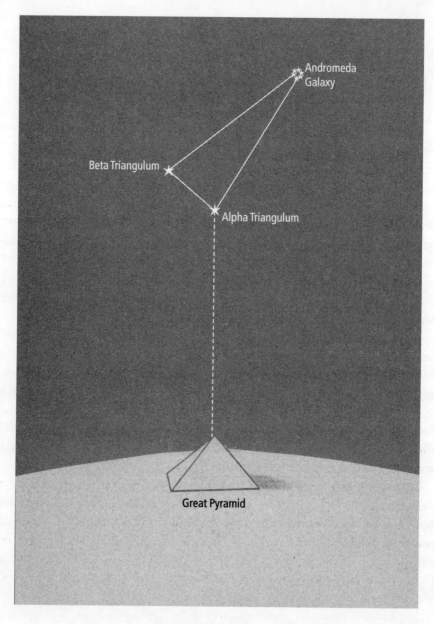

Figure 136: The Great Pyramid, Triangulum, Andromeda.
This alignment is precise when Polaris is most nearly over the pole of the Earth.

THE LAST WORD

'True without deceit, certain and most true.
What is below is like what is above and what is above is like what is below, for
the performing of the marvels of the one thing.'[18]

In this book I have been discussing something I have failed to understand myself. I cannot see how the position of any particular star over the Earth can have any bearing on the Earth itself. There is no apparent physical connection between mountains and starlight other than light itself. Despite this there is clearly a numerical connection between the brightest stars and the highest mountains, and these numbers (defining the parallels on the spheres) do illustrate a straightforward equation where the parallel defined by the brilliant star persistently equates with the parallel of a predominant mountain. The highest mountains therefore 'mirror' the brightest stars in a manner certainly not to be expected from a truly random process, but this has proved hard to illustrate in a book because of the scales involved.

The reader may imagine that by following any chosen parallel on Earth they will encounter a world-dominating summit, but this is certainly not the case when the Earth parallel you are following is but a fraction of a degree in width. It is possible to prove this by choosing at random a series of ten parallel bands each with a width of 0.2°. If you arbitrarily define these ten Earth parallels at intervals on a map of Asia, the odds of chance are set against one of your chosen parallels locating Mt Everest. Thus, to define a world-order summit with each one of your randomly selected parallels would be passing strange.

Yet, as we have seen, when the brilliant Duat stars are employed to define the narrow parallels, each one matches the location of a world-order summit. An emphatic link therefore exists between the brightest Duat stars and the highest points on half the Earth; a series of numerical equations that cannot readily be attributed to serendipity. None the less I am at a loss to describe this union between Heaven and Earth without a symbol for divinity appearing in the equation itself, and no such symbol exists in modern science.

So perhaps the most successful way to communicate this enduring faith intellectually is, after all, to build a great mountain under a brilliant star.

APPENDICES

'There is a principle which is a bar against all information, which is proof against all arguments and which cannot fail to keep a man in everlasting ignorance; that principle is contempt prior to investigation.'[1]

INTRODUCTION

When George Everest surveyed the mountains of the Himalayas he found peak number 15 on the survey to be the highest and so the most elevated summit in the world was named after him. The Times and the Phillip's world atlases differ in their given co-ordinates for Mt Everest by 5' of latitude.

Any study involving a number of precise locations, be they stars or mountains, is bound to involve some error. I have drawn figures from many sources in an effort to be precise, however I apologize for any errors, for whatever reason they might have occurred.

The appendices are divided into four parts:

1. The Great Pyramid alignments in 2450 BC and AD 2080.
2. The vertical alignment of ancient sites and stars today.
3. The alignments between stars and mountains in the present day.
4. Stellar geometry: Orion, Auriga, Lepus.
   (Terrestrial geometry is best studied on Operational Navigation Charts.
   Charts P–13 and Q–13, showing central Australia, provide a fine example.)

Throughout the book I have referred to 'celestial latitude' in place of the correct astronomical term 'declination'. In the appendices I will revert to the use of declination (Dec.), and right ascension (RA) in describing the stars' positions.

The source of figures for the star co-ordinates in stellar epoch AD 2000 is Patrick Moore's *The Guinness Book of Astronomy* (Guinness Publishing, 1995). Stellar co-ordinates for other epochs are found in *SkyMap* computer software. Where these differ I have used *SkyMap* in preference.

In the vast majority of cases the sources used to determine the precise location of mountains and ancient sites are the 1:1,000,000 Operational Navigation Charts.

The Times and Collins world atlases have also been used where information was unclear on the ONC chart.

For work involving Great Britain I have used the 1:50,000 and 1:25,000 Ordnance Survey Landranger and Pathfinder series, coupled with *The Complete Atlas of the British Isles* (Reader's Digest, 1965).

In order to cover the essential ground in the book I have kept the working figures to a minimum in the text. In referring to 'the present day' I have generally been referring to some time in the next 100 years. In attempting to define that time more precisely the Great Pyramid is most accurately aligned to the celestial sphere in AD 2080. I have therefore used this date in Appendix I.

THE GREAT PYRAMID ALIGNMENTS IN 2450 BC AND AD 2080

The pyramid angles are subject to minor differences depending on the source used to define these angles. These agree with most sources within a few arc minutes.[1] Figure 137 provides the key for the star alignments that follow in both epochs.

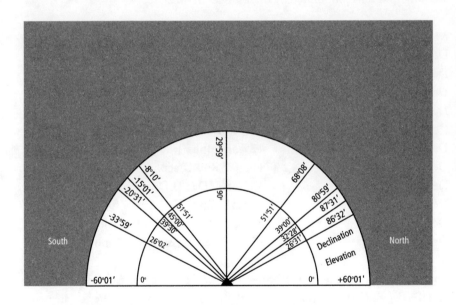

Figure 137: Key for star alignments. The inner circle shows pyramid angle elevations, the outer circle shows the declination on the celestial spheres.

ANGLE

The southern horizon at 0°	Dec. −60°01'
The ascending passage at 26°02'	Dec. −33°59'
The Queen's Chamber southern star shaft 39°30'	Dec. −20°31'
The King's Chamber southern star shaft 45°00'	Dec. −15°01'
The north face angle 51°51'	Dec. −08°10'
The vertical 90°00'	Dec. +29°59'
The south face angle 51°51'	Dec. +68°08'
The Queen's Chamber northern star shaft 39°00'	Dec. +80°59'
The King's Chamber northern star shaft 32°28'	Dec. +87°31'
The descending passage 26°31'	Dec. +86°32'
The northern horizon at 0°	Dec. +60°01'

The brightest stars pinpointed by these angles in AD 2080:

ANGLE	STARS
Dec. −60°01'	−60°07' Beta Crucis
Dec. −33°59'	−34°04' Alpha Columbae (Phact)
Dec. −20°31'	−20°42' Beta Lepus (Nihal)
Dec. −15°01'	−15°03' Gamma Librae and the sun in Libra
Dec. −08°10'	−08°07' Beta Orionis (Rigel)
Dec. +29°59'	+29°58' Alpha Triangulum
Dec. +68°08'	+68°06' Rho Draconis
Dec. +80°59'	+80°58' HD8181 Draconis
Dec. +87°31'	+89°31' Alpha Ursa Minor (Polaris)
Dec. +86°32'	+86°30' Delta Ursa Minor (Yildun)
Dec. +60°01'	+59°36' Beta Cassiopeiae (Caph)

The two angles producing the 'target' around Polaris are the descending passage and the King's Chamber northern star shaft. As the Earth turns, they create two circles on the celestial sphere. One circle measures nearly 5° in diameter, the other about 7°. Polaris now appears to go around the pole defining a circle 1° in diameter at the target centre.

Excluding Polaris, the average discrepancy achieved in the alignments listed above is about seven arc minutes. The alignment to Cassiopeia on the northern horizon appears to *pass through* the triangle created by the three brightest stars in this constellation.

Due to precession many stars move by much more than seven minutes of declination on the celestial sphere over a period of only 50 years. Consequently the alignments listed above appear to be timed to coincide with considerable precision within a single epoch as Polaris reaches its precessional culmination. Polaris makes its closest polar transit in AD 2100.

The *SkyMap* computer programme[2] provides actual stellar co-ordinates on the celestial sphere coupled with stellar positions in the sky from any location on Earth, accounting for precessional motion, proper motion, nutation and atmospheric refraction.

The figures listed below illustrate the synchronization of the Great Pyramid with the stars during the first century of the new millennium. With the exception of Cassiopeia and Polaris, these figures illustrate the precision with which these stars become aligned to the pyramid spotlights during a very short window in history. This window coincides all but precisely with the precessional culmination of Polaris. The close synchronization is indicated by the figures in bold.

STAR	AD 2000	AD 2080	AD 2100	SPOTLIGHT
Beta Crucis	−59°41'	**−60°01'**	−60°07'	**−60°02'**
Alpha Columbae (Phact)	−34°04'	**−34°02'**	−34°02'	**−33°59'**
Beta Lepus (Nihal)	−20°46'	**−20°42'**	−20°41'	**−20°31'**
Gamma Libra	−14°47'	**−15°03'**	−15°07'	**−15°01'**
Beta Orionis (Rigel)	−08°12'	**−08°07'**	−08°05'	**−08°10'**
Alpha Triangulum	+29°35'	**+29°58'**	+30°04'	**+29°59'**
Rho Draconis	+67°52'	**+68°06'**	+68°09'	**+68°08'**
HD8181 (SAO1515) Draconis	+81°19'	**+80°58'**	+80°52'	**+80°59'**
Alpha Ursa Minoris (Polaris)	+89°16'	+89°31'	+89°33'	+87°31'
Delta Ursa Minoris (Yildun)	+86°35'	**+86°30'**	+86°29'	**+86°32'**
Beta Cassiopeiae (Caph)	+59°08'	+59°36'	+59°42'	+60°01'
Delta Cassiopeiae (Ruchbah)	+60°14'		+60°44'	
Gamma Cassiopeiae	+60°43'		+61°15'	

The list above illustrates the precise nature of the synchronization between the pyramid spotlights and stars on the celestial sphere coinciding with the precessional culmination (or tropic) of Polaris over the north pole of the Earth in AD 2080. The stars of Cassiopeia (the queen of heaven) dance around dramatically on the northern Giza horizon during this century, whilst the stars of Crux appear simultaneously on the southern horizon. The three bright stars (Alpha, Beta and Gamma Cassiopeiae) create yet another triangle of stars aligned to the Great Pyramid at this time. But the northern horizon alignment appears to fall within the triangle, just as Polaris also falls within an isosceles triangle formed by the three brightest surrounding stars. However, measures such as these at the horizon are subject to the effects of atmospheric refraction and this actually causes one bright star in Cassiopeia to appear due north on the Giza horizon *(see Atmospheric Refraction below)*.

By focusing and synchronizing these alignments attention is drawn to the period AD 2080–2100. This not only coincides with the culmination of Polaris, but also coincides exactly with the time when Betelgeuse and Eltanim reach precessional culmination on the solsticial colure. (The culmination of a star in the precessional cycle can be likened to the tropic of the sun in the annual cycle.) Thus the first brilliant Orion star culminates within a few years of Polaris (on the dragon line), and all the pyramid angles appear synchronized for this event, when Alpha Aquarius also transits the celestial equator (AD 2065).

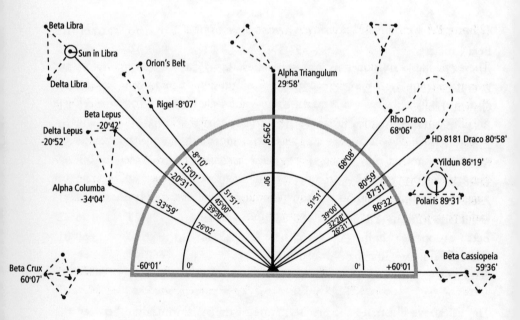

Figure 138: Great Pyramid alignments to stellar triangles AD 2080

FEATURES OF THE SKY OVER GIZA
2550 BC–2450 BC

I have used the date 2450 BC very liberally in the main text, but this date maybe slightly later than the intended synchronization time. A very significant event occurred on the celestial sphere in 2540 BC. At this date the two stars Alnitak and Betelgeuse became aligned on a meridian for the first time in many thousands of years. As the juxtaposition on the meridian took place the two brilliant stars had the following co-ordinates.

2540 BC

Alnitak:	RA 2 hours 0 mins	Dec. −15°15'
Betelgeuse:	RA 2 hours 0 mins	Dec. −05°15'

(2 hours RA is exactly 30° from the equinoctial colure at 0°.)

These two stars in Orion were, and still are, exactly 10° apart, accurate to one arc minute measured on the celestial sphere. Rounding the figures only slightly, the distances between Rigel and Alnitak, Alnitak and Bellatrix, and Mintaka and Rigel are all 9°. And the angular distance from Alnitak to Saiph is about 8°.

The ancient Egyptians were well known for measuring intervals of 10° on the celestial sphere and this remains the angular distance between Alnitak and Betelgeuse to this day. It is the coupling of the alignment of Betelgeuse and Alnitak that suggests synchronicity in the pyramid planning because in the same decade Melkalanin passed vertically over the Great Pyramid.

2534 BC

Melkalanin	Declination +30°00'	Capella Declination	+28°30'
Giza	Latitude 29°59' north	Mt Katherine latitude	28°30' north

(Melkalanin and Capella were the two brightest stars passing over Sinai at this time.)

In the decade when Alnitak and Betelgeuse measure out 10° at 2 hours RA the star Melkalanin found the vertical over Giza and the star Capella found the vertical over Mt Katherine (within two hours of each other). Thus a further interval of 1°30' (or 1.5°) was defined above the mountain and the pyramid.

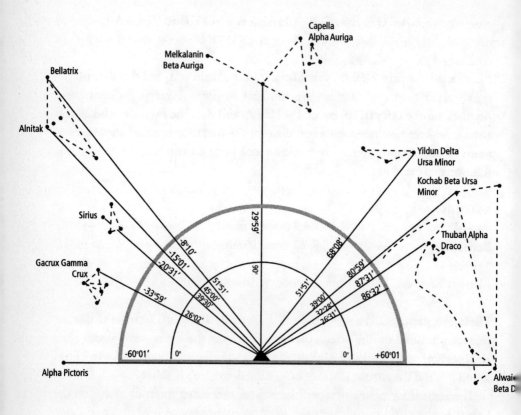

Figure 139: Great Pyramid alignments to stellar triangles 2450 BC

The date 2450 BC used in the main text perhaps defines the end of a century during which the pyramid spotlights synchronized with the stars, and the mountain equals star equation was created by Capella and Melkalanin. The transient nature of this synchronization can be judged from the figures below.

These figures illustrate the precessional motion of stars spotlighted by the Great Pyramid between 2540 BC and 2400 BC. The varying apparent motion of the stars between these dates is due to the gyroscopic motion of the celestial grid (precession). Because the measured effect of precessional motion varies greatly from star to star (shown here in the declination of the star), it is possible to see an era of synchronization with these particular stars and the pyramid spotlights at this particular time.

The deduction that the alignments were created intentionally is made on the following basis. The aligned stars are generally bright and are understood to be highly significant in the mythology and religion of the community that built the monument pointing to them. However this linkage is then provided with a form of geometric confirmation, i.e. an isosceles relationship is found between the stars in the spotlights *(see Appendix IV)*. But above all this, the key to the synchronization is established by the presence of a bright pole star on target.

STAR	2540 BC	2500 BC	2450 BC	2400 BC	SPOTLIGHT
Alpha Pictoris[3]	−59°37'	−59°37'	−59°37'	−59°37'	−60°01'
Gacrux	−33°27'	−33°37'	−33°50'	−34°03'	−33°59'
Sirius	−20°58'	−20°50'	−20°41'	−20°32'	−20°31'
Alnitak	−15°15'	−15°03'	−14°49'	−14°34'	−15°01'
Bellatrix	−08°46'	−08°34'	−08°19'	−08°03'	−08°10'
Melkalanin	−29°58'	+30°11'	+30°27'	+30°43'	+29°59'
Yildun	+67°29'	+67°39'	+67°53'	+68°07'	+68°08'
Kochab	+80°19'	+80°27'	+80°38'	+80°48'	+80°59'
Thuban	+88°33'	+88°19'	+88°02'	+87°45'	+87°31'
Alwaid	+60°38'	+60°31'	+60°23'	+60°15'	+60°01'

The figures above illustrate the era during which the spotlights from the Great Pyramid co-ordinated with the stars discussed in the main text. (Notice the culmination of Alpha Pictoris – the star reached its *tropos*, i.e. its turning point in the precessional cycle, at this time. The same is now happening to the Orion constellation.)

Comparing the above figures with those for the direct alignments in AD 2080, it becomes possible to suggest that the precessional extreme of Polaris (i.e. its tropic in the precessional cycle) was considered to be an event of great substance in prehistory. The pyramid builders were concerned to fix a point in time and that time is the high point of Polaris (coinciding with the tropic of Orion/Osiris).

ATMOSPHERIC REFRACTION

The position of a star seen by the naked eye is not necessarily equivalent to its position on the astronomical celestial sphere. The Earth's atmosphere refracts starlight, causing the image of the star in the sky to appear slightly removed from its true position in space. The aberration of starlight is 0° at the vertical, 1' of arc at 45° elevation, 5.5' of arc at 10° elevation and 37' of arc on the horizon.[4] These figures are subject to atmospheric pressure, air quality, temperature and other factors. Therefore it is generally true to say that the stars are not actually where they are seen in the sky. The atmosphere acts as a slightly distorting mirror. This distortion is sufficient to displace the true position of a star by the width of a full moon at the horizon.

Consequently, all the spotlight alignments discussed in this book require varying degrees of adjustment in order to render the true visual image of the sky witnessed from Giza. For example the alignment to Rigel up the north face of the Great Pyramid today is accurate to about three arc minutes on the celestial sphere, but the starlight will be refracted by about one arc minute at this elevation (or altitude).

The only place where atmospheric refraction has a really notable effect on the position of stars is on the horizon. In perfect viewing conditions certain stars just below the true horizon become displaced upwards, moving above the horizon and becoming visible due to atmospheric refraction.

The apparent exclusion of Cassiopeia from the tight synchronization illustrated by the figures shown for AD 2080 is thus rectified by aberration, resulting in the stars Epsilon Crucis and Beta Cassiopeia appearing almost simultaneously in the present precisely on the horizon lines of the Great Pyramid due north and due south. This balance currently occurs around midnight on the vernal equinox.

The refraction of starlight between little star groups *causes the observed angular distance between the stars to alter.* This means that the visible geometric relationship between points of starlight in the sky also alters!

In consequence the near isosceles relationship between the three brightest stars in Cassiopeia is squeezed at the horizon, appearing more truly isosceles. Further to this, the star appearing at the same time on the southern horizon, Epsilon Crucis, is also subject to atmospheric refraction. This results in the limb of the cross (Crux) being raised about half a degree above the horizon, revealing a perfect isosceles triangle between the stars Gamma, Epsilon and Lambda Crucis directly in the pyramid spotlight due south. Therefore, to the eye, around midnight on the vernal equinox there is one small isosceles triangle on the northern Giza horizon, and one small isosceles triangle on the southern horizon. (The effect of atmospheric refraction is also mentioned in Appendix IV.)

In the illustrations I have used the position of the stars as they appear in the *Institute of Physics Photographic Star Atlas* to establish the isosceles triangles; however, the illustration provides a condensed view of the triangles found in the sky.

THE VERTICAL ALIGNMENT OF ANCIENT SITES AND STARS TODAY

AVEBURY (SEE ALSO SILBURY HILL)

Avebury latitude 51°25'40", Eltanim declination 51°29'20"(AD 2000)

The star Eltanim is now reaching its lower culmination in the precessional cycle. The star crosses the solsticial colure in the next few years and is very closely aligned on the meridian with the four aligned stars in Auriga, now also on the solsticial colure. The star appears overhead at Avebury at midnight on the night of the summer solstice in this epoch (AD 2000). The line of four stars in Auriga stands upright on Avebury's northern horizon on the minute of midnight at the summer solstice as Eltanim passes overhead.

The vertical alignment of Eltanim is displaced by about four minutes of latitude. The same displacement occurs with the mountain alignment between Juza and Ben Nevis, and between Alwaid (also called Rastaban) and Mt Brandon.

Avebury	51°25'40" north	
Silbury Hill	51°24'50" north	51°29'20" Eltanim
Ben Nevis	56°47'30"	56°52'21" Juza
Mt Brandon	52°13'40"	52°18'05" Alwaid

Each alignment is displaced by four or five arc minutes in the same direction. There is then a near perfect uniformity between these parallels accurate to a few yards on the ground. Strangely, the misplacement of about four arc minutes is the same as the slight deviation in the cardinal alignments of the Great Pyramid. Professor Thom noted that the central marker in the stone circles he studied in Britain was always deliberately misplaced from the central point of the ellipses formed by the stones. (The geometric form of the 'stone circles' was found to be one of four or five regular ellipses. These shapes are repeated throughout the stone circles of Britain.) The deliberate misplacement of the precise geometric point is a recurrent feature in this ancient geometry. Rutherford[1] called it 'the displacement factor' when referring to the displacement of the meridian passages in the Great Pyramid from the central axis of the building. In such a symmetrical building one would expect the passages to be aligned on the central axis, likewise one would expect a stone at the centre of a circle (or ellipse), but in both cases the ancient designers chose not to do the obvious.

The Avebury circle is situated on a parallel of latitude 51.428° north of the equator.

The figure 51.428 is very precisely 360 ÷ 7, a number notable for its exclusivity in the mathematics given below:

$$360 \div 1 = 360$$
$$360 \div 2 = 180$$
$$360 \div 3 = 120$$
$$360 \div 4 = 90$$
$$360 \div 5 = 72$$
$$360 \div 6 = 60$$
$$360 \div 7 = 51.428 \text{ (Avebury latitude 51.428)}$$
$$360 \div 8 = 45$$
$$360 \div 9 = 40$$

These figures indicate the 'exclusion' processes discussed in the book. In this case 360 ÷ 7 clearly stands out from the neighbouring whole numbers.

The people who created these sites have gone to considerable lengths to produce this odd numerical 'exclusion'. I believe they have achieved this (to several decimal places) in order to define and communicate their intelligence. Thus they establish their true credentials as highly advanced geographers and astronomers.

The Avebury dragon was constructed from two parallel lines of stones curling away from the massive stone circle at Avebury over Woden Hill to the Sanctuary where the tail of the dragon terminates in a second small circle.

1. The Sanctuary circle at Avebury has a longitude of 1°49' west.
2. The Stonehenge circle (about 17 miles to the south) also has a longitude of 1°49' west.

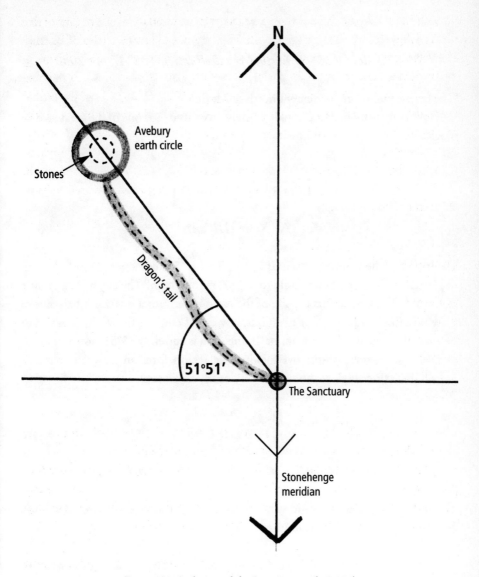

Figure 140: Avebury and the Sanctuary angle 51°51'

Therefore Avebury Sanctuary and Stonehenge are accurately aligned on the meridian 17 miles apart, almost within the width of the circles themselves.

Further to this, a line raised 51°51' from the parallel of the Sanctuary passes directly over the centre of the Avebury circle. (The slope angle of the Great Pyramid is 51°51'.)

CAHOKIA

Monk's Mound 38° 40' north, Vega declination +38° 47' AD 2000

'The largest prehistoric settlement north of Mexico.'[2]

'How strange, then, that Cahokia is rarely given its due as one of the great archaeological treasures of the continent.'[3] (*See plate 8.*)

CHINESE PYRAMIDS

Nr Xi'an (His'an)

The largest of the Chinese pyramids is described as '50 kilometres [31 miles] south west of Xi'an'.[4] One pyramid is said to be '300 metres' high![5] The city of Xi'an is one of the oldest in China. It is the site of the famous Terracotta Army. Little has been written in English about these pyramids, however. I estimate the White Pyramid to be around 33°50' north and Gamma Triangulum is currently 33°51' north.

The three highest points overlooking the region form an isosceles triangle,[6] indeed these three high points appear very nearly equilateral.

CHOLULA

Cholula 19° 03' north, Arcturus +19° 11' (AD 2000)

The site of 'the largest pyramid'[7] known on Earth, spread over 45 acres reaching a height of 210 feet. The pyramid is in a rundown condition overgrown and ill defined.

Cholula is placed very neatly on the line from Citlaltepetl passing through two peaks aligned on the meridian and on to the fourth highest peak in Mexico.[8]

An angle of 51°51' raised from the parallel of Cholula reaches Teotihuacán.

The star Arcturus is now located at declination 19°11'.

Cholula is located at 19°03' north, and Citlaltepetl reaches its summit at 19°02' north, Popocatapetl reaches its summit at 19°02' north, Ixtraccihuatl reaches its summit at 19°11' north and Nevada de Tahoca reaches its summit at 19°06' north. Thus the four highest mountains overlooking North America (from the south) share a parallel only 10 arc minutes broad. The line from end to end measures over

150 miles. The great Cholula pyramid also rests on this notable Earth parallel, beneath Arcturus in AD 2000.

EASTER ISLAND

27.5' south, 109.20' west

Nano Kao, Terevaka and Katik are the three volcanoes creating an isosceles triangle on this island. The star alignment to Antares is not as accurate as other alignments to mountains, none the less Antares now appears to pass directly overhead if you are living on Easter Island.[9]

The outer extremes of Easter Island form an isosceles triangle. These are North Cape, Cape Cumming and Cape te Manga.

Antares declination −26°26' AD 2000
Antares declination −26°36' AD 2080

The island can be located by following the meridian due south from the extreme fingertip of the lower Californian peninsula.

GLASTONBURY TOR

Latitude 51°08'40" north

A very pronounced natural peak rising to 518 feet. The hill, once called the 'Isle of Glass', the 'Island of Apples' or 'Avalon', has strong associations with the legend of King Arthur, but is also rumoured to be the place visited by Joseph of Arimathea carrying the Holy Grail.

The star Eltanim passes over Avebury as given above. Eltanim is the only bright star to occupy the fifty-first parallel (Dec.) at present, and Glastonbury Tor, Stonehenge, Silbury Hill and Avebury all share this parallel.

Tintern Abbey (another ancient holy site) is directly north of Glastonbury, and the distance between Stonehenge and Glastonbury is the same as that between Glastonbury and Tintern Abbey. The same distance reaches Dunkery Beacon, the highest point on Exmoor to the west, and the same distance again reaches High Willhays and Yes Tor, the highest points in the south west of the British Isles.

Glastonbury Tor is on a straight line joining the fingertip of Land's End with Avebury. When extended, this is the longest line overland that it is possible to draw east to west across the British Isles.

GIZA

Latitude 29° 59'

This is the plateau overlooking Cairo at the apex of the Nile Delta, the site of the Great Pyramid and its two large companions.[10]

The continent of Asia is joined to the continent of Africa near this location by a strip of land measuring about 1° on the meridian. (The Suez Canal now creates a waterway over this land.)

The great rift of the Red Sea reaches its northerly extreme on the thirtieth parallel as does the Persian Gulf and the Gulf of Mexico. This parallel also defines the Nile Delta, the Mississippi Delta and the triangular peninsula at the mouth of the Yangtze river. The intervals between these three delta shapes on the thirtieth parallel are 90°, 120° and 150°.

The single great circle on the planet covering the greatest distance over land passes through Giza.

Alpha Triangulum is currently passing directly above the pyramids at Lisht, to the south of Giza. The precessional motion of Triangulum carries the Alpha star directly over Giza in AD 2080 (when the 11 angles of the Great Pyramid are most precisely synchronized to the stars; *see Appendix I*).

The precessional motion of Alpha Triangulum:

AD 2050 = 29°50'
AD 2100 = 30°04'
AD 2450 = 31°43'

NAZCA

Nazca Town 15.8' north, 74.59' west

The lines at Nazca represent one of the greatest unsolved mysteries on Earth, but after 30 years of research Maria Reiche suggested that the great spider depicted on the Nazca plain was connected with the progress of Orion's Belt on the celestial sphere.

When the 45° star shaft from the Great Pyramid located Alnitak in 2450 BC, the stars of Orion's Belt were passing over Nazca. The Belt has subsequently travelled about 15° to the north on the celestial sphere, reaching the celestial equator today.

THE SANCTUARY (AVEBURY)

51°24'35" north, 1°49'35" west

The end of the dragon's tail is currently outlined by a circle of modern markers defining a much older circle believed to have been made with wooden posts. A chapel may have been built on this site, which shares the meridian of Stonehenge. A line from the Sanctuary drawn 51°51' north of west defines the centre of Avebury circle.

SILBURY HILL

51°24'50" north, Eltanim Dec. 51°29'

Much like the Giza pyramids, Silbury Hill was thought to be a tomb, but no body was found within when it was excavated. In light of the star alignments linking Silbury Hill to Giza and the other pyramids around the world, it may be possible to imagine Silbury Hill as it looked on completion: a vast chalk-white mound glaring in the sun. The meridian through the heart of Silbury Hill defines the tangent to the Avebury ring ditch. The geometry between the earthworks on Salisbury Plain further to the south adheres to the principle of using the perimeter ditch as a geometric marker.[11] The easternmost and westernmost extremities of the Avebury perimeter ditch are defined by the meridian alignments of Silbury Hill on the west side and the Kennett Longbarrow on the east side. The massive headstone marking the entrance to the Kennett Longbarrow is precisely aligned on the meridian, creating a tangent with the easternmost extreme of the Avebury ditch.

Silbury Hill is located beside a violent loop in the River Kennet flowing to the east. The river actually follows the meridian until it reaches Silbury Hill, then it diverts by 90° and travels due east. Thus Silbury Hill marks the right-angled turn in the local River Kennet.

STONEHENGE

51° 10'40" north, Alheka (+30°) +51° 09'

Stonehenge is one of the most famous ancient sites in the world. The stones are placed in a slowly undulating landscape with the River Avon running from north to south a few miles to the east. The river takes a dramatic kink at the town of Amesbury east of Stonehenge, near the site of the older Woodhenge.

The Cursus runs a few hundred yards north of the Stonehenge circle crossing the land from east to west and leading to Glastonbury Tor.

The 20-mile radius from Stonehenge takes in one of the most dramatically changed areas of land in the world. Many millions of tons of earth have been moved over this landscape, creating a vast complex of earth barrows, ditches, mounds and enclosures punctuated by a series of more than 20 great ancient sites defined by equally large earthworked ridges and ditches marking their extremities.

The huge earth-moving operation in the orbit of Stonehenge takes in Silbury Hill and Avebury 17 miles north, and terminates at Barbury Castle four miles to the north of Avebury. (The star Eltanim currently passes over Barbury Castle most precisely.)

The earthworks in this area are often referred to as 'forts'. (But, for example, the earth wall surrounding Martinsell Hill 'Fort' is clearly not built for fortification.) Though the ditches were perhaps used for protection at some stage, the entire area has been organized geometrically on the Earth's grid in such a manner that the earthworks are related on the meridian and parallels of the Earth very precisely. The edges of the earthworks are used to define straight lines joining these sites over many miles. For example a straight line joins Sidbury earthwork, Stonehenge, Grovely Castle and Haredene Wood earthwork. Another joins Rybury Camp, Stonehenge, Old Sarum and Clearbury Ring, etc.

The isosceles triangle and the straight line are very clear features in this geometry and the majority of the earthworks are placed on high points with extensive vistas affording a flat horizon most suitable for astronomical observations. The geometry between these points appears remarkable well oriented on the Earth grid.

The key meridian running through the area is clearly defined by Avebury, Stonehenge, Silbury Hill running north to the Peak (High Peak or Kinder Scout). The fingertip of Lindisfarne (Holy Island) defines this meridian precisely.

When the Duat stars are shifted by 30° to the north the star Alheka passes over Stonehenge as follows:

Alheka +30° = 51°09' north (AD 2000)
Stonehenge = 51°11' north

The passage of Eltanim over Avebury occurs almost exactly 12 hours later. (In other words the star Alheka +30° aligned over Stonehenge is on the same celestial meridian as the head of the dragon. Thus the two sites, and the two stars now marking the sites, are joined on their respective meridians.)

TEOTIHUACÁN

19°42' north, 98°51' west [12]

This is the site of the pyramids of the Sun and the Moon, a 'map of heaven'.[13]

On Tactical Pilotage Chart J–24C 1:500,000 it appears that San Martin de las Pyramides at Teotihuacán is placed equidistant between the two local highest peaks. These summits create an isosceles triangle with the next high point to the east. More easily seen on this scale is a substantial isosceles triangle based on two of the highest mountains in Central America, forming a line on the Earth parallel.

The star Arcturus currently passes over these mountains as shown in Figure 141.

Notice how the site of Teotihuacán is incorporated into the star alignment process by its triangular relationship with these mountains. (The same process draws K2 into the alignment process when Procyon passes over Nanga Parbat, likewise Mt Elbert under Vega.)

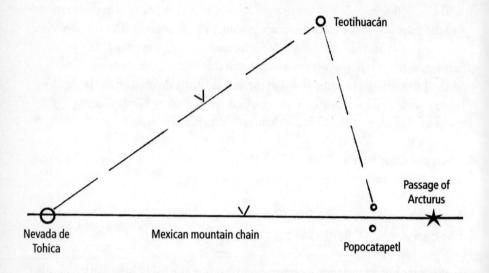

Figure 141: Teotihuacán and the Mexican mountains

TIAHUANACO

16° 32' south, Sirius -16° 43'

This is the site of the Akapana pyramid and the Gateway of the Sun.

The backbone of South America takes a pronounced bend at this point. The mountainous Andes sit astride a large elevated area of Salt Flats, with the main Cordillera Real overlooking Lake Titicaca giving way to the Cordillera Oriental, so named because this range turns south following the Earth meridian for several hundred miles.

The star Sirius currently has a declination of –16°43'.

The high point just south of Tiahuanaco has a latitude of –16°40'.

See Sirius, Appendix III.

3

THE ALIGNMENTS BETWEEN STARS AND MOUNTAINS IN THE PRESENT DAY

MOUNTAIN LATITUDES

In the following list the latitudes of mountains are compared with the declination of stars in AD 2000. In many cases the declination of stars changes by several arc minutes on the celestial sphere during one epoch (50 years). The figures below therefore illustrate the narrow band of latitude within which stars and mountains are currently aligned. In all cases (at the appropriate time) these stars will appear perfectly vertically overhead to the naked-eye observer at the named location.

The figures listed are taken from *The Guinness Book of Astronomy (AD 2000)* by Patrick Moore (Guinness Publishing, 1995) and the mountain latitudes are found on the 1:1,000,000 Operational Navigation Charts.

In most of the cases listed below the brilliant stars are found to pass over one corner of an isosceles triangle, or point created by mountains or land extremities. These are detailed in the main text.

It is only possible to sail a boat along one band of latitude on the Earth without encountering an obstruction. The perfect circle of ocean passes between Tierra del Fuego (Cape Horn) and the northernmost extreme of the Antarctic peninsula. The sea channel between the two landmasses (allowing unrestricted sailing on the parallels approximately 56° to 61° south) is marked on each extreme by the vertical passage of the second and third brightest stars in the sky *(see overleaf)*. This single small circle is therefore the only open mouth of water on the planet allowing the sailor a perfectly circular sea passage without beginning or end, i.e. an Eternal Return. By coincidence, the constellation Crux currently passes over this channel (called Drake's Passage) and the cross itself (brought down to Earth) provides a bridge over the mouth of water between the two continents. The Orion constellation forms a similar bridge between the Milky Way and Eridanus. I will discuss these events in the context of the Adze of Upuaut and the ancient Egyptian opening of the mouth ceremony in my next book.

SEVEN BRIGHTEST STARS AD 2000

	STAR	DECLINATION	LATITUDE AT LOCATION
1	Sirius	−16°43' (AD 2000)	Mt Illimani −16°38'
			Tiahuanaco −16°32'
2	Canopus	−52°42' (AD 2000)	Strait of Megallanes
			(Tierra del Fuego) Southernmost
			extreme of mainland South America.
3	Rigel Kentaurus	−60°50'	Elephant Island (Antarctica)
		−60°50'	(Northerly extreme of Antarctica)
4	Arcturus	+19°11'	Mt Ixtraccihuautl +19°11'
			Cholula +19°03'
5	Vega	+38°47'	Antero peak +38°40'
			Cahokia +38°40'
6	Capella	+46°00'	Mt Adams +46°11'
			Mt St Helens +46°11'
7	Rigel	−08°12'	Recife −08°12' (Easternmost
			city in the Americas, easternmost
			tip of the American continent)

DRACO STARS AD 2000

Eltanim (Beta)	+51°29'	Silbury Hill	+51°25'	(+04' = 51°29')
Juza (Zeta)	+56°52'	Ben Nevis	+56°48'	(+04' = 56°52')
Alwaid (Gamma)	+52°18'	Mt Brandon	+52°14'	(+04' = 52°18')

LIBRA STARS AD 2000

Zubenelgenubi (Alpha)	−16°02'	Mt Ancohuma	−15°54'
Zubenelchemale (Beta)	−09°23'	Mt Hauscaran	−9°08'

ORION AD 2000

The span between the three stars of Orion's Belt defines the width of Lake Victoria. All three stars now appear simultaneously (daily) over the lake. Lake Victoria shares the meridian of Giza, thus the reflection of Orion's three Belt stars simultaneously in Lake Victoria today occurs 30° south of their terrestrial counterparts on the Giza plateau. Thirty degrees north of Giza Lake Ladoga balances the equation. The Belt stars likewise appear simultaneously over the delta of the River Amazon.

Orion figures for AD 2000 are broken up into two lists:

List A: The Orion stars declination +30° are compared with terrestrial latitudes.
List B: Other brilliant Duat stars +30° are compared with terrestrial latitudes.

List A: Orion

THE EYE
Mountain
Mt Ararat, Turkey (5,165 metres) +39°.42'n
(The mountain is over 30 miles broad at the base i.e. about half a degree.)
The three brightest stars in the eye of Orion encircle Mt Ararat.

Star
Heka +39°56'; Phi 1 +39°29'; Phi 2 +39°17'
(The summits of Aragats, El Brus and Cilo Dagi form an isosceles triangle. Mt Ararat is displaced from the triangle apex.)

THE SHOULDERS
Mountain
Mt Bukadaban Feng and Ulugh Muztagh +36°26'n

Star
Bellatrix +36°21'

Mountain
Mt Cilo Dagi, Turkey +37°30'n

Star
Betelgeuse +37°24'

THE BELT
Mountain
Mt Kun Ka Shan +29°47'

Star
Mintaka +29°42'

Mountain
Dhaulagiri (Himalayas) +28°39'n

Star
Alnilam +28°48'

Mountain
Mt Everest +27°59'n

Star
Alnitak +28°03'

THE DAGGER/PHALLUS
Mountain
Mt Nezzi +25°35'

Star
Ori 1981 +25°34'

Island
Philae +24°01' Elephantine +24°06'

Star
Lota Ori +24°05'

THE LEGS
Mountain
Mt Tarso Ahon +20°23'

Star
Saiph +20°21'

Delta
Mouths of the Ganges Delta +21°40'

Star
Rigel +21°42'

List B: Other Duat stars +30° compared with mountain latitudes

Mountain
Mt Rasdajan +13°15'

Star
Sirius +13°17'

Mountain
Nanga Parbet +35°14'

Star
Procyon +35°14'

Site
Stonehenge +51°11'

Star
Alheka +51°09'

Extreme Points
Burifa Hill +58°40'
   (John O'Groats 58°38', Cape Wrath 58°38' and Strathy Point +58°36' – these three northern extremities of mainland Britain form an isosceles triangle on the Earth's parallel.)

Star
Elnath +58°36'
   (Alheka and Elnath are the two bright stars in Taurus symbolizing the Bull's Horns. They form an isosceles triangle with the star Ain in the Hyades. In turn the brightest five stars in the Hyades form two isosceles triangles. These formations are easily seen in a clear night sky.)

4

STELLAR GEOMETRY: AURIGA, ORION, LEPUS

Recently improved software allows angular distances between stars to be established by moving a cursor across a computer screen. My current software performs this function extremely accurately over short angular distances, but the accuracy is reduced over larger spans of the sphere.

For example, the stars of Orion's Belt are separated by angular distances as follows:

Alnitak to Alnilam	1°21'
Alnilam to Mintaka	1°22'

The isosceles relationship has remained unchanged over the past 5,000 years due to the very small proper motion of these stars.

The same accuracy is found with the beautiful triangle of stars beside Capella. Just like Orion's Belt, this isolated trio creates an equally accurate isosceles triangle. Rigel, Alnitak and Mintaka likewise and again three brilliant stars in Crux and in Auriga and in Lepus all create the same perfect geometric form.

Using stars to provide geometric markers requires that each star should be established as a point with a given radius. There is nothing known to be stationary in the universe and consequently to define a geometric point on the celestial sphere I have assumed that each star should be covered by a point about the size of a match head held at arm's length (approximately five arc minutes in diameter). Thus with these small points established on the sphere we can calculate whether a truly perfect geometric isosceles triangle can be drawn between them using angular measures. In this exercise the three perfectly isosceles points must fall within five arc minutes radius of the stellar point.

Using this method the following perfect isosceles triangles can be drawn between the brightest star points on the celestial sphere discussed in this book (angular measures are approximate):

Alnitak–Alnilam 1°21'	Alnilam–Mintaka 1°22'
Bellatrix–Alnitak 9°09'	Alnitak–Rigel 9°03'
Alnitak–Rigel 9°03'	Rigel–Mintaka 9°03'
Alnitak–Mintaka 2°44'	Mintaka–Beta Orionis 2°48'
Betelgeuse–Elnath 22°14'	Elnath–Bellatrix 22°14'
Bellatrix–Aldebaran 15°44'	Aldebaran–Heka 15°48'
Beta Lepus–Alnitak 19°08'	Alnitak–Delta Lepus 19°11'
Alpha Lepus–Delta Lepus 5°20'	Delta Lepus–Beta Lepus 5°21'
Beta Lepus–Alpha Columbae 13°30'	Alpha Columbae–Delta Lepus 13°29'
Capella–Elnath 17°36'	Elnath–Melkalanin 17°36'
Capella–Melkalanin 7°36'	Melkalanin–Theta Auriga 7°44'
Delta Lepus–Alpha Lepus 5°21'	Alpha Lepus–Gamma Lepus 5°20'
Alpha Lepus–Alnitak 15°55'	Alnitak–Mu Lepus 15°51'
Alpha Triangulum–M32 18°10'	M32–Beta Triangulum 18°10'
Delta Crucis– Beta Crucis 4°16'	Beta Crucis–Alpha Crucis 4°15'
Gamma Crucis–Beta Crucis 3°22'	Beta Crucis–Epsilon Crucis 3°22'

When the length of Orion's Belt is measured without atmospheric refraction the angular distance is 2°44'. But atmospheric refraction can reduce the measure of Orion's Belt to 2°41' on the horizon. The precise geometry of lights in the night sky is therefore permanently slightly flexible, and altering all the time.

The geometry can be seen by using dividers on a retinal image photograph, or by using a cursor on the computer, or by judgement with the naked eye. In either event the true isosceles geometric point is found not on the mobile point, but fixed right beside it.

The book describes how the stars appearing in the pyramid spotlights create geometry in a simple join the dots fashion.

The most notable example of this occurs between the Belt stars, the three spotlighted stars Alnitak, Bellatrix and Rigel, and again with Delta Lepus, Alpha Columbae and Beta Lepus. The measure of these triangles (with all three corners spotlighted by the Great Pyramid) are given above.

Three star maps taken from the Institute of Physics *Photographic Atlas of the Stars*.

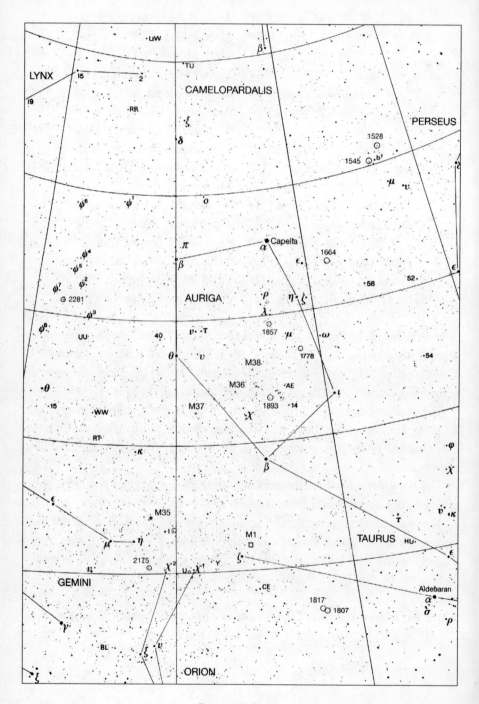

Figure 142: Auriga

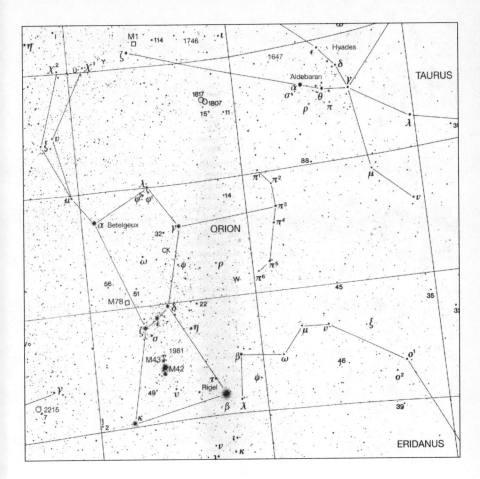

Figure 143: Orion

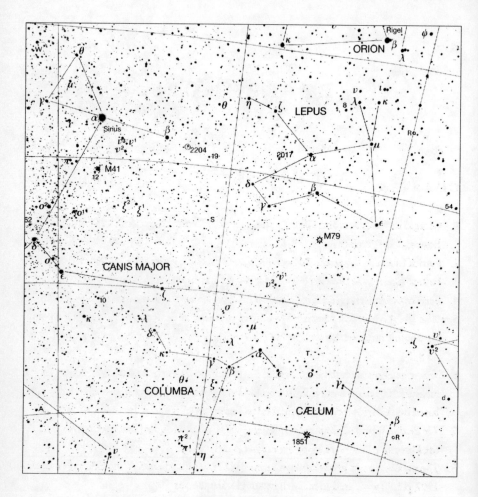

Figure 144: Lepus

REFERENCES

CHAPTER I

1. Giorgio de Santillana and Hertha von Dechend, *Hamlet's Mill*, Gambit International, Boston, 1969, Preface
2. Patrick Moore, *Stargazing: Astronomy without a Telescope*, Aurum Press, 1985
3. Patrick Moore, *The Guinness Book of Astronomy*, Guinness Publishing, 1995, p.164
4. See *The Orion Mystery*, Robert Bauval and Adrian Gilbert, William Heinemann Ltd, 1994.
5. 'The so-called "Orion Mystery": A rebuttal to New Age notions about ancient Egyptian astronomy and funerary architecture', *KMT: A Modern Journal of Ancient Egypt*, Vol.7, no.3, 74
6. Ten years of research has been conducted in telekinesis using the odds of chance as a measure. The researchers at Princeton University reached their conclusions entirely based on the knowledge of 'normal odds' in a series of random distributions.
7. *The British Museum Dictionary of Ancient Egypt* concurs with Mr Chadwick and so does the Director of the Giza Mapping Project, Mark Lehner.
8. The measurements given in Mark Lehner's *The Complete Pyramids* (Thames and Hudson, 1997, p.109) were used to make these rough calculations.
9. Sir Norman Lockyer, *The Dawn of Astronomy*, Macmillan, 1894
10. *The British Museum Dictionary of Ancient Egypt*, 1997
11. Astronomers have chosen to use the terms 'longitude' and 'latitude' to define a sphere focused on the ecliptic poles rather than the celestial poles. Throughout this book I have ignored these facts and simply referred to 'celestial longitude and latitude' as the direct mirror image of the reciprocal lines on the Earth. The correct astronomical terms are right ascension (RA) (for longitude) and declination (Dec.) (for latitude).
12. Robert Bauval refined Virginia Trimble's earlier estimate of 2500 BC when more accurate measures for the shaft angles were made by laser. However these estimates may need revising back to 2500 BC *(see Appendix I)*.
13. Every 23 hours, 56 minutes and 4 seconds a star returns to the same location on the observer's meridian.

14. As mentioned (*see note 11*), the correct astronomical terms are right ascension (RA) (for longitude) and declination (Dec.) (for latitude).

15. See *The Stairway to Heaven*, p.253, 'Forging the pharaoh's name', Zecharia Sitchin, Bear & Co., 1992

CHAPTER 2

1. Giorgio de Santillana and Hertha von Dechend, *Hamlet's Mill*, Gambit International, Boston, 1969, Preface

2. I have used 30° throughout the text of the book. The precise location of Giza is 29°58'51".

3. R. H. Allen, *Star Names: Their Lore and Meaning*, Dover Publications, 1963

4. The true tropic is mobile, but this alignment falls within half a degree.

CHAPTER 3

1. Bertrand Russell, quoted in Giorgio de Santillana and Hertha von Dechend, *Hamlet's Mill*, Gambit International, Boston, 1969, Preface

2. See J. L. E. Dreyer, *A History of Astronomy from Thales to Kepler*.

3. An American Naval Survey team attempted to locate the precise apex of this massive geographic triangle and found the Great Pyramid there. C. Piazzi Smythe, *Our Inheritance in the Great Pyramid*, 1880, p. 86

4. David J. Nemeth, 'Ancient and Modern Geomancies' in *The Power of Place*, ed. James A. Swan, Gateway Books, 1993, p.216

5. R. T. Rundell Clark, *Myth and Symbol in Ancient Egypt*, Thames and Hudson, 1959, p.48

6. Such is the prevailing view. See I. E. S. Edwards, *The Pyramids of Egypt*, Penguin, 1949. In this 'definitive work' Cheops is a foolish man.

7. The account of Cheops given by his grandson Menkaure, quoted in Adam Rutherford, *Pyramidology*, C. Tinling & Co. Ltd., 1961

8. The Greeks at the time of Ptolomy were unable to define the sky within one part in 2,000 on the meridian. (See *A History of Astronomy* from Thales to Kepler, J. L. E. Dreyer.)

9. J. G. Bennett, *Sacred Influences*, quoted by Adrian Gilbert, *Magi*, Bloomsbury, 1996, p.257

10. Adrian Gilbert, *Magi*, Bloomsbury, 1996, p.256

11. Giza latitude 29°59'

12. Operational Navigation Chart H–5 1:1,000,000

13. On Operational Navigation Chart H–5 these two mountain peaks, Az Zud and Al Lawz, are perfectly aligned on the meridian, but a study reveals the point Ras Muhammad as the focus for this terrestrial geometry, which extends down the Red Sea coast.

14. Proper motion over this period noticeably alters the position of a few stars, but the overall pattern appears the same for many thousands of years.
15. As already mentioned, called 'right ascension' and 'declination' respectively by astronomers.

CHAPTER 4

1. Giorgio de Santillana and Hertha von Dechend, *Hamlet's Mill*, Gambit International, Boston, 1969, Preface
2. 'This divinity was later the Chadaeo-Assyrian sun god Dumu-zi, the Son of Life, or Tammuz, widely known in classical times as Adonis.' R. H. Allen, *Star Names: Their Lore and Meaning*, Dover Publications, 1963
3. Sahu: a stellar title for Osiris.
4. 'To much high heaven the Androgyne bewails/New born aloft the sky where blood is sprayed.' Peter Lemesurier, *Nostradamus: The Next 50 Years*, Piatkus, 1993, p.259
5. Heather Couper and Nigel Henbest, *The Stars*, Pan Books, 1988, p.60
6. *Night Sky*, Collins Gem, HarperCollins, 1995, p.166
7. The summer solstice sun appears at 6.00 RA, spanning half a degree.
8. Closest transit 89.30' in AD 2100.
9. See Robert Bauval and Adrian Gilbert, *The Orion Mystery*, William Heinemann Ltd, 1994.
10. Sir Norman Lockyer, *The Dawn of Astronomy*, Macmillan, 1894.

CHAPTER 5

1. Giorgio de Santillana and Hertha von Dechend, *Hamlet's Mill*, Gambit International, Boston, 1969, Preface
2. Piazzi Smythe, *Our Inheritance in the Great Pyramid*
3. Quoted in Wm. R. Fix, *Star Maps*, Octopus Books, 1979, p.95
4. Dr Kurt Mendelsson, *The Riddle of the Pyramids*, Thames and Hudson, 1974, p.29
5. Kurt Mendelssohn received his doctorate from the University of Berlin, where he studied physics under Planck, Nernst, Schrödinger and Einstein. He was elected a Fellow of the Royal Society in 1951 and received its Hughes Medal. The Institute of Physics awarded him the Simon Memorial Prize. Dr Mendelssohn is the author of over 200 articles and papers in scientific journals and magazines and has written a number of books. In addition to travelling widely throughout the world, he has been Visiting Professor at Rice University, Texas, and a large number of other American universities; at Tokyo University; the Academia Sinica, Peking; the Tata Institute, Bombay; Kumasi

University, Ghana; and the Bulgarian Academy of Science, Sofia and Coimbra University. He was Emeritus Professorial Fellow of Wolfson College, Oxford.

6. Mark Lehner, *The Complete Pyramids*, Thames and Hudson, 1997, p.100
7. Mendelssohn, op. cit.
8. I. E. S. Edwards, *The Pyramids of Egypt*, Penguin Books, 1949
9. Ibid.
10. Concerning Aratus, *Phaenomena*, quoted in R. H. Allen, *Star Names: Their Lore and Meaning*, Dover Publications, 1963
11. Stellar epoch AD 2000, from *The Guinness Book of Astronomy*, Guinness Publishing, 1995, p.228
12. See Robert Bauval and Graham Hancock, *Keeper of Genesis*, William Heinemann, 1996.

CHAPTER 6

1. Humboldt, quoted in Giorgio de Santillana and Hertha von Deschend, *Hamlet's Mill*, Gambit International, Boston, 1969, Preface
2. *Hamlet's Mill*, ibid.
3. Ibid.
4. Gerald S. Hawkins, *Stonehenge Decoded*, Fontana, 1973
5. Or −15° and one minute.

CHAPTER 7

1. Giorgio de Santillana and Hertha von Dechend, *Hamlet's Mill*, Gambit International, Boston, 1969, Preface
2. Aratus, *Phaenomena*, trans. Stanley Lombardo, North Atlantic Books, n.d., p.20
3. See Arthur Norton, *Norton's Star Atlas*, Longman, 1986
4. At the precise time of solar alignment the Alpha star is 1° lower than the centre of the sun's disc. The true occultation thus takes place when the sun has fallen by 1° on the sphere. On both occasions an accurate isosceles triangle can be drawn between the balance stars and the sun's disc.
5. There are said to be about 4,000 individual stars visible on the celestial sphere.
6. Michael E. Bakich, *The Cambridge Guide to the Constellations*, Cambridge University Press, 1995, p.232
7. Star HD8181. Figures at the tip of the tail of Draco.
8. Full details of the close synchronization with Polaris are given in Appendix I.
9. J. L. E. Dreyer, *Astronomy from Thales to Kepler*
10. R. H. Allen, *Star Names and their Meanings*, Dover Publications, 1963

11. Adrian Gilbert, *Magi*, Bloomsbury, 1996, p.152
12. R. T. Rundle Clark, *Myth and Symbol in Ancient Egypt*, Thames and Hudson, 1993, p.41

CHAPTER 8

1. Giorgio de Santillana and Hertha von Dechend, *Hamlet's Mill*, Gambit International, Boston, 1969, Preface
2. All three Draco alignments fall within five arc minutes of the target *(see Appendix II)*.
3. The name still referred to by the National Trust literature at the site. The Dragon Ring is on the Dragon Line.
4. OS Landranger 1:50,000 Swindon, sheet 173
5. John Michell, *A View over Atlantis*
6. See Appendix II for the precise alignments.

CHAPTER 9

1. Giorgio de Santillana and Hertha von Dechend, *Hamlet's Mill*, Gambit International, Boston, 1969, Preface
2. In Egyptian mythology Set sends a scorpion to kill Horus.
3. Due to the slightly non-spherical nature of the Earth there are slight aberrations on the grid.
4. *The World's Last Mysteries*, Reader's Digest, 1977
5. −15°1'
6. *The Times World Atlas, comprehensive edition*
7. Source of figures *The Times World Atlas* and *The Guinness Book of Astronomy*, Guinness Publishing, 1995
8. *The World's Last Mysteries*, op. cit., p.131
9. Ibid.
10. Graham Hancock, *Fingerprints of the Gods*, William Heinemann, 1995, p.75
11. *Proper motion:* Stars appear to move uniformly in relation to the Earth, but they also move in relation to one another. Proper motion is the actual movement of a star as it travels in space viewed from Earth.
12. Machu Pichu 13°09' south, Lambda Lepus −13°10' (AD 2000).

CHAPTER 10

1. Giorgio de Santillana and Hertha von Dechend, *Hamlet's Mill*, Gambit International, Boston, 1969, Preface
2. *The Guinness Book of Records*, Guinness Publishing, 1998
3. Graham Hancock, *Fingerprints of the Gods*, William Heinemann Ltd, 1995.
4. Chris Morton and Ceri Louise Thomas, *The Mystery of the Crystal Skulls*, Thorsons, 1997, p.139
5. Cahokia Mounds State Historic Site circular, 1998; 30 Ramey St, Collinsville, IL 62234
6. Paul G. Bahn (ed.), *Lost Cities*, Weidenfield and Nicolson, 1997
7. Operational Navigation Chart G-18 1:1,000,000
8. John Michell, *A View over Atlantis*
9. Edward Stanford Ltd, 13-14 Long Acre, London WC2E 9LP
10. Whether the code was cognized without being consciously understood is not discussed in this book. I have presumed, for the purposes of this book, that the pyramid builders were fully conscious of the pattern they created across the globe.
11. John Anthony West, *Serpent in the Sky*, Harper & Row, 1979, p.179

CHAPTER 11

1. Giorgio de Santillana and Hertha von Dechend, *Hamlet's Mill*, Gambit International, Boston, 1969, Preface
2. An expression used by Prince Charles in a speech in 1997.
3. Graham Hancock, *Fingerprints of the Gods*, William Heinemann Ltd, 1995, p.471
4. The crucial point concerning precession here is that this relationship between Alnitak and Mt Everest only arises when Orion culminates, erect on the meridian, as Triangulum passes over Giza, as the solstice sun crosses the galactic equator, as the Great Square aligns to the Earth's grid and as Polaris transits the pole, etc. In other words it is the *synchronization* of the terrestrial and celestial sphere at this particular point in history that we are directed to observe.

CHAPTER 12

1. Giorgio de Santillana and Hertha von Dechend, *Hamlet's Mill*, Gambit International, Boston, 1969, Preface
2. Mt Rasdajan is the highest point overlooking all North Africa from 1° north.
3. Mt Stanley is higher than Mt Rasdajan, but the mountain is considered within the central African (Rift Valley) mountains. Mt Rasdajan is therefore the highest point north of 1° north in Africa.

4. These figures have been produced using the present day star atlas (*The Guinness Book of Astronomy*) and the relevant Operational Navigation Charts. They have been rounded up or down by only one tenth of a degree in order to produce this extraordinary series of equations. *See Appendix III.*

5. Heather Couper and Nigel Henbest, *The Stars*, Pan Books, 1988

6. See ONC J-4.

7. Robert Graves, *The Greek Myths*, Penguin, 1960

8. E. A. Wallis Budge (ed.), *The Book of the Dead*, Penguin Arkana, 1989

9. *The Guinness Book of Records*, Guinness Publishing, 1997, p.216

CHAPTER 13

1. T. S. Eliot, 'Four Quartets'

2. Marmaduke Pickthall, *The Meaning of the Glorious Koran*, Dorset Press, n.d.

3. Quote attributed to 'Edkins'; David J. Nemeth, 'Feng-shui as Terrestrial Astrology' in *The Power of Place*, ed. James A. Swan, Gateway Books, 1993, p.227

4. Mazzoroth, although of uncertain derivation, may come from a root meaning 'to watch', the constellations thus marking the watches of the night by coming successively to the meridian; but Dr Thomas Hyde and the learned translator at Oxford in 1665 of the *zij*, or tables, of Ulug Beg, and of Al Tizini's work, derived them from Ezor, a girdle; while the more recent Dillman referred to them as Zahir, from Zurah, a glittering star, and so signifying something specially luminous.

5. *The Complete Atlas of the British Isles*, Reader's Digest, 1965

6. John Michell, *A View over Atlantis*

7. Joseph Campbell, *Occidental Mythology*, Arkana, 1991

8. Charles H. Hapgood, *Maps of the Ancient Sea Kings*, Turnstone Books, 1979

9. Graham Hancock, *Fingerprints of the Gods*, William Heinemann Ltd, 1995

10. Andrew Bayuk, 'Cyber journey to Egypt: spotlight interview with Dr Zahi Hawass', *Guardian*, 22 March 1997 (Internet)

11. Pierre Grimal, *The Dictionary of Classical Mythology*, Blackwell, 1996, p.363

12. *Timaeus* quoted in W. T. Olcott, *Star Lore of All Ages*

13. Ibid.

14. Quoted Giorgio de Santillana and Hertha von Dechend, *Hamlet's Mill*, Gambit International, Boston, 1969, p.260

15. British Museum, WA K2847

16. Masoudi, Akbar Ezzeman manuscript, quoted by Rutherford in *Pyramidology*, Book 4, C. Tinling & Co. Ltd., 1961

17. Aratus, *Phaenomena*, trans. Stanley Lombardo, North Atlantic Books, n.d.

18. *The Emerald Tablet of Hermes Trismegistus*

APPENDICES

1. Herbert Spencer, quoted in Giorgio de Santillana and Hertha von Dechend, *Hamlet's Mill*, Gambit International, Boston, 1969, Preface

APPENDIX I

1. More recent measurement by laser suggests the King's southern star shaft is angled at 45°14'.
2. The *SkyMap 3.1* programme source: *The Smithsonian Astrophysical Observatory Star Catalogue*, 1990 machine readable version, as supplied on NASA's National Space Science Data Centre's *Selected Astronomical Catalogs, Vol.1*, CD–ROM.
3. In the text I found Alpha Horogulum in this spotlight, but Alpha Pictoris may have been the intended target. With improved software developed during the course of writing this book I have found Alpha Pictoris to be the brightest star on the southern horizon at this time and it was also then crossing the solsticial colure. In every other case, the improved software has resulted in an increased apparent accuracy in the pyramid spotlights. I now believe Alpha Pictoris was the intended target around 2500 BC, not Alpha Horogulum, as suggested in the text.
4. *Larousse Encyclopedia of Astronomy*, Paul Hamlin, London, 1966 p.98.

APPENDIX II

1. Adam Rutherford, *Pyramidology*, C. Tinling & Co. Ltd., 1961
2. Cahokia Mounds State Historic Site circular, 1998; 30 Ramey St, Collinsville, IL 62234
3. Paul G. Bahn (ed.), *Lost Cities*, Weidenfield and Nicholson, 1997, p.163
4. Internet. http://hawk.hama-med.ac.jp/dbk/chnpyramid.html
5. Ibid. 22/1/98
6. Operational Navigation Chart G–9 1:1,000,000
7. *The Guinness Book of Records*, Guinness Publishing, 1997
8. Tactical Pilotage Chart J–24C 1:500,000
9. International Travel Map no.308 1:30,000
10. Operational Navigation Chart H–5 1:1,000,000
11. This was noted in 1925 by Alfred Watkins in *The Old Straight Track*, Abacus, 1987
12. Operational Navigation Chart P–26 1:1,000,000
13. Stansbury Hagar, Department of Ethnology, Brooklyn Institute of Arts and Sciences.

BIBLIOGRAPHY

BOOKS

R. H. Allen, *Star Names: Their Lore and Meaning*, Dover Publications, 1963

Aratus, *Phaenomena*, trans. Stanley Lombardo, North Atlantic Books, n.d.

Anthony Aveni, *Stairway to the Stars*

Paul G. Bahn (ed.), *Lost Cities*, Weidenfield and Nicholson, 1997

Michael E. Bakich, *The Cambridge Guide to the Constellations*, Cambridge University Press, 1995

Robert Bauval and Adrian Gilbert, *The Orion Mystery*, William Heinemann Ltd, 1994

J. Bronowski, *The Ascent of Man*, BBC Books, 1974

Robert Burnham Jr, *Burnham's Celestial Handbook*, Dover Publications, 1978

Joseph Campbell, *Occidental Mythology*, Arkana, 1991

Joseph Campbell, *Oriental Mythology*, Arkana, 1991

Joseph Campbell, *The Masks of God*, Penguin Arkana, 1991

The Cartographic Satellite Atlas of the World, ROBAS BV, Netherlands, 1997

The Cereologist (journal), Pub Global Circles Research

Peter A. Clayton, *Chronicle of the Pharaohs*, Thames and Hudson, 1994

The Complete Atlas of the British Isles, Reader's Digest, 1965

R. J. Cook, *The Pyramids of Giza*, Seven Islands, 1992

Geoffrey Cornelius and Paul Devereux, *The Secret Language of the Stars and Planets*, Pavilion, 1996

Heather Couper and Nigel Henbest, *The Stars*, Pan Books, 1988

John Cox and Richard Monkhouse, *Phillip's Colour Star Atlas Epoch 2000*, 1991

Erich von Daniken, *Chariots of the Gods*, Corgi, 1969

Richard Dawkins, *River out of Eden*, Science Masters, 1995

Serena Roney Dougal, *Where Science and Magic Meet*, Element Books, 1991

J. L. E. Dreyer, *A History of Astronomy from Thales to Kepler*

Lowell Edmunds, *Approaches to Greek Myth*, Johns Hopkins University Press, 1990

I. E. S. Edwards, *The Pyramids of Egypt*, Penguin, 1949

Dan Escott, *Cathedrals and Churches*, Oliver and Boyd, 1965

Wm. R. Fix, *Pyramid Odyssey*, Jonathan-James Books, 1978

Wm. R. Fix, *Star Maps*, Octopus, 1979

Rand and Ross Flem-Ath, *When the Sky Fell*, Stoddart, 1995

Michel Gauquelin, *The Cosmic Clocks*

Adrian G. Gilbert, *Magi*, Bloomsbury, 1996

Adrian G. Gilbert and Maurice M. Cotterell, *The Mayan Prophecies*, Element Books, 1995

Stephen Jay Gould, *Questioning the Millennium*, Jonathan Cape, 1997

Robert Graves, *The Greek Myths*, Penguin, 1960

The Guinness Book of Records, Guinness Publishing, 1997

Pierre Grimal, *The Dictionary of Classical Mythology*, Blackwell, 1996

Graham Hancock, *Fingerprints of the Gods*, William Heinemann Ltd, 1995

Graham Hancock and Robert Bauval, *Keeper of Genesis*, William Heinemann Ltd, 1996

Charles H. Hapgood, *Maps of the Ancient Sea Kings*, Turnstone Books, 1979

Gerald S. Hawkins, *Stonehenge Decoded*, Fontana, 1973

Gerald S. Hawkins, *Beyond Stonehenge*, Arrow, 1977

Murry Hope, *The Sirius Connection*, Element Books, 1996

Christopher Knight and Robert Lomas, *The Hiram Key*, Arrow, 1997

Ervin Laszlo, *The Creative Cosmos*, Floris Books, 1993

Mark Lehner, *The Egyptian Heritage: Based on the Readings of Edgar Cayce*

Mark Lehner, *The Complete Pyramids*, Thames and Hudson, 1997

Peter Lemesurier, *The Great Pyramid Decoded*, Element Books, 1977

Peter Lemesurier, *Nostradamus: The Next Fifty Years*, Piatkus, 1993

Peter Lemesurier, *Gods of the Dawn*, Thorsons, 1998

Norman Lockyer, *The Dawn of Astronomy*, Macmillan, 1894

Morris Marples, *White Horses and other Hill Figures*, Allan Sutton Publishing, 1981

John Matthews (ed.), *A Glastonbury Reader*, The Aquarian Press, 1993

Kurt Mendelssohn, *The Riddle of the Pyramids*, Thames and Hudson, 1974

John Michell, *A View over Atlantis*

John Michell, *A Little History of Astro-archaeology*, Thames and Hudson, 1977

Patrick Moore, *Stargazing: Astronomy without a Telescope*, Aurum Press, 1985

Patrick Moore, *The Guinness Book of Astronomy (AD 2000)*, fifth edition,
    Guinness Publishing, 1995

Chris Morton and Ceri Louise Thomas, *The Mystery of the Crystal Skulls*, Thorsons, 1997

Otto Neugabauer, *The Exact Sciences in Antiquity*, Dover, 1969

Arthur Norton, *Norton's Star Atlas*, Longman, 1986

W. T. Olcott, *Star Lore of All Ages*

Naomi Ozaniec, *The Elements of Egyptian Wisdom*, Element Books, 1994

Nigel Pennick, *The Ancient Science of Geomancy*, CRCS Publications, 1979

Nigel Pennick, *Leylines*, Weidenfield and Nicholson, 1997

The Photographic Atlas of the Stars, The Institute of Physics, 1997

Charles Piazzi Smythe, *Our Inheritance in the Great Pyramid*, 1880

Marmaduke Pickthall, *The Meaning of the Glorious Koran*, Dorset Press, n.d.

R. T. Rundell Clark, *Myth and Symbol in Ancient Egypt*, Thames and Hudson, 1959

Adam Rutherford, *Pyramidology*, C. Tinling & Co. Ltd., 1961

Giorgio de Santillana and Hertha von Dechend, *Hamlet's Mill*, Gambit International, Boston, 1969

Walter Scott (ed. and trans.), *Hermetica*, Solos Press, 1997

Jane B. Sellers, *The Death of the Gods in Ancient Egypt*, Penguin, 1992

Ian Shaw and Paul Nicholson, *The British Museum Dictionary of Ancient Egypt*, 1997

Zecharia Sitchin, *Earth Chronicles (The 12th Planet, The Stairway to Heaven, The Wars of Gods and Men)*, Bear & Co., 1992

Ian Stewart, *Nature's Numbers*, Weidenfield and Nicholson, 1995

James A. Swan (ed.), *The Power of Place*, Gateway Books, 1993

Robert K. G. Temple, *The Sirius Mystery*, Destiny Books, 1976

The Times World Atlas, Comprehensive Edition, Times Books

Guy Underwood, *The Pattern of the Past*, Abacus, 1977

Arthur Versluis, *Song of the Cosmos*, Prism Press, 1991

Christopher Walker (ed.), *Astronomy before the Telescope*, BCA, 1996

E. A. Wallis Budge (ed.), *The Book of the Dead*, Penguin Arkana, 1989

Sir Wallis Budge, *Egyptian Religion*, Carol Publishing Group, 1997

Alfred Watkins, *The Old Straight Track*, ABACUS, 1987

John Anthony West, *Serpent in the Sky*, Harper & Row, 1979

Colin Wilson, *From Atlantis to the Sphinx*, Virgin, 1997

World Mythology, Larousse Encyclopedia, 1995

The World's Last Mysteries, Reader's Digest, 1977

MAPS AND CHARTS

1:1,000,000 Operational Navigation Charts
D–11
E–15, E–16
F–2, F–16, F–17, F–18
G–4, G–7, G–8, G–9, G–18, G–19, G–20
H–4, H–5, H–9, H–10, H–11
J–4, J–5, J–6
K–5
L–4, L–5
M–4, M–5, M–25, M–26
N–26
P–13, P–26
Q–13, Q–27
R–23
T–18

1:500,000 (Mexico City) TPC J–24C

Israel Physical, 2 Sheet, 1:250,000
Easter Island 1:30,000 International Travel Map No. 308, second edition (1998)
Bartholomew. Egypt 1:1,000,000

Landranger Series 1:50,000 Ordnance Survey
Sheets 41, 67, 74, 75, 80, 81, 173, 174, 180, 181, 182, 183, 184, 185, 193, 194, 195, 200, 203, 204
Pathfinder Series 1:25,000 Ordnance Survey
Sheets 1169, 1185

INDEX

and the Rockies 157–61, *160*, *161*
in the Sierra Nevadas 162–3
in South America 143–7, *144*, *145*, *146*, *148*
stellar 104, 249–52
and the sun in Libra 109–11, *109*, *110*
in Taurus/the Hyades 247
at Teotihuacán 153–4, *154*
and Triangulum 218–19, *219*, *220*
in the UK 118–29, 206, 208, 247

Kangchenjunga 181, *182*
Katherine, Mt 36–8, *37*, 40, 44, 46–8, *47*, *52*
Kochab, and ancient Egypt 11
Kun Ka Shan, Mt 183–5, *185*, 191, 246

legominisms 43, 76–7, 97, 135
Lehner, Mark 73
Lepus, isosceles geometry 99–104, *99*, *101*, 108–9, *108*, 147, 159, *159*, 248, *252*
Libra 108–11, 136–8, *136*, *139*, 141, 159, *159*, 244
Lindisfarne 129, 241
Little Bear 18, 20, 31
Lockyer, Sir Norman 4, 9, 91, 209
longitude 209

Machu Pichu 147, *148*, 159, *159*
Mayans 113
Melkalanin 21–2, *22*, *24*, 25, *25*
mountain correlation 36–8, 44
Mendelssohn, Dr Kurt 73
meridian 10, 12–13
correlations 50–1, 128–9, 206
Mexico, pyramids in 151–6, *151*, *153*, *154*, *155*, *156*, 236–7

Michell, John 129, 168, 207
Milk Hill 123, *124*, 125
Milky Way 106–7
Mintaka 65, 66–7
Giza pyramid alignment 5–6, *5*
Kun Ka Shan alignment 183–6, *185*, *186*, 191, 246
mountains:
correlations 35–9, 42, 143
and isosceles geometry 38, 204
vertical stellar alignment 36–40, *37*, 50–1, 149–68, 178–203, *194*, *200*, 243–7
see also specific names
Muztag, Mt 193–5, *194*, 245

Nanga Parbat 189–90, *190*, 241, 247
NASA message 173
Nazca lines 137, *148*, 159, *159*, 239
Nezzi, Mt 51–3, *52*, 191–2, 246
Nile Delta, terrestrial geometry 44–53
Nissan, Prof. 4
Nut and Geb concept 1–2, *2*, 38, 41, 135, 205–6

Olympus, Mt 197
Orion *3*
in AD 2000 245–7
Belt:
angle with Polaris 177
30° displacement 175–86, *186*
concurrence above in AD 2000 68, *68*
culmination date 60
dagger 62–6, *64*, 191–2, *193*, 246
foot 94, *95*
Great Pyramid alignment 105
isosceles geometry in 30–1, *31*, 65, 83, 93, *94*, 96–7, *217*, 248–51, *251*